FAITHFUL *of* HEART

Books by Tracie Peterson

A Minnesota Legacy

Faithful of Heart

The Hope of Cheyenne

A Constant Love
Designed with Love
A Moment to Love

The Heart of Cheyenne

A Love Discovered
A Choice Considered
A Truth Revealed

Pictures of the Heart

Remember Me
Finding Us
Knowing You

The Jewels of Kalispell*

The Heart's Choice
With Each Tomorrow
An Unexpected Grace

Love on the Santa Fe

Along the Rio Grande
Beyond the Desert Sands
Under the Starry Skies

Ladies of the Lake

Destined for You
Forever My Own
Waiting on Love

Willamette Brides

Secrets of My Heart
The Way of Love
Forever by Your Side

The Treasures of Nome*

Forever Hidden
Endless Mercy
Ever Constant

Brookstone Brides

When You Are Near
Wherever You Go
What Comes My Way

Golden Gate Secrets

In Places Hidden
In Dreams Forgotten
In Times Gone By

Heart of the Frontier

Treasured Grace
Beloved Hope
Cherished Mercy

The Heart of Alaska*

In the Shadow of Denali
Out of the Ashes
Under the Midnight Sun

Sapphire Brides

A Treasure Concealed
A Beauty Refined
A Love Transformed

For a complete list of Tracie's books, visit TraciePeterson.com.

*with Kimberley Woodhouse

1

A MINNESOTA LEGACY

FAITHFUL of HEART

TRACIE PETERSON

a division of Baker Publishing Group
Minneapolis, Minnesota

Published by Bethany House Publishers
Minneapolis, Minnesota
BethanyHouse.com

Bethany House Publishers is a division of
Baker Publishing Group, Grand Rapids, Michigan

Printed in the United States of America

Library of Congress Cataloging-in-Publication Data

Names: Peterson, Tracie author
Title: Faithful of heart / Tracie Peterson.
Description: Minneapolis, Minnesota : Bethany House Publishers, a division of Baker Publishing Group, 2026. | Series: A Minnesota legacy ; 1
Identifiers: LCCN 2025016489 | ISBN 9780764244285 paperback | ISBN 9780764246159 cloth | ISBN 9780764246166 large print | ISBN 9781493452576 ebook
Subjects: LCGFT: Fiction | Romance fiction | Christian fiction | Novels
Classification: LCC PS3566.E7717 F35 2026 | DDC 813/.54—dc23/eng/20250603
LC record available at https://lccn.loc.gov/2025016489

Scripture quotations are from the King James version of the Bible.

This book is a work of fiction. Names, characters, places, and incidents are the product of the author's imagination or are used fictitiously. Any resemblance to actual events, locales, or persons, living or dead, is coincidental.

Cover design by LOOK Design Studio, Peter Glöege

Baker Publishing Group publications use paper produced from sustainable forestry practices and postconsumer waste whenever possible.

25 26 27 28 29 30 31 7 6 5 4 3 2 1

PROLOGUE

August 1866
Philadelphia, Pennsylvania

"It is important to remember that your gifts will be used to change the lives of those who cannot do so for themselves. Their numbers are high, especially since the war has left a great many women widowed and children orphaned. Remember, no matter your donation, it will be a blessing," the speaker declared to thunderous applause.

Judith Ashton Stanford was among those in the approving audience. She clapped and rose to her feet. The long, hot afternoon of lectures had come to an end, and she was rather anxious to return home.

"I was quite impressed with the speakers," the bearded man standing next to her said almost like they'd been in previous conversation. He was a handsome man with a hint of mischief in his smile. His dark eyes searched her face as if for answers to some unspoken question. "I'm Dr. Roman Turner."

"Judith Stanford." She extended her gloved hand. "I agree, the speakers were wonderful. I've long desired to help the poor in whatever way possible."

Her passion for widows and orphans had come about partly due to her own situation. She and her husband, Alden Stanford, had married June third in 1862, and the next day Judith had waved with the other wives and daughters as their men marched off to fight for the North. She had never seen him again. He perished in the war during the Battle of Gettysburg in July 1863.

At twenty-two, Judith had been naïve about the risks. Now twenty-six, she felt as though she'd gained far more knowledge than she ever wanted. Losing her husband was one of many losses. Her brother died in the war as well, and her mother and father died in a riverboat accident the very next year. Her entire life had been altered.

Had it not been for her charity work and taking over her father's steamboat service, Judith might have despaired. Other women certainly had. Every day she learned of widows who had given up, sinking deeper into their loneliness and seemingly impossible circumstances.

"There's so much to be done. I am from Minnesota, and we are dealing with a growing number of widows and orphans there too," Dr. Turner said.

"We have so many due to the war that it has become the focus of several charities."

"I can well imagine. I served on the battlefield as a surgeon and saw many a good man breathe his last."

Judith had seen so many families devastated by the loss. Sorrow alone was enough to cause hopelessness, but add poverty to this and they were helpless to fight back. Rarely did a woman have any means of supporting herself. Losing their men left women with an immediate financial void that was difficult, if not impossible, to overcome. Families did what they could to watch out for one another, and good men sent home money from their pay. But as the fighting war dragged on, the needs of those women and their children mounted, and battlefront postal services were often not available.

Judith and her mother had gotten involved in helping as a means of healing from their own personal losses. There were multiple agencies striving to create assistance for the widows and orphans of war. Judith and her mother had also seen the need to help those whose husbands and fathers were still living, still fighting. They had created a charity to provide food and clothes for these families. Even after her mother died, Judith continued the good work, urging local churches to care for their own as a service unto God.

"I find that helping those less fortunate has done much to bless me." Judith's collar seemed to tighten as the heat in the room grew more unbearable. "Women are at a great disadvantage to earn their own living, even more so while taking care of a family. If we do not show compassion on them, I feel they will never be able to make their way to thriving, rather than merely surviving."

"You speak quite eloquently. We have some wonderful folks in Minneapolis but could certainly use someone with your beauty and grace to stir their hearts to action."

"We need women like Judith to stir the hearts of people everywhere, Dr. Turner." This came from an older woman Judith had known for many years. Harriet Silverman was a formidable fund raiser with all sorts of creative ideas for bettering the plight of the poor. "I am doing what I can to convince her to take on larger roles in our various charities. She has impressed me with her attention to detail."

"You are too kind." Judith smiled at the older woman. Mrs. Silverman had been working quite feverishly to entice her to join a committee overseeing housing for widows with children.

"Mrs. Silverman, I was encouraged by your speech. Thank you for inviting me," Dr. Turner said. "There is a definite need to better the living conditions of the poor. Getting the stray animals off the streets alone will greatly improve health conditions amongst the people."

"I've said as much for years, Dr. Turner. And I will continue to advocate cleanliness. However, it is difficult to choose soap over soup when your child is hungry."

It was true. Hunger was a nagging need.

The older woman tapped Judith on the arm. "If you'll excuse me." Mrs. Silverman was distracted by a couple of wealthy-looking men and left Judith and Roman to continue their conversation.

"You mentioned Minneapolis. Is that where you live?" Judith asked, wishing the temperatures would abate.

"For the last few years, yes. Prior to that, my family was in Maryland."

"And the war sent you west?" She drew her fan and began to use it.

"Not at all. My father inherited property in Minnesota. I remained in Baltimore to finish my education and training, but before I could return to my family, the war broke out, and doctors were very needed in the army."

"I can well imagine. The numbers of wounded must have been difficult to deal with. My own husband was lost at Gettysburg."

"I'm sorry to hear that." His expression changed to one of concern. "I thought I heard it mentioned that you had lost your parents recently."

She continued to wave the fan. "Two years ago. My father owned a steamboat service on the river, transporting goods and people. They were on a trip, and the boiler blew up. Their cabin was just above, and they were killed instantly."

"Was it sabotage?"

"No. At least, those who investigated said there were no indications of such. My father had expressed concerns about the boiler days before the accident. He thought he'd dealt with the problem, but obviously he was mistaken." She reattached the fan's cord to a button on her waistband. The lacy piece hadn't helped cool her at all and, in fact, waving it about had only served to make her hotter.

"Your losses have been great. My father also passed away during the war."

"In battle?" she asked.

He shook his head. "It's a long story, but he died in Minnesota." Dr. Turner glanced past her into the crowd behind them. "It was one of those senseless and unnecessary things."

"I'm so sorry." She couldn't help but notice something about his expression that suggested his grief was still strong, but she didn't feel the situation warranted the intimacy of her questioning him.

"I realize it's quite forward of me, but I wonder if you might consider having dinner with me tonight? Mrs. Silverman has known me for years and can vouch for my character."

The idea of attending supper with the dashing doctor enticed Judith, though she probably shouldn't even consider accepting an invitation from a stranger. Before she could answer, Mrs. Silverman put an end to any romantic notions.

"Judith! Judith!" Mrs. Silverman called, motioning her to come.

"If you'll excuse me, I believe I'm needed elsewhere. It was a pleasure to meet you, Dr. Turner."

"For me as well, and if you come to Minneapolis, please be certain to look me up."

She nodded and gave him a smile. "I'd like that."

Roman watched the young woman move through the throng of people. She was as graceful as a swan swimming among the reeds. He found himself mesmerized for a long while. She was beautiful, there was certainly no doubt about that. Her voluminous brown hair had been carefully pinned into place, held by ebony lacquered combs. Her gown, although trimmed in black, was not that of mourning. The dark green suited her complexion, and the lightweight material was sensible for an extremely warm day.

But there was something more to her—something that attracted him in a way he'd not felt before. Judith Stanford had a heart for the very things he did. She cared about those around her who were suffering and in need, and she put others first.

His mother and sister were always after him to find a wife and settle down, but until this moment, he'd never met a woman with whom he could imagine himself married. Judith Stanford, however, was easily a match for the bride he had imagined. She was soft-spoken, yet firm in her opinions and confident in doing the right thing. Just the fact that she was here spending her free time listening to lectures on helping the destitute spoke volumes about her character.

But even as he thought these things, Roman chided himself. He didn't really know anything about Judith Stanford other than the information Mrs. Silverman had shared in their brief conversation earlier. Certainly not enough to think favorably toward a lifetime together. No doubt it was just the heat.

Sweat trickled down the side of his neck. The temperatures were almost unbearable, and Roman felt he'd had more than enough of crowds and lectures. He made his way toward the back of the room where the exit doors would lead him outside into the hopefully cool night air. As he drew near to where Judith stood listening to Mrs. Silverman, he sensed there might be a problem. Judith seemed strangely silent, almost distracted.

As he came abreast of her and the others, Judith turned. The look on her face was one he'd seen on the battlefield just before men lost consciousness. Reaching out, he caught her as she fainted.

"Oh dear! Oh my!" Mrs. Silverman waved her gloved hands in exclamation. "What has happened!"

"I believe the heat has overcome the poor woman," one of the men declared.

Roman lifted Judith into his arms. "Let's get her outside. The open air will be better. Mrs. Silverman, please find us a way through the crowd."

Outside the air was cooler, but heavy with humidity. Roman stood holding Judith in his arms and wondering what he should do next.

"I believe there is a marble bench to the side, just over there." Mrs. Silverman pointed.

Roman caught sight of the bench and nodded. He crossed the portico and wondered whether to seat Judith on the bench or continue holding her. She was light enough he could have held her forever, or so he told himself, but propriety was important. He gently lowered her to the bench and, while still holding on to her, grabbed the fan attached to her waistband. He didn't see how it was fastened and gave a hard yank. The button holding it danced across the stone floor.

Roman opened the fan while balancing Judith and began to use it quite vigorously. "If someone could get her a glass of water, that would help," he said, not even bothering to look up.

She started to rally as he continued to fan her face. When she opened her eyes and met his gaze, she smiled. Roman was certain she had no idea of where she was. He smiled back.

Then at once, his nearness seemed to alarm her. She jerked and sat up straight, pulling herself out of Roman's arms with surprising strength.

"Oh goodness. What happened?"

"You fainted, my dear," Mrs. Silverman announced. "The heat was positively abominable. Thank God for Dr. Turner. He just happened to be passing by and caught you as you fell."

Judith looked into Roman's eyes. For a moment, he lost the

ability to reason. He had never met a woman who so completely captured his thoughts. He'd long prayed for a wife, but could it really be this easy? Could she be the one?

"Thank you for helping me, Dr. Turner." She reached over and took the fan.

"I'm afraid I pulled rather hard and sent a button flying across the way." He motioned with his head but refused to look away from the glance that kept him spellbound.

She smiled. "It's of no concern, given the service you rendered me." She fanned herself a few times. "It's usually not so hot in the evening, but the room seemed quite confining."

"Yes, there were simply too many people in one small space," Mrs. Silverman agreed. "I will call for my carriage and see you safely home."

Roman thought to offer that himself but knew it would be inappropriate. However, accompanying them would be completely fitting.

"I could go with you," he offered.

"Nonsense. I have my driver and two footmen. We'll be just fine, Dr. Turner. Please return to the fund raiser. I know it is important for you to meet with several of our larger donors."

The wonder of the moment ended with that. He straightened and stood. "I hope you'll be feeling better soon, Mrs. Stanford."

"Again, thank you for your help." She drew in a deep breath. "I am much revived and quite myself again."

Roman smiled and gave a bow. He certainly wasn't exactly himself. The encounter had left him more than a little shaken. Something important had happened, but exactly what, he couldn't say.

May 1870
Philadelphia, Pennsylvania

Comfortably seated in her home office, Judith perused the list her secretary Helen had just given her. "There are just so many needy souls in the world."

In the four years that had passed since Harriet Silverman had begged her to come on board a committee to help poor widows, Judith had immersed herself in concerns for the destitute. With Harriet's help, she had mastered the ability to influence those around her, and she was known for her fund-raising parties and speeches. Most every women's group in the Philadelphia area had hosted her to speak on more than one occasion. Church ladies' groups were especially fond of bringing Judith to their special events, where she could offer them insight and encouragement, as well as suggestions for how best to benefit the less fortunate in Philadelphia.

"As you can see by the names put together from the area churches, the number of widows and orphans continues to grow. The churches that offer food goods tell me that they are nearly depleted. Their donations have been quite minimal."

Judith nodded. "Oh, Helen, it is a sorrowful sight to see. I visited one of the orphanages yesterday, as you know. There must have been at least twenty infants at that location alone. The staff are overworked, and the funds to support those precious lives are at a minimum. I must find a way to send more money."

The nearly forty-year-old assistant nodded. Helen was a plain-looking woman with brown hair and eyes. She was short and of petite frame, but to Judith there was nothing small about Helen Jessop. The woman worked just as tirelessly as Judith and shared her employer's deepest concerns.

Judith put the list aside. "I'll simply have to host a party to get more donations."

Helen reached into her pocket for the leather-bound journal she kept ever at the ready. "What type of party would you like to give?"

"Well, the weather has been quite nice, and the garden is starting to bloom in full. I suppose we could plan a garden party with the provision to host indoors if the weather turns bad. Or even a riverboat excursion. You know how the well-to-do seem to enjoy that diversion."

"There are benefits to both," Helen assured.

"Well, we can decide that later today."

Helen jotted notes in a furious fashion. Without looking up, she posed additional questions. "Shall we invite from the red list or the blue? Or shall we include both?"

"Both, I think. I haven't been pressing any one of them since the Christmas season. It's time for them to step up and do their part."

Judith got to her feet and went to the large window that looked out on the upper-class neighborhood. The house she lived in was not overly grand, but the area surrounding her was, and her neighbors were affluent and more than capable of donating to the cause. Elsewhere in the city, the very rich were more than aware of the growing problems in their community. But, while knowledgeable about the situation, they were rather slow at times in coming to the aid of their poorer brothers and sisters. Like a church minister, Judith would simply have to bring to light the fact that they had been blessed and needed to bless others.

A carriage pulled up to the curb of her property, immediately capturing her attention. Judith tried to place the rather handsome man who stepped down. For a moment, her thoughts went back to the dashing young man who'd caught her after she'd fainted years earlier at a fund raiser. Dr. Roman Turner had drifted around in her dreams and thoughts ever since. She'd never had the opportunity to visit Minneapolis, but she had considered it several times, especially when she thought of once again meeting the distinguished doctor.

The man at the carriage conversed with the driver for a moment and then proceeded up her walkway. It wasn't Dr. Turner.

"I believe I have company," she said, turning away from the window.

Helen looked up. "I shall see who it is. Are you receiving?"

"Of course." She smoothed down the overskirt of her bustled blue gown. "Show him in. He may come bearing gifts." Judith came to stand at the edge of her desk. She had no idea who the well-dressed man was, but perhaps he represented a new donor. She could only hope.

She listened as Helen greeted the man. Helen had been such an asset to her work. They'd first met at church shortly after Judith's parents had died. The requirements of dealing with her parents' business had been almost too much in the wake of her grief, and Helen had volunteered to help Judith put things in order. She had been a godsend.

"Mr. Norbert Black is calling," Helen announced, pausing at the door. She gave Judith the man's card.

Judith read that he was an attorney from Minneapolis, Minnesota. There were only two things she knew for sure about Minneapolis. First, it was where the elusive Dr. Turner lived. Second, it was the home of her estranged grandfather, someone she'd never met.

The handsome black-haired man stepped into the room, with a twinkle in his eyes and a smile on his lips. Judith sized him up, determined to guess why he'd come. It was something of a game to her. Seeing him take charge of the moment and extend his hand in greeting, she couldn't help but like him.

"Mr. Black, I'm Judith Stanford. How may I be of service?"

He shook her hand. "It's a pleasure to finally meet you. As you probably noted from my card, I am an attorney. I have but one client, by choice, I assure you," he quickly added. "I work for your grandfather, James Ashton Sr."

Judith wasn't quite sure how to take the news, but she was quite certain that she would never have guessed these details on her own.

"Please sit down." She motioned to the same leather chair Helen had recently vacated. Moving behind her desk, Judith reclaimed her seat and waited.

Mr. Black hesitated, as if studying the situation. Judith had watched people all her life—a helpful habit in soliciting donations for her charities. She could read people very well and always knew when they were ready to move forward. Mr. Black was showing all the signs of a man trying to choose between two paths.

"Helen, would you please ask Mrs. Meachem to arrange tea?"

"Of course." The secretary left the room to speak to the cook, leaving Judith alone with Mr. Black.

"Please sit, Mr. Black, and tell me why you've come today. You seem rather at a loss for words."

He took a seat and gave her another broad smile. "I'm just

rather taken aback. I had no idea you were so young and beautiful."

"What a bold thing to say." His words put Judith on guard. She'd had men attempt to speak words of admiration and love before.

"I know, and I apologize. You have taken me by surprise. I beg forgiveness."

"Surprise hardly entitles you to be intimate where intimacy is not called for." Judith knew she'd taken a degree of severity that perhaps wasn't merited, so she smiled. "Let us start anew. Why don't you tell me why you have journeyed here from Minnesota?"

Mr. Black leaned back in the chair and nodded. "Thank you for being so gracious. I am here at the direction of your grandfather."

"Well, that's quite a shock. I didn't even know if the man was still alive. You see, he long ago cut us out of his family."

"I am familiar with the circumstances."

She frowned. "Then you know that my grandfather removed himself from the company and correspondence of his son many years ago. Cut him off without a dime and left him to his own survival. Therefore, I have very little interest in whatever my grandfather might want to say."

"And Mr. Ashton told me that I might expect this type of reaction from you." He smiled. "But you seem like such a generous soul. I've heard about your good works here in Philadelphia. I made it my task to investigate the things that you were involved with. Your charity work speaks of the tenderness you hold for the less fortunate in your community."

"My mother had a heart for such ministries. I merely followed in her footsteps."

"Still, it reveals a kindness and compassion that might surely allow you to consider what your grandfather is requesting of you."

"He's requesting something?" She chuckled. "And here I thought perhaps he was extending an apology. I should have known better."

"He would like for you to come and visit him."

Judith shifted her weight as her bustle bit into her skin. "I have no desire to visit him. He made it clear that we were nothing to him."

"He's old and approaching the end of his life," Mr. Black countered. "The mistakes of his youth are no doubt haunting him."

"So he admits he made a mistake in separating himself from his family?"

It was Mr. Black's turn to shift. "He hasn't said as much, but I do believe that is his thought on the matter."

Helen gave a light knock and wheeled in the tea cart. She rolled it to a point near Judith and waited for instruction.

"You may go, Helen. I'll pour."

The woman exited the room without a word as Judith rose to prepare the tea. Mr. Black also stood. "Do you care for cream or sugar, Mr. Black?"

"Nothing, thank you."

She handed him the cup and saucer, then extended a small plate of cookies. "Would you care for further refreshment?"

He chose one and balanced it on the side of the saucer.

Judith poured cream into her cup and then tea. She added sugar, then took up a spoon and gave the contents a delicate swirl as she took her seat. Mr. Black did likewise. It was all done with the greatest formality, and yet it seemed oddly casual.

"I know that my grandfather is old. However, I feel the time has passed for us. I'm thirty years old and have never known the man, nor his affections. I see no reason to strike up an acquaintance now."

"He's quite wealthy, as you might know. Furthermore, he is

intent on knowing you and determining if you are worthy of inheriting his vast fortune."

Judith shook her head. "I do not want his money. He left my father to struggle on his own when he was but twenty-one. And while he was a man full grown, he would have benefited from fatherly kindness and love. He received neither. You may not know the full story, but let me enlighten you.

"My parents met soon after Father graduated college and found himself drawn to riverboats. My mother's father was a riverboat captain and hired my father as a roustabout who handled deck chores. James Ashton Sr. was greatly displeased. He saw nothing of value in hard labor.

"My mother was but sixteen and already working hard to cook and clean on the same boat. They fell in love rather quickly, and when my father proposed marriage, there was a great celebration amongst the workers and my mother's father. He could see how clearly in love they were and wanted only happiness for his daughter. Mr. Ashton wanted happiness only for himself. He forbade my father from marrying her."

She sipped her tea and then continued. "Of course, my father's love for her was greater than anything he felt for my cold and indifferent grandfather. They married, and Mr. Ashton cut all ties with the only son he had. So you see, I have no interest in turning back time to assuage his conscience. You may tell him for me, the only thing he now needs is the Lord. Let him cultivate a relationship with God Almighty before he faces Him in death."

She fixed Mr. Black with a look that had been known to whither lesser men. The attorney quickly considered his teacup. For a long moment, neither said anything at all.

Judith hoped that would be the end of it. She had much to accomplish in planning her garden party, and Mr. Black was of no benefit to her needs.

"I can understand," he finally said, "that your father was

grieved by his father's rejection of the woman he loved and his plans for the future. However, that is in the past. If you are a Christian woman, as I have heard you are, then might I suggest that forgiveness is called for. After all, you and your grandfather have never had opportunity to speak or share your interests."

"I do not hold anything against the man, and I certainly do not wish for God to judge him harshly." Judith sipped her tea and gave a shrug. "I simply have no interest in him whatsoever. He has never been a part of my life, and I see no reason that he should be so now."

"He has no heir."

"And that was his choice, Mr. Black. Just as it's my choice to remain here in Philadelphia."

Black glanced around as if worried that he might be overheard. "He's very wealthy. His money could help your charities considerably. To inherit his wealth would allow you to be quite generous."

Judith didn't want to consider that, even for a moment. She knew Mr. Black was no doubt right in suggesting such things, but she likened it to Satan tempting Christ in the desert. She would stand her ground with Scripture.

"Matthew six, verses nineteen through twenty-one admonishes us, 'Lay not up for yourselves treasures upon earth, where moth and rust doth corrupt, and where thieves break through and steal: But lay up for yourselves treasures in heaven, where neither moth nor rust doth corrupt, and where thieves do not break through nor steal: For where your treasure is, there will your heart be also.' My treasures are in heaven, Mr. Black, not this earth."

"But you work to make a better life for those less fortunate. To do so, you need the money that wealthier men might give."

"That is true, but I will entrust the Lord to lay it upon the hearts of those men, rather than go chasing after my grandfather's approval for an inheritance."

She stood. “Now, Mr. Black, if there is nothing more, I have a full schedule and have already yielded enough of my valuable time to this matter. I must bid you farewell.”

The man jumped to his feet and extended his empty cup. “I had hoped we might be able to further discuss the matter. Perhaps I could be allowed to call on you tomorrow? I must admit that after meeting you, I am intrigued to know you better.”

“As I said, my schedule is quite full, Mr. Black. Thank you for coming.”

As if knowing that her mistress was ready to dismiss the man, Helen appeared. “Right this way, Mr. Black. I have your hat.” She gave it a little shake toward him, as if enticing a dog with a bone.

Judith took his cup and saucer and offered a brief hint of a smile. “Good day, Mr. Black.”

He looked as if he might say something, then gave a nod and bowed. Helen hurried him from the room and out the front door. Judith went to the window and watched him reboard his carriage. He was a very pleasant sort of fellow and quite nice in his appearance. Perhaps one might even call him extraordinarily attractive.

She frowned, though, thinking of the reason he had come. She’d had no idea her grandfather was still living, much less that he was considering her as an heir.

Her father had never truly spoken against him, but he’d made it clear that their values in life were quite different. When her father had gone away to further his education, he had fallen into the company of Christian men who mentored and guided him to accept Jesus as his Savior. In turn, he had led her mother, his soon-to-be father-in-law, and eventually Judith to Jesus.

As Judith remembered, Father had told her that her grandfather had no use for another to be God when he considered himself qualified for the role. And while he hadn’t lied about the treatment he'd received from the man, Father had never been given to cruel comments or condemnation. Instead, he held great pity for his father and made it clear to Judith that he prayed daily for his salvation and that she should as well.

And she had.

But she had no desire for there to be anything more between them. And while it would be nice to have vast amounts of money at her disposal, she wasn't about to sell her soul to the man who had so deeply wounded her parents.

No, it wasn't an issue of forgiveness. It was a matter of keeping evil at bay. The Bible admonished Christians in the fourth chapter of James to "Submit yourselves therefore to God. Resist the devil, and he will flee from you."

Surely the same was true for those who served him.

May 1870
Minneapolis, Minnesota

At thirty-seven, Roman Turner was still not overly content with his life. He was highly regarded for his skills and the amazing feats of surgery he performed during the war. But life had dealt him several unsatisfactory blows, and he was still coming to grips with them years later. By this age, he had expected to be a husband and father, perhaps to have a large clientele of paying patients.

Even now, as he attempted to read one of his medical books while awaiting the supper his mother and sister, Claudette, were preparing, Roman couldn't push aside his frustration. Their home was the best he could buy on his meager physician's wages. Had he settled back east instead of in Minneapolis, he might be making enough money to provide them a better life, perhaps even an affluent one. Had he moved to Philadelphia, he might have met up with the beautiful Judith Stanford again. Instead, he'd chosen to remain in Minneapolis, where his father moved the family in 1860 after being gifted a large parcel of land from an aging uncle.

When his family moved west, Roman remained in Baltimore to finish some specialized training, but the thought of joining them was one that held great appeal. The frontier needed doctors, and he was excited to work with people from all walks of life. Then the war came. Roman volunteered to serve in the Union Army and found himself separated from friends and colleagues as the country chose sides.

He was almost immediately relocated to a hospital in Washington. While there, he received a letter from his mother, telling him that his father had been swindled out of most of his land. Of course, Roman could do little about it. He prayed and waited to hear more about their circumstances as the war continued.

The news that came wasn't good. His father had taken the loss of his property quite hard. His health had slipped away, and his mother wrote of concern that he would not live long. And then the end had come, leaving his mother and ten-year-old sister alone in a land of uncertainty and assured poverty. Roman had tried to gather enough money together to relocate them to New York City, where he had friends, but nothing ever came together.

Then in 1862, terrible news had come of the Sioux uprising in Minnesota, and Roman had feared for his family. He'd pressed his mother to take Claudette and flee. He even tried to get leave, but his services were too desperately needed on the battlefields. Thankfully, the uprising remained at a distance from Minneapolis.

The rest of the war had been a time of desperation for Roman. He had done what he could to provide for his family, but he couldn't go to them. Not when the war was more intense than ever.

When the end finally came and Roman was able to return

to Minneapolis, he found his mother and sister quite destitute. Friends were doing what they could, and their pastor kept an eye on them, but even with the money Roman had sent, they were worse off than he'd ever imagined.

"Dinner's nearly ready, Roman," his mother called, pulling him out of his melancholy thoughts. "Your Aunt Mary is coming to join us tonight. She should be here shortly."

"Thanks for letting me know."

Mother smiled and returned to the kitchen. It wasn't fair. She and Claudette both worked far harder than any other women he knew. These days, they did it out of their love for the poor more so than for their own welfare. As Roman's presence and his war bonus helped to bring them financial stability, they had wanted to help in his endeavors to better the lives of others.

Most evenings after supper, they could be found making baby blankets or diapers. Sometimes they sewed nightgowns for the older children and knit slippers for the adults. They were good Christian women who wanted to serve God as best they could with the only skills they had to offer.

Roman felt the same and used his medical knowledge to treat the less fortunate. He particularly liked visiting the orphanage. The children there were so happy to have anyone show them affection and attention. The city had reached a population of over thirteen thousand people—more than double what it had been just ten years earlier—and with that growth, the number of impoverished had increased as well. It seemed especially true for the orphans.

A knock on the door sent Roman to welcome his aunt Mary. She smiled and stretched up to give him a kiss on the cheek. "Roman, you're as handsome as ever. When are you going to take a wife?"

For a brief moment, the image of the brown-eyed woman he'd met four years ago in Philadelphia came to mind. Judith Stanford. But just as quickly, it passed, and Roman laughed.

This was Aunt Mary's usual questioning. He gave her a hug and reached out to take her shawl and bonnet.

"I'm far too busy to take a wife, as you well know. Now come in and enjoy a quiet evening with your family."

"It's so good to see you. I feared you might be too busy. Your mother mentioned there was an accident at one of the mills yesterday."

"Yes, one of the sawmills. Three men were injured, but they're doing well today."

"I'm glad to hear it."

Roman hung her belongings on a peg by the door. "Mother says dinner is nearly ready."

"I'll go see if she needs my help," Mary said, heading toward the kitchen.

She looked quite tired, and Roman worried about her health. She had taken a job with James Ashton's household five years ago and worked her way up to housekeeper. As a widow, she had to support herself, but that wasn't her real reason for going to work for the horrible old man. Roman could hear her explanation even now.

"He's the reason your father is dead. By working in the house, perhaps I can find proof of the way he swindled poor Andrew. If so, then we can take it to the legal authorities and see justice done."

But justice could never be done. Justice wouldn't bring back his father after being cheated by the man who claimed to be his partner.

"Let's be seated," Mother called as she brought a large pot to the table.

Mary followed with a platter of biscuits, and nineteen-year-old Claudette brought the butter and serving ladle.

"Mother has made the best stew. It's perfection," Claudette announced.

Roman took a seat at the head of the table and waited for

the women to join him. "Let's pray." He bowed his head and offered thanks for the food and a blessing on those who had gathered to share it.

"How was your day, Mary?" Roman's mother asked.

As much as Roman hated her working for Ashton, he always listened closely for any details that might help them see the old man condemned for the things he'd done.

"It was long and tiring. Mr. Ashton insists on having the stairs polished weekly. It's a never-ending job, and the maids resent the additional task. I did find the opportunity to work in his office, however. He went out for meetings, and I took the task of cleaning there, hoping I might be able to search through his papers."

"He'll never leave anything condemning him out in the open," Roman said, accepting a bowl of stew his mother had just portioned out.

"He has a locked room on the third floor. That's where he keeps the old records. I have recently acquired the key, but there's rarely an opportunity to go there. Even if I did, I'd truly have no excuse for being there if I were found out." Mary placed a biscuit on her plate and accepted the butter from Claudette.

"Aunt Mary, you've been there for five years with nothing to show for it," Roman said, grabbing a couple of the biscuits. "I would much rather you quit and get away from him. James Ashton is a vile and abominable man who cares nothing about anyone but himself. I fear if he finds out who you are, he'll cause you great pain."

"I fear that as well," Mother said, handing Claudette and Mary their bowls of stew.

"I need to work to support myself. You both know that. Mr. Ashton provides me room and board, as well as a small salary. It isn't the best arrangement, but it might merit us some answers one day. Until then, I'll simply keep to myself and do what I must. The way that man swindled Andrew and others should be known."

"It is known, but it was just legal enough that no one can do anything about it," Mother replied. "We've known this for nearly ten years. Nothing is going to change now. We must accept that it was the will of God and move forward. We're doing all right. Claudette and I have just made twenty dollars, I'm proud to say."

"Creating a traveling wardrobe for Mrs. Cooperton was a lot of work. And that woman had more than enough money to pay you better than twenty dollars for it," Roman countered. He sampled the stew and marveled at his mother's skills. She had always been able to put together a hearty meal.

"It wasn't an entire wardrobe, and twenty dollars is a large sum of money, Roman. It will allow us a few extras, as well as enable us to further your cause. Claudette and I plan to make several dozen diapers as soon as we can purchase white flannel."

"And we will need your help making my wedding dress, Aunt Mary. Daniel and I are planning to marry as soon as his promotion comes through this fall."

"I should have plenty of time to help with that," Mary promised.

Roman listened as Claudette described the type of dress she wanted. He wanted her to have the wedding of her dreams but knew their resources would be limited. He would have to see if he could take on some additional patient work. More than once he'd been asked to serve as surgeon to some of the wealthier families. Perhaps he could work out something. But even though he considered this, he knew it would be almost impossible. He was already working from sunup to past sundown. His hours were consumed with those who couldn't afford to pay. Were he not receiving money from various charities, he wouldn't even be able to care for his mother and sister. Some provider he had turned out to be.

He sighed and breathed a silent prayer, begging God to deliver them—to avenge his father and bring justice to their family. James Ashton had been responsible for robbing them of their future. No doubt he'd done it to others as well. Why didn't God stop him?

"Roman, you need a haircut," his mother said.

He startled, then ran his hand back through his wavy dark hair. "I do. I've been putting off asking you."

"We'll get to it right after dinner," she promised and then gave him a loving look. "You must keep up your appearance. You are quite handsome."

"You're prejudiced," Roman teased and tore pieces of biscuit up into his stew.

"Nevertheless, it's true, and you really should consider taking a wife."

Roman nodded but didn't have the heart to remind his mother that taking a wife would mean one more mouth to feed, and they were having a hard enough time keeping proper meals on the table as it was.

He lowered his head to hide the frown that came unbidden. Nothing was as he wished it could be. He knew, however, that God had called him to the tasks at hand. The poor needed a good doctor, same as the rich. Perhaps a wife wasn't in the plan at all.

"She what?" James Ashton Sr. paced the room as he listened to his private attorney explain his encounter with Judith Ashton.

"She said she wasn't at all interested in your money and she wouldn't come," Norbert Black repeated. "I suppose because she has her own money."

"Everyone wants more money, and while I've seen the records of her various investments and business dealings, she has nothing compared to what I can give."

The old man finally stopped pacing and went to his desk. He plopped down in the leather chair and pressed his hand to his heart. "Ring for Mrs. Deeters to bring my tonic, Bert."

"She has the evening off," Black replied. "Let me fetch it for you."

"No, call for Winchell. He knows where everything is."

Black rang the bell and explained things to the maid who responded. Despite Winchell being at least sixty-five years old, the man was there in moments. He had always been reliable.

"Yes, sir?" He came to stand beside Ashton.

"I need my heart tonic. Bring it and a cup of hot tea." Ashton didn't bother to ask if Black wanted anything. The man was his employee. Let him get something on his own time.

"Now where were we?" Ashton could feel his heart pounding rapidly and wanted to focus on anything else.

"I liked your granddaughter," the lawyer continued. "She has a sterling reputation for a widowed woman. She has managed to oversee her father's investments and interests without being compromised. Her reputation speaks for itself. She is highly esteemed in the community for her charitable works."

"But she says she doesn't care about my money?"

"Yes, sir."

James found this ironic. How like her father she must be. He, too, had turned up his nose at wealth beyond his understanding. And all because he didn't want to yield his will to James. And for what? The love of a woman, nay . . . a girl. She had been barely sixteen and the daughter of a riverboat owner. James Ashton Jr. might have had any number of wealthy socialites, but instead he fell in love with a working man's daughter.

"She's also known for her Christianity. She attends church regularly and tithes."

"Do-gooders often do." James could hardly see the attraction to such things. Still, the idea of anyone turning away from the possibility of inheriting millions was something unfathomable to him. Money was the most important thing in the world. One could not better himself in any way without it.

"And she flat out refused to even consider coming to Minneapolis?"

"Yes, sir. She wouldn't allow me to go into detail or even share information about you. I'm sorry, but I did try."

James nodded and rubbed his chin. "She intrigues me. Tell me, what does she look like?"

"She looks a great deal like the painting of your wife, sir. She has thick, wavy brown hair and brown eyes with lovely arched brows. Her features are delightful."

"So were her grandmother's."

"Yes, sir. Your sitting room painting of her is stunning."

"That was painted the year after we married." James remembered the outrageous cost of it as well. The portrait man had insisted on fifty dollars. Had the painting been anything less than perfection, James would have thrown the man out on his ear. But he had superior references and was highly regarded with paintings that hung in the better homes of society, so what else was there to be done?

"So she's beautiful and kind of heart. What else can you tell me about her?"

"She married in 1862, and her husband died in the war. There were no children. She's not remarried, nor does it appear she's sought to do so. She is educated and knowledgeable. She seems to be well-read and attends a great many lectures. I would venture to say she enjoys learning new information."

"She must come to me. She must!" He pounded his hand down on the desk just as Winchell returned with his medicine and a steaming cup of tea on a silver tray.

"Ah, Winchell, thank you." James waited as his valet placed the cup and saucer in front of him. Winchell took up the bottle of tonic next and looked to his employer.

"Should I put it in the tea?" he asked.

"Yes."

Winchell nodded and uncorked the bottle. Using a silver spoon, he measured out two spoonfuls of the medicine and stirred them into the tea before recorking the bottle.

"Will there be anything else, sir?"

"Return the medicine to my room and that will be all."

"Very good, sir." The salt-and-pepper-haired man turned with great formality, taking the bottle with him.

Once he was gone, James lifted the cup to his lips and took a long drink. The temperature was just perfect, and the medicine, although bitter, was tempered by the sugar Winchell had thoughtfully added.

In a few moments, James could feel his heart slow to a less frantic beat.

"You will make another trip there, Bert. You will convince her that she must come. Use whatever means necessary. In fact, tell her that I will donate to her favorite charity if she will but come visit me immediately."

"That might convince her. What amount should I offer?"

"Something she'll find impossible to refuse. Let's say, ten thousand dollars. Get a bank draft for that amount to take with you. Pull it from my bank in Boston. If her heart is so pure and her desire truly to help those less prosperous, then she'll be unable to refuse my request."

The attorney smiled. "She'll be able to help a great many people with that kind of money. Perhaps even build them a place to find shelter and care."

"Whatever she decides is fine by me, so long as she comes to Minneapolis before the end of the month. Do you understand me?"

Black nodded. "I do, sir, and I will see to it that this happens."

"Then go now. Take my private train car and convince my granddaughter to come."

Once Black left the room, James took his tea and made his way to the sitting room, where the painting of his wife was displayed over the fireplace. A footman appeared almost the moment James sat down.

"Would you care for a fire, sir?"

"Yes. Make a big one. I intend to be here a while." He finished his tea and placed the cup on the side table. "In fact, tell Mrs. Markle I will take my supper here."

"Very good, sir." The young man hurried to make the fire and waited just long enough for it to catch before leaving to relay the request.

James watched the dry logs begin to burn, and only once they were burning well did he lift his gaze to the portrait of his young wife, commissioned when she was just twenty-one and had given him a son. He remembered the delight he felt at the news. Every man needed an heir, and his son would fulfill that destiny. Or so he'd thought.

Now, however, he was once again in need of an heir, and the only one able to fill those shoes was a self-sufficient, stubborn woman who, from the sound of it, was more like her grandmother than she realized.

"Oh, Caroline," he murmured, studying the painting. The woman who looked back at him was glowing in pride and accomplishment. She had told him she would bear him a son, and she did exactly that. Sadly, she was never able to bring another baby full term, but it hadn't mattered at the time. James had been pleased with the boy who bore his name. For years he had taken instruction from his father, as well as correction. They had sent him to the best schools in Boston and kept him in the best company. Later, when he asked to go to Philadelphia for college, Caroline insisted they allow James Jr. to make his own choice.

What a mistake that had turned out to be.

And now James Sr. was forced to continue dealing with that mistake.

Heaving a sigh, he lowered his gaze to the fire. He could still see his wife's tear-filled eyes as he announced they would no longer have anything to do with their only son. She had begged him to reconsider, but he had refused. No one acted in the way their son had done and got away with it. James Jr. had been willful and disrespectful. He had chosen a mate from an unworthy family, ruining all his father's plans for the future.

The boy could have married anyone. He could have merged his line with royalty, but instead he chose a pauper's daughter.

James Sr. looked back up at the painting and could almost swear the woman who stared back was judging him. All his life, he had been able to control people with exception to two—his wife and son. Now it appeared that his granddaughter would be number three.

Unless, of course, he could find her price.

Bert was delighted with his new assignment. Returning to spend time in the company of Ashton's beautiful granddaughter was a delightful prospect. Having spent the last ten years working for the old man and enduring his tyrannical ways, Bert felt it was only fair that he have some kind of enjoyment at Ashton's expense.

Judith Ashton was more than fair pay. He imagined the possibility of spending wonderful evenings together. He wouldn't press too hard at first, but rather convince her to give him a chance to explain her grandfather. Perhaps he could take her to fine dinners or even the theater or a concert. She might feel it unnecessary, but Bert was sure he could find a way to convince her. Sometimes the only thing a woman desired was a little attention. Judith had been a widow for nearly seven years. And while she was older than he might have considered for a wife, she was still quite lovely.

There was also the matter of her bank account, which was even lovelier.

He rid himself of most of his clothes, then stretched out on top of his bed. The windows were open, and even though the air was a bit chilly, he enjoyed the feel against his skin.

"I must find a way to convince her to come," he said to no one. "Then I need to convince her to be mine."

He smiled to himself at the thought of the beautiful Judith Ashton in his arms. She would make him the envy of every man in the city, despite her connection to her wretched, ill-tempered grandfather.

Two weeks after dismissing Mr. Norbert Black, Judith found herself in his company once again. For reasons beyond her understanding, she had allowed Mr. Black to talk her into dinner. Now as they finished their main course of baked flounder with crab stuffing, she questioned the sanity of having said yes. All he wanted to do was convince her that she must come to Minneapolis and see her grandfather. And he seemed unwilling to take no for an answer.

"You need to understand. Frankly, it's a matter of gravest concern," Mr. Black reasoned. "Your grandfather is an old man and not long for this world."

"Why do you say that? Many men have lived well past seventy-five," Judith said, putting her fork aside.

Mr. Black pressed the napkin to his mouth, then returned it to his lap. "That is true; however, the doctor has made it clear that will not be the case with your grandfather. He has a heart condition that will not allow him to live much longer."

"I see." She drew a deep breath. Why did this situation have to fall upon her? Her grandfather had caused nothing but pain to her parents. Why should she yield to his request?

"He knows that you have reason to doubt the sincerity of his invitation, but he truly wants to know you. He has no one left."

"That was his choice." She waited for the waiter to take their plates before continuing. "My grandfather made his decision and now regrets it. Why should that matter to me?" She hated how callous her response sounded but didn't attempt to soften her tone.

Mr. Black leaned forward with a smile. "I know that you have been taught to hate him, but let his mistakes be forgotten."

"I was never taught to hate my grandfather." Judith's brow furrowed. She could feel the tension in her face and forced herself to calm. "My parents never hated him, nor will I. They felt sorry for him and pitied him for the loss in his life."

Mr. Black looked at her oddly. "Pitied James Ashton Sr.? That isn't something I have heard said before. Why pity one of the wealthiest men in the country?"

"Because while he might have money, he lacks what is truly important in life. First and foremost a relationship with God. My father said he never had time or interest for God. From what I've heard from you, that attitude remains unchanged."

"It's true. Mr. Ashton has never been a religious man."

Judith shrugged. "I feel sorry for anyone lacking a relationship with God. How does a person deal with the sorrows of life without God? How does my grandfather face his own demise without knowing what awaits him in eternity? He must be terrified."

Mr. Black chuckled. "Your grandfather is a great many things, but I hardly think terrified is one of them. I've never known a man with less fear. He cares not for what happens after this life. He's only driven to see this one well-lived."

"But it's not well-lived. Having served only himself and his ambitions, my grandfather forfeited the only things that truly mattered. He had a family but cast us all aside. He might have known love for a lifetime. As I understand it, my grandmother and father showed him great affection, and he turned away from them."

"He was a man of business. He was driven to provide for his family."

"At the cost of a relationship with them. Don't you find that sad?"

Mr. Black leaned back against the chair and seemed to really consider her words for a moment. "I suppose I do. I am not like him in the way that he doesn't need affection and affirmation in his life. I would cherish the love of a wife and child . . . children."

Judith smiled. "Most men would. Most women as well. We were not made to face life alone. Even so, a person can hardly be tied so completely to their job and bank account and still have anything left to share with another. My father longed for a relationship with his father. He had to turn to others to fill that void because his own father would have nothing to do with him. And why? Because he married the woman he loved, rather than allow my grandfather to assign him a mate by way of a beneficial financial arrangement."

"Still, it seems that he is seeking to make amends now. A Christian is called upon to forgive and forget."

"Forgive, yes. But forgetting is far more difficult, and I might say, both require divine assistance. People are not easily given to forgetting the wrong done to them."

"True, Mrs. Stanford. Very true. It is hard to forget those things people have done to us . . . hurtful and devastating things. I, too, struggle to let go of the past. That's why I can understand your hesitancy to forgive your grandfather. The two go so closely hand in hand. It must be difficult for you to let go of the wrongs he has done to you and your family."

Judith didn't care for the implication that she couldn't forgive her grandfather. Before Norbert Black had shown up, she hadn't given the old man much thought. The poor in Philadelphia consumed her time and efforts, and James Ashton Sr. was but a vague consideration. Until now.

"I'm sorry, Mr. Black. I suppose I seem harsh. Believe me, I am not. Since your first visit, I have thought of my grandfather and wondered whether I made the right decision. Seeing you back here so soon sends me yet again down a path of contemplation. It wouldn't be that difficult to board a train and go west to at least speak to him."

"I truly don't think you would regret it, and he has authorized this to sweeten the deal." Mr. Black reached into his coat and produced what appeared to be a bank draft. When he handed it to her, she realized that was exactly what it was. She was shocked by the amount of money represented there.

"What is this for?"

"Mr. Ashton knows that taking you away from your charity work is something that concerns you and affects your decision. He offers this donation as a means to provide for those charities while you're gone. Now you can come to him unconcerned by what your absence might mean to them, having already provided for their needs."

"I see." She studied the draft for a moment. Ten thousand dollars was a great deal of money. Certainly more than she had to share on her own. The benefits it could provide for the destitute were too great to ignore. She couldn't allow her pride and frustration with one old man to determine whether or not someone in need had a meal or warm place to stay.

"Very well," she said, looking up at Mr. Black. "It would appear that I can be bought."

He shook his head. "I don't see it that way at all. I see that you regard the needs of others above your own desires. That makes you quite admirable in my thoughts."

"Well, I'm not sure I'm deserving of your praise, but I can hardly allow such generosity to be forsaken."

"We can leave tomorrow. I have your grandfather's private train car at the ready."

"I will need a couple of days to put my affairs in order. I couldn't possibly leave until Friday." Judith was already making a mental list of things that would have to be done. Leaving for any great amount of time would require putting additional responsibilities on Helen.

By Friday, things were set in motion to allow Judith to leave Philadelphia without great concern that others would suffer in her absence. Helen would distribute her grandfather's money according to her instructions. Thankfully they hadn't yet sent invitations for the garden party and would wait until Judith's return to move forward on their plans. It would make for a good midsummer event.

Helen had readily accepted the additional responsibilities. She would oversee the charities as well as Judith's household. Judith knew that Mr. Barnes, her business manager, would be more than capable of handling all the riverboat financial affairs and her other investments. Oh, the blessing of having capable assistants.

Norbert Black was on her doorstep precisely at the agreed-upon hour of ten. Judith had her staff load her trunks onto his hired carriage. She'd had little idea of how long she'd be gone and so planned as concisely as possible. Still, it was difficult to know exactly what to bring.

Her grandfather was known to have one of the finest houses in Minneapolis, according to Mr. Black. Therefore, she was certain they would dress formally for the evening meal. Black had also told her that her grandfather was not given to evenings on the town or social gatherings. She'd decided against bringing any of her finer things for events like operas and ballroom parties. If such occasions arose in the short time she planned for her visit, Judith would simply beg off.

At the train station, the crowds were overwhelming. The rush of people coming and going was enough to make Judith question her sanity. Thankfully, James Ashton Sr. had a well-appointed private rail coach for travel, and she wouldn't find herself packed into the overcrowded passenger cars. The Ashton coach would allow for comfort and privacy. Perhaps too much privacy, where Mr. Black was concerned, but given that the porter would be constantly checking in with them, Judith felt it would be acceptable. Thankfully he would be sleeping elsewhere.

"I think you're going to like traveling this way. It's quite refined, and your grandfather spared no expense."

She was rather impressed by the car, though for its sensibility rather than its opulence. The walls were paneled in walnut, and the upholsteries were done in a sturdy damask. The sage-green background with cream-colored fleur-de-lis patterns made a stately, almost regal appearance.

At one end of the main room was a dining table and four chairs. At the other end were several overstuffed chairs and a small sofa. The row of windows on either side of the car had heavy green velvet draperies and shades for complete privacy.

"This is quite lovely," Judith said, observing every nook and cranny.

"Mr. Ashton hates traveling and figured if he had to go back and forth to Boston to attend his business affairs, he might as well do so in comfort. This particular car is only a year old. He had read that Queen Victoria was getting a new railcar and paid to learn the details. Her car has lighting and a bathroom of its own. He demanded no less."

"I do hope he finds some pleasures in life. It would be a shame to know nothing but work and distrust of others."

Mr. Black surprised her by laughing. "You so amply describe him. It's as if you have known him your entire life. He is definitely not a man of pleasures. He allows himself luxuries; however, I cannot say he finds any joy in such things. If he does, he certainly never says as much."

"How very sad. Again, I find great pity in my heart for such a man."

A knock sounded at the door, and the conductor came in. "We're ready to leave the station. Your lunch will be served once we're on our way. The porter will check on you regularly to see if there is anything else you need. Mr. Black, your sleeping quarters are directly ahead in the next car."

"Thank you." Mr. Black smiled. "See? All prim and proper. Your reputation will suffer no loss."

The conductor gave Judith a nod before leaving the room. It wasn't long before the train gave a series of jerks and groans as it pulled slowly from the station. Judith took a seat by the window to watch Philadelphia pass from view. She had traveled plenty in her adult years. Raising money for her charities had taken her to numerous places to offer encouraging speeches and solicit monies. She was well-known in the East for her passionate pleas to the wealthy on behalf of the poor. How very different this trip would be.

"I hope you're comfortable," Mr. Black said, joining her in the chair opposite. "I've traveled several times with Mr. Ashton, and this car allows for the best comforts."

"So it would seem. I've never known anything quite like it."

"Yes, well, Mr. Ashton wanted to make certain you were able to travel in style."

"Why?"

He looked at her oddly for a moment. "I beg your pardon?"

"Why should he care? He doesn't even know me."

"He knows you well enough. He had me learn what I could about you."

Judith didn't like the idea of being studied by strangers, but she supposed there was nothing to be done about it.

"A person can learn a lot about the day-to-day activities of someone and still not know them. I am doubtful that either of you have a true understanding of my nature."

"Well, it is obvious that you're generous and compassionate," Black countered.

"I suppose anyone involved with charities could be considered such, Mr. Black."

"Please call me Bert. Even your grandfather does on most occasions. Mr. Black is far too formal."

"Very well. And you may call me Judith." She studied the handsome man for a moment. His black hair and mustache were carefully coiffed, and his clothes were obviously tailored for his tall, slender frame. There was truly no fault in his appearance. However, there was something about his attitude that gave her pause.

"Thank you, Judith. I will enjoy that very much. I find your company to be . . . well, delightful."

"How did you meet my grandfather, Bert?" She hoped to keep him from focusing too much attention on her.

"My father was his solicitor in Boston. Before that, I believe he worked with my grandfather. They had a legal firm that handled all your grandfather's business dealings. When Mr. Ashton came to Minnesota in 1857, he encouraged my father to extend his services. I moved to Minnesota to become Mr. Ashton's private attorney. He even managed to keep me out of the war."

"But the war was brought on by many concerns and injustices. Were you not of a mind to see an end to slavery and the country unified?"

"It mattered little to me one way or another. I did not own slaves but could certainly not fault those who did."

"I could and did. Slavery is an abominable thing."

"Even the Bible made provision for slaves," he argued.

"Perhaps provision, but not approval."

"Either way, it wasn't for me to impose my desires on another."

Judith had much less respect for him with that statement. "Sometimes we must take a stand in order to help our fellow man." She could see that she wasn't going to change his mind easily. "Well then, you are my grandfather's lawyer. Do you also have other clients?"

"No. I handle all of his legal affairs and only his. It commands all my time."

"I'm sure it does."

"Your grandfather is not one to sit idle and allow others to arrange his affairs. He's very active in his business."

"And what is his business?"

"Making money." Bert gave a laugh and crossed his legs. "Your grandfather has his hand in just about anything that turns a profit. He has vast forests that are being logged and sawmills to turn those logs into lumber. He's invested in the brickyards, railroads, steel and flour mills, and a bevy of smaller businesses, as well as shipping out of Boston and textile mills."

"And what does he do with that fortune of his?"

"Invests it wisely and makes even more money."

"But to what purpose?"

"I don't follow you." Bert truly looked confused.

"For what purpose does he continue growing his fortune? He doesn't help anyone with it, nor does it sound as if there has been any great benefit to himself or his family."

"He lives in luxury. That's a great benefit, given so many others live in poverty and have little."

"My point exactly. How can one live happily knowing that they have the means to make life better for others, but then do nothing? It seems to me that though my grandfather has accumulated vast earthly treasures, he now finds himself at the end of his life. He cannot take such treasure with him, and yet he has no one to share it with. He could give it to charities and bless thousands, but that is not his heart either."

"Which is why he's considering you."

Judith glanced back outside as the train picked up speed. Had she made the right decision? Perhaps she should just get off at the next station and make her way home. This entire affair troubled her in ways she couldn't begin to explain, and she couldn't shake the feeling that her entire life was about to be turned upside down.

"You look a great deal like your grandmother," Bert said, turning the conversation back to Judith. "She was a great beauty. I didn't know her personally, but there's a portrait of her in your grandfather's house. You could be her twin."

"My father told me as much." She had always liked that she resembled her grandmother. Her father held deep affection for the woman, and not just because she continued to sneak correspondences and money to him after Grandfather had removed them from his life. She was a woman of faith who offered sage counsel and godly encouragement. Father had always maintained that his mother was a prized jewel among women.

"She had the same wavy, dark brown hair and even arranged it in a similar fashion like you with the part in the middle and the two sides swept back. But not tight. Some women pull their hair back so tightly that it appears unnatural. Yours is fashioned in such a manner that seems refined and yet almost casual."

Judith laughed and touched her hand to the back of her neck. "Yes, well it's hardly casual. There's so much of it that it takes a little bit of time to see it all put in place. But enough of that. Tell me more about my grandfather's home in Minneapolis, please."

"His estate is actually on the St. Anthony side of the river."

"And what river is that?"

"The Mississippi, of course. It is a vital part of our city. Congress is even considering all manner of projects for bettering that waterway. I've heard it said that one day, everyone will use the river for travel."

"I would love to see that. I grew up on riverboats."

The conversation continued until lunch was served, and after that the porter suggested perhaps Judith would like to rest. He opened a door beyond the dining area to reveal a lovely bedroom that had a private washroom. On a stand not far from the door, someone had deposited a few pieces of her luggage.

After the porter left, Judith closed the door and locked it. She had no desire for anyone to just walk in on her while she rested. Despite what Bert claimed to know about her, Judith was an extremely private person. People might well know about her charitable work, but few knew much about Judith Ashton the woman. And frankly, she intended to keep it that way.

Life had dealt her some heavy blows. Death had come too early and often in her life. Her heart was quite scarred from those visits, and she was determined to refrain from close relationships.

While she cherished many of her riverboat memories, her first encounter with death had been on one when she was seven and her little brother Franklin was four. At the time, her father owned and piloted a paddle-wheeler. Despite their parents' warnings to stay away from the railing and never go near the water without one of them at their side, Franklin fell from the paddle-wheeler and drowned in the river.

Her youngest brother, Jonathan, was just a year old at the time. Death came for him seventeen years later during the War Between the States, shortly after she had lost her husband and just before she lost her parents. Death was more than a casual acquaintance, and Judith wasn't at all certain she could bear to lose even one more person she loved.

Perhaps that had been the reason she'd never ventured to Minneapolis to inquire about Dr. Turner. She had definitely been attracted to him, but thoughts of losing her heart to him, and the price that might have to be paid, prevented her from taking any action.

But seeing Grandfather Ashton wasn't something she felt would cause her pain. She supposed that was the only reason she had finally agreed to go see her dying grandfather. That and his generous donation to her charities.

She'd like to say that indifference was all she could offer James Ashton Sr., but there was unfortunate regret when she thought of him. The grandfather she'd never known. The man who rejected his own son all for the sake of pride and social standing. What was she to do with such a man?

Was this all a mistake?

Judith's first thoughts of Minnesota were quite positive. The place was in full spring bloom, and the air, although a bit humid, was filled with a variety of scents. Bert had explained that her grandfather lived on the east side of the Mississippi River in a community called St. Anthony. Minneapolis, on the west side of the river, was where her grandfather conducted most of his business.

Judith had never seen the Mississippi River but knew from what Bert told her that only a fraction of its volume ran through Minneapolis. Still, it was a busy river, with falls that aided the mills and small islands that had been utilized for rich and poor alike. Bert shared that there was a wealthy community of folks who had built extravagant homes on Nicollet Island, while at the other end were sawmills. One of which her grandfather owned.

Her grandfather's neighborhood in St. Anthony was well groomed with lovely homes. Nearby, the wealthier folks had spared no expense to cultivate impressive grounds. Her grandfather's acreage had lush lawns with perfectly trimmed bushes that lined the circle drive of carefully positioned paving stones. The house itself was a three-story masterpiece done up in blond-colored brick.

"As you can see for yourself, Mr. Ashton has put quite a bit of money and effort into having one of the most beautiful homes in the area," Bert said as they drove up the lane.

"I was just admiring the color of the bricks. I must say I find them charming."

"People all over the country demand that brick. It's produced in the brickyards of Chaska, just a few miles from here. Your grandfather owns one. He quickly saw the value of the product and has used it on multiple occasions. His home is considered one of the finest examples of the brick's quality."

"It is lovely." Judith let her gaze travel the full length of the house as the driver came to a stop at the front door. There were four cream-colored circular columns supporting an entryway portico. The windows were all trimmed out with arched embellishments and dark green shutters.

"There's a beautiful garden in the back for strolling. Your grandfather takes daily walks, even in the winter. At least he used to," Bert corrected himself. "His health has not allowed him to do that of late. But you'll find that the gardeners have created quite an oasis. There are fountains and flowers of every kind. Just wait until you see it in full summer bloom."

"How nice." Judith drew a deep breath. She was more than a little bit nervous about meeting her grandfather.

The footman came to open the door to the carriage. Bert jumped down and quickly offered her a hand. Judith descended the steps and kept what she hoped was a calm expression on her face, just in case her grandfather was watching from one of the windows. She neither wanted to seem too eager, nor indifferent to the situation.

She ran her gloved hand down the side of her burgundy-colored jacket. The traveling suit was quite smart. She had ordered it made in a durable but lightweight material and found it most comfortable for long journeys.

"I suppose I'm as ready as I'll ever be," she said, looking at her companion.

"You look lovely, and remember, you favor his beloved wife. He's going to be quite taken with you, I'm sure."

They climbed the three steps to the landing, and Bert went to the door and knocked. "I will say this much. He can be quite intimidating, but you have a strong spirit. I know you'll be able to hold your own."

Judith nodded, and it was only a few moments before a rather attractive woman opened the door. She nodded and stepped back.

"This is Mrs. Deeters, the housekeeper," Bert announced.

The woman glanced at Bert. "Mr. Black."

"How is he today?"

"Quite well. He's been anxious for your arrival." Her tone betrayed a hint of discomfort. Perhaps she felt the anxiety of the moment.

"Well, this is Mrs. Stanford, the woman he's been waiting for."

"I'm pleased to meet you, Mrs. Stanford." Mrs. Deeters ushered them farther into the foyer and closed the door.

"The pleasure is mine." Judith smiled, hoping the woman would relax.

Judith took the time to glance around. There was far too much to take in. The highly polished staircase was to one side of the foyer, while a hallway ran down the other side. To her left and right were pocket doors that were closed as if to keep prying eyes from making an examination.

The foyer itself was a stately receiving room with fine art hanging on the walls and an entryway table gracing the center of the room. Upon this, there was a lovely arrangement of flowers—white peonies, lilacs, and a variety of other blooms.

"This is all so beautiful," Judith whispered.

"Mr. Ashton would like you to be seated here. He will join you momentarily." Mrs. Deeters opened the door to the left and revealed a well-appointed sitting room.

Judith followed Bert into the room, once again trying to take it all in at once. It was obvious that her grandfather demanded the finer things of life. The furnishings were of the highest quality. Judith was used to being in opulent homes, as she spent her life convincing the wealthy to donate to her causes for the poor. She recognized the Axminster rug in its regal hues of cream, red, and orange with just the right splashes of green and blue—one of the few types of rug whose origins were English rather than oriental.

Equally impressive was the array of Hepplewhite tables and stuffed-back chairs. The chairs' carved tapered legs and intricate scrolling left little doubt to their value. She claimed one for herself, while Bert took an identical chair across from her.

Judith had just caught sight of a marble statue in the far corner when an old man entered the room. His gaze rested upon her. She returned his stare without thought. He was balding with snowy white hair encircling the lower half of his head. A white mustache was neatly trimmed beneath a slightly bulbous nose. But it was his eyes that drew Judith's attention. They were deep-set and dark. Even though he said nothing, she felt that James Ashton Sr. was passing judgment upon her.

Bert rose. "Mr. Ashton, may I introduce you to your granddaughter, Judith."

"I know who she is." Her grandfather might well be dying, but his voice did not betray any weakness. It was strong and bore the tone of a man used to giving orders and being annoyed with the world.

"I'm pleased that you arrived without incident," he said, giving Judith yet another once-over. "Mrs. Deeters will show you to your room, where you may rest until dinner this evening. Mr. Black, you may go."

The old man turned to leave, but Bert was clearly disturbed by being dismissed. "I thought you might want to discuss the trip with me."

The older man looked at him for a moment as if trying to decide what to do with him. He shook his head. "There will be time. Go now. I have business."

"I can aid you in that."

Judith wasn't sure why Bert was trying so hard to remain in her grandfather's company, but it was clear he was unneeded.

"Just go," her grandfather commanded, leaving the room.

Mrs. Deeters immediately entered and went to Judith. "I will show you to your room. I've already had your trunks taken upstairs, and two of the maids are attending to your wardrobe. You'll be in the Lilac Room."

Judith turned to Bert, who seemed at a complete loss. "I suppose we shall meet again. Farewell for now."

"Yes." He smiled. "I should very much like to continue seeing you."

"I'm sure you will, since you work for my grandfather." She left the matter at that and followed Mrs. Deeters from the room.

As they climbed the stairs, the housekeeper began to explain some of the workings of the household. "Your grandfather keeps an office on the first floor. It is forbidden for anyone to step foot in that room without the specific invitation of Mr. Ashton. Otherwise, the house will be at your disposal on the first and second floors. The third floor contains servant quarters and storage, so there is no need for you to concern yourself with it."

They reached the top of the grand staircase, and Mrs. Deeters crossed to the left. Here again the furnishings were of the finest quality.

"To the right of the stairs is the hall that takes you to your grandfather's suite. He despises noise and asks that the house be shrouded in silence from ten at night until eight o'clock in the morning. Therefore, please refrain from singing or any type of noisemaking that might disturb him."

"He sounds rather difficult to please." Judith offered her comment without thinking. Still, she didn't apologize.

"Here at the far end of the west wing is your suite. We call it the Lilac Room because your grandmother appointed it as such."

They entered through double doors, and Judith immediately found herself in a calming sea of femininity. The walls were both papered and painted in a soft lavender hue. White trim edged the windows, and beautiful crown molding highlighted the ceilings. On the oak floors were a variety of rugs woven in hues of purple and all the shades it could offer. Some were done in flowery designs, while others were more geometric in their patterns.

"As you can see for yourself, you have a fine sitting room here. It's still quite chilly in the evening, so a fire will be laid while you're at dinner. Should you want one any other time of the day, simply ring." Mrs. Deeters pointed to the dark purple cord. "In fact, should you require anything, you have but to ring and I will attend you."

Just beyond a rather comfortable-looking sofa, a door opened and two young ladies dressed in black with white aprons appeared. In their arms they carried Judith's best dresses. They curtsied in front of Judith.

Mrs. Deeters made the introductions. "This is Harriet and Beth. They will be available to help you dress and arrange your hair. They will also make certain that your room is to your liking. Should you need anything at all, just let them know."

"Thank you. I'm pleased to meet you both."

The girls bobbed again but said nothing. Mrs. Deeters

quickly took over. “Girls, go get those dresses pressed. Miss Ashton will need something to wear for dinner this evening.” The girls hurried from the room. It was clear they were well trained and used to working fast.

“I have arranged a bath for you,” Mrs. Deeters continued. “Through this door you have your bathing and dressing room. Beyond that is your bedroom. I had the girls lay out your nightgown and robe.”

A hot bath sounded wonderful. The long days of travel, even in a beautiful private train car, were beginning to catch up with her. She suppressed a yawn.

“I shall be quite blessed to have a hot bath,” Judith said, smiling. “Thank you for such thoughtfulness.”

Mrs. Deeters looked at her for a moment with a hint of a frown. “We are here to serve. You have only to let your needs be known.”

Judith wasn’t sure what had caused the older woman displeasure, but she decided to say nothing. Her only focus for the moment was a bath. After that, she could give more thought to her grandfather and his household. No doubt there would be plenty to consider.

“Will you require help bathing?”

“Goodness no.” Judith shook her head. “I can manage just fine on my own.” After all, she’d been doing exactly that most of her life.

“I’ve heard that Mr. Ashton has company coming to stay,” Claudette told her brother as he finished doing up the buttons of a clean shirt.

Roman had come home to change after a feverish child threw up on him. Such were the risks involved in treating children, and he took it in stride.

“Poor Aunt Mary will no doubt have her hands full and

get little time away from the house." Roman remembered other times when Ashton had business associates come to stay. His aunt had spoken of the disruption and problems such visits caused. It seemed Mr. Ashton was not a man who desired to play host to anyone, yet found himself obligated at times.

Claudette brought Roman a clean black tie and helped him knot it in the front and tuck the ends under his shirt's collar. He quickly pulled on his suit coat, which thankfully he'd not been wearing when the child became ill. Through the years he'd learned to discard his jacket as soon as he started looking at patients in the orphanage. It had saved his coat on more than one occasion.

"Did Daniel mention how the men are doing after that accident at the sawmill?" Roman asked.

"Only that they're already back at work. They can't afford to miss more. The money is too important to their families."

"They'll heal faster if they give themselves time. I understand the need for financial support, but those were some seriously deep cuts I stitched."

Claudette brushed the back of his coat, then came around to the front to touch up the lapels. She smiled. "There. You're perfect. Where are you off to now?"

"I have a meeting with Reverend Knickerbacker." He kissed the top of her head. "I should be home early. Maybe I'll have time to fix the roof." The last thunderstorm had lifted some of the shingles and caused damage that needed to be repaired. Roman had been waiting for a free moment to get to the task.

Heading off down the street, Roman tried to focus on the positive. The neighborhood was a decent one where he didn't worry about his mother and sister being by themselves on nights when he was delayed in getting home. Their house, although small, was paid for in full thanks to a bonus Roman had received after the war. They did what they could to get by, and for all purposes, their lives were good. So why did he feel so overwhelmed and frustrated?

It seemed impossible to rid himself of the heaviness that seemed to weigh him down each day. His father had once been so successful. They'd lived well and enjoyed plenty. Roman knew this wasn't the life his father had desired for his family, and yet when his fortunes had changed due to the corruption of James Ashton, rather than fight . . . he'd given up.

Sometimes remembering that his father had willed himself to die was more than Roman could consider. His father's death was still talked about in hushed whispers. The Turner family had been well received in Minnesota. Having invested in the area with a confidence that he intended to make his mark, Andrew Turner had been highly regarded. He owned numerous pieces of property, as well as investments in several businesses. Roman had known his father to be a risk taker of the very best kind. He put great thought into any project, weighing the good and bad, the possible with the improbable. He had been prudent, but willing to see beyond the immediate to what the future could hold.

Then James Ashton came into the picture and changed everything. Roman clenched his fists just thinking about the man. How could God have allowed his father to be so clearly duped? It wasn't in Andrew Turner's nature to act the fool, but he'd somehow been convinced to sign over his holdings to a ruthless land baron like James Ashton. Roman had never had a chance to speak to his father on the matter, and his mother had never fully understood what happened except that Ashton stole everything in a manner that was just this side of legal.

God, I pray for deliverance every day. How can that man be allowed to continue as he does—hurting others and robbing people blind? When will You give us justice? My mother and sister deserve more. My meager salary keeps food on the table, but there's never anything left for more.

He heaved a sigh and paused to cross one of the busier streets. How could God remain silent on the matter for so long? Was God even listening?

Judith had dressed in her freshly pressed gown of salmon-colored silk with cream braid trim. She'd taken extra care with her hair and spent nearly half an hour before dinner in prayer. She didn't know what to think of this man who had greeted her with but a few words, then left her on her own until dinner. She hadn't even spoken to him.

Even now as she sat at one end of his dining table while he sat at the other, Judith was completely uncertain of her decision to come to Minneapolis. Perhaps it had all been a big mistake. Maybe she was wrong to take his money, even if it had already benefited so many.

The servants came and placed course after course in front of them. It was some of the most delicious food Judith had ever consumed. Still, she remained silent. She was determined to say nothing until her grandfather initiated the conversation. Guarding her mouth was something she had learned at an early age. Mama had always told her that it was a wise person who had self-control over their tongue. Judith had learned to listen first and speak later, and it had served her well.

After almond torte for dessert, Judith dabbed her napkin to her lips. Her grandfather got to his feet and rang for one of the servants.

"We'll take coffee in the sitting room," he told the young man who appeared. The servant gave a curt nod and left the room without a word.

Judith got to her feet and was surprised to find another man at the ready to assist her with her chair.

"The sitting room is just through the archway and across

the hall," her grandfather instructed. He headed that way, not even bothering to wait for her to catch up.

She followed at a leisurely pace, glancing around at the dining room she'd already studied throughout the meal. She didn't want to seem too eager. Her grandfather was something of a puzzle to her. Aside from what Bert had told her, she knew only what little her father had shared. The man was very nearly a complete mystery to her.

"Have a seat. I'm sure you have questions, and I have some of my own." The old man motioned her into the room. Judith chose the throne chair nearest to the fireplace. She had been chilled all evening and relished the warmth that spread over her body.

James Ashton seemed surprised by her choice. He watched her a moment and then snapped his fingers. Just like that, the same young man who'd helped her earlier was there to draw up a matching chair, placing it surprisingly close to her own. She thought it strange that this man who had kept them at a distance throughout the meal would now seek more intimate seating.

She glanced upward and caught sight of the painting. Judith gasped. It might have been a portrait of herself.

"Yes, you look just like her," her grandfather said, lifting his gaze to the picture. "I was quite startled by it myself, despite Mr. Black having warned me."

"He mentioned it to me as well, but I had no idea of it being such a close match." Judith was surprised by the joy in her grandmother's expression. "She seems so happy."

"She had just given birth to your father some months prior. She was happy."

"She loved him a great deal."

Her grandfather said nothing. Perhaps the memories of such things caused him discomfort and even pain. Judith wasn't completely without sympathy.

"I've done my research on you, Judith. I know quite a bit about you."

"I'm afraid I know very little about you." She watched to see how he might take that news.

The firelight reflected in his eyes as he gave a curt nod. "As I suspected. I'm sure that my son was probably severe in his opinions of me, but there's nothing that I can do about that. He was always willful and opinionated."

Judith had no desire to listen to this stranger disparage her father. "Why have you asked me here?"

Her grandfather chuckled. "I've been told you have no difficulty in speaking your mind. Well, good for you. I have asked you here because my health is failing me."

The footman appeared with the coffee. He poured a cup for Judith's grandfather and then asked her if she would care for any. She declined and waited for the old man to continue.

He seemed to be in no hurry. He sipped the steaming liquid, then placed the cup and saucer on the table beside him. It was clear he would set the pace for their conversation.

"I know that Mr. Black informed you about my health. The fact is simply that my heart is giving out. I have no heir, and as you can see and have probably heard, I have a great deal of wealth that I've accumulated over the years. I've asked you here so that I might know you better and deem your worthiness to be my successor."

"I see. I suppose it would do me little good to reiterate what I said when Mr. Black first came to see me."

"That you aren't interested in my money?"

Judith met the man's skeptical expression. "Exactly so."

"I find, Judith, that everyone has their price. You gave in for a ten-thousand-dollar donation to help your charities."

"I could hardly deprive the poor and suffering. This trip is an inconvenience, but the benefits to those in need mattered a great deal more than my comfort."

"So you despise me?"

Judith couldn't help the smile that touched her lips. "I neither despise you, nor care for you. You have no place in my life."

The old man frowned. "You must be of some opinion toward me."

She nodded. "As I mentioned to Mr. Black, I feel pity for you."

"Pity!" He practically roared the word.

Judith had anticipated his reaction and sat unmoved. "Yes. Pity. It was the emotion my father associated with you as well. We felt sorry for you."

"Sorry? So-sorry? You—you cannot—" The old man sputtered and cleared his throat. "I am not someone to be pitied. I have everything that a man could possibly want."

"Except an heir, apparently."

"You are as willful as your father."

She laughed. "I am, after all, an Ashton."

"No!" he declared, jumping to his feet. "You cannot call yourself that until you earn the right. It might be the name given you at birth, but as I told your father, that name holds with it much responsibility and esteem. You must prove yourself."

"I'm afraid I am no one's puppet or performer." She stood. "I'm sorry, but it was a mistake for me to come. However, I'm certain your money has blessed a great many people in Philadelphia, and for that I am grateful."

"I desire you to stay."

She looked at him for a long moment. "I realize you are a man used to getting whatever you want; however, I see no reason to remain. I am a Christian woman, and you find no value in such things. I'm a worker of charities and desire to better the lives of the poor. You apparently have no interest in that either. There's very little we have in common, and I can only suppose that this makes me a poor choice for your heir."

"I'll give you another ten thousand for your charities if you'll remain with me until I die. The doctor is convinced that it won't be longer than a couple of months. Perhaps the end of summer."

Judith was surprised by this but said nothing. She knew he was sick, but he seemed so strong and obstinate that it was easy to forget. Still, the last thing she wanted was to spend her summer in his company. The money was hardly worth it.

"Make it twenty thousand," he said, seeming to read her mind.

She was nothing more than a business transaction to him. If that's the way he wanted it, Judith could play the game. "Thirty thousand, and I will consider it prayerfully and give you an answer in the morning."

He smiled as if knowing he'd won. It nearly caused her to take back her words, but if he agreed to it, then Judith could arrange to have homes built for quite a few families in Philadelphia.

"Very well. Thirty thousand dollars will be given to you at the end of the summer, whether or not I choose you to be my heir. I'll have a contract drawn up tomorrow that you can sign if you agree to stay."

Judith nodded. It would take a great deal of prayer to know if she was making the right choice. It could benefit so many, but then again, the Bible admonished her to flee the devil. At the moment, she wasn't at all convinced that the man standing before her wasn't the very incarnation of that entity.

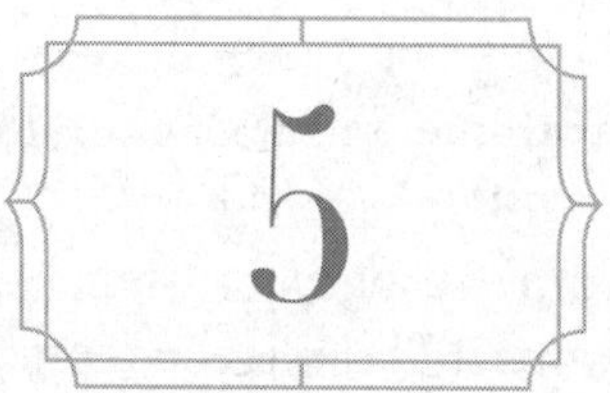

Sitting across from her grandfather the next morning, Judith noted the space between them wasn't nearly as extensive as it had been the night before. It was clear that several leaves had been removed from the massive table, and now they were only a dozen or so feet apart. Whether this was regularly done for the purpose of a less formal breakfast, or her grandfather had hoped to show her that he was willing to draw her closer, Judith had no idea. It was, however, a more comfortable setting, and after such a restless night, she found herself grateful.

When James Ashton appeared and took his seat, the servants immediately brought breakfast to the table. Judith was not surprised to be served rather than given a choice. It seemed to be her grandfather's fashion. Thankfully, his choices were like her own. Scrambled eggs, bacon, and toast.

The footman appeared at her side with a cup of tea, a small pitcher of cream, and a sugar bowl. She thanked him and then bowed her head to pray over the meal, knowing her grandfather wouldn't concern himself with such things. When she finished, she looked up to find him watching her.

"So have you decided?" he asked, wasting no time.

"I have." She saw no reason to draw out the matter. "I will accept your offer on two conditions. One, the money will be released immediately. I want it sent directly to the charity I set up for widows and orphans in Philadelphia. This way houses can be built for them prior to winter. Second, you will agree to attend church with me on Sundays, so long as your health allows."

He fixed her with a glaring expression. "And how do I know you'll keep your word if I release the money now?"

"How do you ever know if your investments will come to fruition? You must take a chance. I am a woman well-known for keeping my word. You will simply have to accept that, or we have no deal . . . sir." She added the title of respect, hoping to show that she wasn't without regard to his position.

"You know I'm not a religious man."

"I do, but frankly that is unimportant to me at this point. It is a condition of my staying, and I won't be moved on this matter."

He frowned and lowered his gaze. She could see that he was wrestling with the decision. He wasn't used to anyone making demands of him.

Judith picked up her fork and began to eat. There was no sense in further discussing the matter. She didn't want to fight with him, yet as she prayed about what to do, she felt convinced that requiring his church attendance was of the utmost importance. The man was desperate for her to remain, so she had a bit of an edge.

She sampled the eggs and found them light and fluffy. The bacon was crisp, and the toast a perfect golden brown. She had to admit that whoever the cook was, they were quite capable, and she was determined to enjoy her meal.

"I will attend Sunday services with you, but do not ask me to participate in any other way. I will not tithe monies, nor be drawn into any position of service."

"Nor would I expect you to be, sir." Judith waited for him to continue.

"And I suppose I have no choice but to send the money immediately. You seem determined to have your way."

She almost chuckled at the resignation in his voice. He might not like having conditions put on his demands, but he knew when he'd been defeated. Still, she remained silent. Judith had no desire to further antagonize the man.

"I will have Mr. Black make the arrangements and see the money forwarded. He'll be by this morning, so if you would be so kind as to write down instructions for mailing, I will see to the rest."

"Thank you, sir."

He looked up at her for a long silent moment. "You may call me grandfather."

She couldn't help the smile that formed on her lips. "I will call you that when you have earned the right."

His brow arched in surprise, then he gave a slight nod. "Quite clever. You have a quick wit." He picked up his coffee cup. "You're very much like your grandmother. She wasn't afraid to confront me or stand up to me when convinced she was right."

"I'm glad to hear that. My father said his mother loved you very much. One cannot love another when their relationship is burdened with fear. I will do my best to respect your position, but I will not fear you nor be bullied by you. There can be nothing of quality in our endeavor to know one another if fear is the foundation."

"It has been a long time since anyone stood up to me. I believe your father might well have been the last to attempt such a thing, and I refused his attitude in full."

Judith shrugged. "You see where that got you."

He nodded, then took a long sip from his cup. Judith wondered what he was thinking. Her defiance and strong will weren't things she offered merely to be obstinate. She felt confident that standing her ground was important. They would never be able to have a true understanding of each other, nor any kind of friendship, if they didn't offer mutual respect and consideration.

"I'm sure your father had little regard for me. However, his upbringing was good, and we were quite close at one time."

"I know. He often told me. He said you were never given to common pleasures or playfulness, but you were good and patient in teaching him a variety of things that served him well."

"I'm surprised that he was so generous in his comments."

"My father loved you," Judith countered, not bothering to look up. "He said there was a time when he was certain you loved him as well, but then another replaced him."

"Another? What nonsense are you speaking?"

She continued to focus on the food and picked up another piece of toast. "Money. Your desire for money replaced your love of him."

"The one had nothing to do with the other. Unless you consider that making money was important to maintain the welfare of the family. That is the duty and responsibility of the head of any household. It was my task to provide a good life for my wife and child, and I did exactly that. Your father never wanted for anything. Neither did his mother."

"Except love." She met his gaze and saw the look of confusion. "Your focus on provision robbed them of your tenderness and love. You became cold and indifferent, but they never gave up hope that you would somehow return to them."

"This is not an accurate accounting. I was not harsh, nor was I cruel toward them."

"No? Perhaps not to your way of seeing it, but you abandoned them when they refused to yield to loving the only thing you loved. Money was not what my father needed. He needed the love of his father. He needed your presence in his life to encourage him and offer guidance in matters that pertained to more than just finance."

"I tried to offer him guidance when he chose a poor man's daughter to marry."

"He was in love with my mother and she with him. It's true she brought little financial wealth to the table, but her heart was given completely, and for that he benefited far more than if he'd been given a wagonful of gold. You never knew him or his life after that. You couldn't see how he took the principles you taught him about hard work and made a good living for himself."

"He could have had so much more if he'd just been willing to do things my way," her grandfather said with apparent regret.

Judith shook her head. "He had it all and was quite happy. And, despite your lack of belief in God, we were heaven-blessed. God's hand was upon us, and Papa's business dealings reaped great reward. When he died, he left me quite comfortable."

"He could have left you more if he'd done my will."

"I'm glad he sought God's will instead. He lived by example, and through his instruction and beliefs, my faith grew and matured. I will never regret that he sought his heavenly Father at the abjuration of his earthly one. It was to his blessing and benefit, as well as mine."

If her words caused pain, James Ashton didn't reveal it. He remained stoic in his expression, and after a moment of contemplation, he lowered his gaze and went back to eating. Judith wondered at his thoughts but let the matter drop.

They finished breakfast in silence, but as her grandfather stood, he took out his watch and addressed her once again. "I wish to take you for a ride around town at ten. Be ready." He left without another word.

Judith breathed a heavy sigh. She felt as if she'd just done battle. If every breakfast was this exhausting, she might well have to plan for a time of rest afterward. She smiled nevertheless. She had gotten what she wanted. Her grandfather would attend church, and the women and orphans of Philadelphia would have lodgings and food. So far, she'd done a good day's work.

James Ashton was more than a little impressed with his granddaughter. She was able to hold her own with him, and that alone made her unique. Bert had told him she was quite intelligent, handling all sorts of business dealings for her various charities. Bert had also dug up some information on her personal investments. Unlike many others who relied upon financial advisors, Judith was known to investigate matters for herself and make her own decisions. James liked that about her, even though he would advise her in the future to seek his counsel.

Of course, he wouldn't be around much longer if the doctors were correct in their assessment of his health. That would necessitate acting fast, pushing her to learn the things that he had in mind to teach her. They barely knew each other, and although he had maneuvered her into spending the summer in his company, there was no telling if she would willingly take instruction.

Bert Black showed up at eight thirty as usual. He appeared at the office and was announced by Mrs. Deeters.

"Come in, Bert. Let's get right down to business. I need you to attend to several things for me today."

"That's why I'm here." He opened his case and pulled out a small book. "What would you like to discuss first?"

“I have made an arrangement with Judith. She’s going to remain here for the summer. In return, I am donating thirty thousand dollars to her widows and orphans fund. See her for the address and arrange for the money to be wired from the bank in Boston.”

Bert jotted down notes. “Very good, sir.”

“When am I meeting with the new architect regarding my block?” His plans for the Ashton Block had been delayed when the original architect moved to Chicago.

“You have a meeting scheduled with them tomorrow at ten.”

“Very good. I expect you to be there. Oh, and I want Judith there as well. It’s important she learn the plans and know what my wishes are since she will most likely be the one to see them carried out.”

“Yes, of course.” Bert continued writing.

“And as much as I detest the idea, we should probably plan some sort of engagement to introduce Judith to our society. Speak to Mrs. Deeters and Mrs. Markle regarding the arrangements. Perhaps we could host a dinner party.” He frowned. “I hate such affairs. It vexes me to even think about strangers making their way through my house.”

“Maybe someone in the community might be encouraged to host a gathering on Judith’s behalf,” Bert suggested.

“She has insisted that I join her for Sunday church services. She might meet someone there who might do the job.”

“I could attend with you and keep a view toward such a goal.”

“Yes, yes. That might work. Let’s delay on hosting, then, and see what might develop.”

“Yes, sir.” Black looked up. “Which church has she chosen to attend?”

James scowled. He hadn’t even thought to ask her if she had some place in mind. Then again, why should she? It wasn’t like she was from the area.

"I have no idea. I suppose she'll tell me when she has decided."

"Most likely. She's probably already researched the matter. Is that all the new business?"

"Yes. Now what have you brought me regarding the old?" James knew the man would have a variety of business dealings for him to manage.

"I have the contract you wanted to put together with the Redford Logging Company. I believe you'll find the changes you requested have been made. I've brought it for your review." Black produced a stack of papers from his case.

Black prattled on regarding various investments that needed James's attention. The man was worth the money he paid, but James wasn't of a mind to focus on business. Judith's presence had somewhat disoriented him. His entire world seemed turned upside down. Even given the way Black had described his granddaughter, James had not expected the woman who showed up at his door.

Then again, maybe it was just his growing heart problem. He gave a light rub to the center of his chest. He didn't like knowing that his time was short. The doctor had made it seem that no matter what he did at this point, James could not stop the inevitability of his passing. Having been in control of himself for nearly sixty years, James found it inconceivable that he should have that power stripped away without warning. But all the money in the world could not buy him extra time, and that reality was only starting to sink in. It was a rather empty feeling.

Roman left the patient he'd been checking on and headed down the street. He had promised his mentor, Dr. Lester, that he would meet him and Reverend Knickerbacker at eleven so that they could further discuss plans for the charity hospital Knickerbacker was determined to see built.

He started to cross the street when he spied Ashton's carriage. The ornate golden *A* on the side door left no doubt as to whom the carriage belonged. Not only that, but the old man himself was sitting there as large as life. He was pointing out something to his companion, a woman. Roman couldn't imagine who she might be or, frankly, what woman would even wish to keep company with the old man when he had quite the reputation as a curmudgeon. Roman remembered hearing that Ashton was going to have company. Perhaps she was some distant family member. Poor woman.

Ashton seemed to be caught up in telling her something, and neither noticed Roman as the carriage moved down the street.

That was the way Ashton had been all the time Roman's family had known him. The man simply didn't care enough to notice anyone or their needs. Roman wished the matter didn't continue to trouble him as it did. His father was dead, and no amount of contemplation would bring him back. Holding a grudge wouldn't change the heart of his enemy.

But it was so easy to remember that Ashton had duped his father. Mother had said the entire matter was finished before his father had even attempted to explain to her what was going to happen. For reasons beyond her understanding, Ashton had convinced her husband to temporarily sign over the properties he possessed in Minneapolis. Supposedly this was an action done in good faith to secure a large loan. Everything was legal. But problems haunted the project at every turn, and in the end, things had fallen apart rather quickly. When Ashton decided to put an end to the arrangement, there was little Roman's father could do but accept his fate. The property remained in Ashton's hands, and Andrew Turner learned a hard lesson about dealing with the ruthless man.

Though it wasn't as if his father had sought counsel or even took time to discuss the project with his friends, and by the time he did take the matter up with a lawyer, it was too late. The lawyer studied the contracts and could find no chance of seeing the property returned to Roman's father. Mother had sent letters telling Roman about the situation and of his father's attempts to convince the older man to do what he called "the Christian thing." But Ashton would hear nothing of it, and his lawyer made it clear that the matter wasn't based on religious nonsense but on contractual agreements that were legal and binding.

Roman watched as the carriage disappeared down the street. Even after all these years, he couldn't shake his desire for the man to get his comeuppance. So often he had prayed for justice, but none ever came.

He made his way to Dr. Lester's home office and tried to put the matter from his mind. Everyone in Minneapolis knew to beware of Ashton. At least, they knew it now. After ruining the lives of many of his rivals, James Ashton had a reputation that no one ignored. Unfortunately, many still found it necessary to do business with him. He was rich, probably richer than anyone else in the area, and he was known to invest in building projects, land development, and railroads. People sought his help whenever there was no one else brave or rich enough to help. Even banks needed his help from time to time. Of course, such help came at a price.

"Enough!" Roman muttered. He was determined to forego further thoughts that only served to discourage and defeat. It was a beautiful day, and he was not going to allow anything or anyone to cause him grief.

He drew in a deep breath and remembered his morning devotions from Ephesians chapter four.

"Let all bitterness, and wrath, and anger, and clamour, and evil speaking, be put away from you, with all malice: And be ye kind one to another, tenderhearted, forgiving one another, even as God for Christ's sake hath forgiven you."

Roman took another deep breath. "I will put it away from me." He smiled, hoping no one had overheard his declaration. Already his spirit felt renewed as he reached the doctor's office.

Dr. John Lester's door was always open to anyone who needed him. Roman opened the door and stepped inside. The room was empty at the moment, and Roman called out to announce his arrival. "John, are you here? I've come for our meeting."

"Roman!" A man some thirty years Roman's senior stepped into the small waiting room. "I'm glad you could come. The reverend isn't here yet, so come on back and share a cup of coffee with me."

They made their way through a door and down the short

hall. To the right was a small examination room, currently empty, that had doubled as a convalescing room for badly injured patients. The rest of the house held private quarters for John, a widower of nearly thirty years.

John took down a mug from a peg beneath his cabinet and grabbed the pot of coffee and brought it to the table, where his own cup sat. He motioned for Roman to take a seat. "I was hoping we'd have a little time to talk. How are you? I haven't seen you for a couple of weeks, except for briefly at church."

Roman took the chair, still trying to forget about Ashton. "I know, I've had my hands full. There's been a lot of late-spring sickness in the poorer quarters."

John nodded and poured Roman a cup of coffee. "I've been busy as well. How's your mother and sister?"

"They're doing well. They've managed to remain healthy, for which I'm most grateful to God. My sister is planning for her fall wedding. I believe most of the town will be invited."

The older doctor chuckled. "Oh, to be young again."

Roman laughed and took the offered mug. "Frankly, I'm glad to be nearly forty. People take me more seriously and figure I'm mature enough to be sound of mind and judicious in decisions."

"Still, I recall to mind those days of youth when nothing wearied me or gave me second thoughts." He joined Roman at the table and poured more coffee into his own mug before placing the pot between them on a woven pad. "Back then I could stay awake for days, and did on occasion. Now I'm fit to be tied if I miss one night's sleep."

"Have you heard from your daughters?"

There had been a time when they'd all lived in Baltimore that John Lester had thought his youngest might have made a wife for Roman. She had been pretty and surprisingly sensible, but Roman found no desire to marry at the time, and she went on to find another. Sometimes he wondered what his life might have been like had he pursued her.

“They’re both doing well in Baltimore. Their husbands are quite successful in their various roles. I must admit it was hard to leave them there, but your need for me here far outweighs theirs. I don’t regret coming to offer my skills in Minnesota.”

“And we’re mighty glad you decided to come as well,” Roman said before sipping the steaming brew. It was strong, almost too strong, but he didn’t show his dislike. Instead, he gave it another sip before setting the mug on the table.

“Do you ever miss Baltimore, Roman?”

“I suppose there are times that I miss the larger cities with the availability of more amenities. We’ve both seen times when a decent hospital and operating surgery would have benefited us. It’s hard to believe that in a city of thirteen thousand people we don’t have a hospital.”

“But soon. The reverend and our men’s group, the Brotherhood of Gethsemane, are making great strides, as you well know. We’ll have a charity hospital by next year if we can manage to get more money than chickens and jars of preserves donated for our services.” He gave a laugh. “Although, I must say that the mint jelly I was given in lieu of payment last week was some of the best I’ve ever had.”

Roman chuckled. He’d received everything from loaves of bread to knitted mittens to the promise of pick of the litter when the owner’s hunting dog had pups.

“That hospital is going to be focused on mill and railroad workers, John. We could use a good facility for the other citizens in town.”

“True, but most would rather remain at home when sick or injured. They prefer loved ones to care for them and doctors to merely visit. The charity hospital is for those poor, single men who have no one to care for them.”

"I know, but proper medical care makes all the difference in the world for a city. That's what I miss most about Baltimore."

John nodded. "You'll get no argument from me." A knock sounded faintly, and John got to his feet. "That will be Reverend Knickerbacker."

He disappeared out of the kitchen and down the hall. Roman waited, uncertain where John planned for them to discuss the hospital business. To his surprise, John brought the reverend back to the kitchen.

"We are meeting rather informally," he told the reverend. "I hope you don't mind."

"That suits me just fine. Roman, it's good to see you. I'm glad you could spare the time."

Reverend Knickerbacker, a balding man of Roman's age, took a seat at the table and smiled. He had a neatly kept beard without a mustache and wore his priest's collar and black suit like a uniform. Roman had always liked the kindly man who knew well the sorrows of life. He and his beloved wife Sarah had lost their children to both disease and accident and now worked to help the orphaned and poorer children of Minneapolis.

"John. Roman. I'm so glad we could meet on this fine day. I know you're both quite busy. I know, too, that there have been many sick in the poorer neighborhoods. Have you any idea of the illness?"

Roman picked up his coffee. "There's a variety of problems being passed around. Most are the usual issues. Hopefully we'll not see any epidemics."

"I've had quite a few patients suffering from the grippe. Seems the change of seasons sometimes brings it about," John relayed, "but as Roman said, there's been a variety of other issues as well. Keeps life interesting, don't you know."

"I do, only too well. Roman, how are those men who were injured at the mill?"

"Recovering well, Reverend. They'll be back on their feet soon."

"Good to hear. Have you given any more thought to the list of needs that we should keep in mind for the charity hospital? I count on you two to give more than just a little consideration to this project of ours. Before we have plans drawn up, I want every need addressed."

"We are always quite thoughtful on the matter," John Lester said, bringing the reverend a mug. He took a seat before he poured the coffee. "Roman and I were just bemoaning the lack of a good surgery. Having the ability to operate in a clean environment with plenty of available medical supplies and qualified help is of the utmost importance."

"We've gone over this before, but more and more attention is being given to cleanliness," Roman added. "Sinks with available hot water would be a tremendous bonus in surgical areas. Plans for good plumbing is critical."

"I have been in touch with several folks back east who have been actively involved in putting together other charity hospitals. Some of the Episcopal nuns have taken extensive training as nurses and are open to relocating here." The reverend took the cup of coffee. "Thank you, John.

"If we can just get a few more regular supporters," the reverend continued, "things would shape up quickly. We need to convince some of the wealthier men to give more. I personally plan to speak to Washburn and Pillsbury. James Ashton as well." He sampled the coffee, then put the mug down.

Roman hid his look of disgust as he bowed his head toward the table. Reverend Knickerbacker could talk to Ashton all he wanted, but there was no chance that stingy old man would give a cent to see the less fortunate benefited.

"We can hardly start a hospital unless we have solid pledges to keep it running. My goal is to get as many faithful supporters as possible. Even if their donations aren't all that big, it will add up. We must encourage the community to see the benefits. We can also advertise that patients from any walk of life can stay for a fee. That way those who don't believe in charity, might also be persuaded to find value in our plans."

"I agree it's good to make it available to all," John said, looking at Roman.

"I do, as well. Soon enough someone with a good amount of money is going to feel the same way as we do, and a hospital for the community will be built."

The reverend nodded. "Until then, we will focus on the poor. I've recently been speaking with Sarah about the need to make a proper orphanage. I want to challenge the state to see it through and have plans to meet with the governor and others in St. Paul next month."

"I second the need for that. We've seen more and more children neglected and deserted." Roman's voice betrayed his enthusiasm. "I would very much like to see the local churches do more in the meanwhile. Perhaps in one of your meetings with other men of God, you could encourage them to create their own local support groups. If congregational members were willing to take in a child or two, or donate to others who are willing, we'd see fewer children on the streets. That would go a long way to stemming disease and injuries."

"I agree. Believe me, the poor and neglected of all ages deserve our concentrated effort," Reverend Knickerbacker declared. "We will see to it that Minneapolis takes care of its own."

"Mrs. Deeters, I wonder if I might ask you a question?" Judith stopped the housekeeper after she finished laying wood for a fire in Judith's hearth.

"Of course. What is it?"

"I need your advice on a church to attend. My grandfather

has agreed to go with me, so it should probably be one of the larger congregations. I want him to feel comfortable, and if he's just one man in a sea of many, then perhaps he won't feel so out of place."

The housekeeper's eyes widened. "Mr. Ashton is going to attend church?"

Judith nodded, suppressing a laugh. "Yes, I know it is shocking, but it's part of my agreement to remain here through the summer. He's promised he will attend church with me so long as he's physically able."

"I see." Mrs. Deeters momentarily bit her lower lip. "Well, many of the wealthier families attend the Episcopal church. We call it Gethsemane, after the garden where our Lord prayed before He was crucified. I attend there myself, along with my sister and her two children, so it's not all wealthy folks."

"That sounds good. We will plan to be at the services there on Sunday. Perhaps you could write instructions as to how to get there for the driver."

"I'd be happy to. It's quite close once you cross the bridge," Mrs. Deeters replied, looking rather askance. "I do hope that Mr. Ashton will join you as he's promised."

"I believe he will," Judith said, smiling. "He knows it's important to me, and in order to get what he wants, he will need to yield on this matter. It's that simple."

Mrs. Deeters gave a nod and then moved rather quickly to the door. Judith could tell she was more than a little bit uncomfortable. Perhaps in time she'd come to realize that Judith was nothing like her grandfather. In fact, she'd like very much if she and the housekeeper could form a sort of alliance to deal with the older man.

She supposed, however, that would take time. Mrs. Deeters had no reason to trust Judith. No one did. She noticed the looks from the rest of the staff. They tiptoed around her grandfather and did the same with her. She couldn't really blame them.

Judith began to pull the pins from her hair. Her grandfather had been quite exhausted from the day and their trip around town. When he told her he would take a tray in his room for dinner, Judith asked if she might as well. He had told her to do as she liked, and Mrs. Deeters had taken care of the rest. Now with dinner behind them and the evening to herself, Judith decided to get comfortable and pen a letter to Helen. She would no doubt be quite curious as to what was happening and why Judith had decided to remain in Minneapolis. Not only that, but Judith needed to detail what she wanted Helen to do with the money her grandfather had sent.

She smiled to herself as she brushed out her waist-length hair. The day hadn't gone all that badly. Her grandfather had been a bit testy at times, but they'd gotten through. She couldn't guess what the implications of spending time with James Ashton Sr. would be. Her life was certain to be altered, but whether for the better or worse was still in question.

A thought came to mind that she'd been pushing aside since agreeing to come to Minnesota. Dr. Roman Turner lived in Minneapolis. At least, he did four years ago. Was he still around the area? Should she make an effort to see him?

It seemed silly, but he did tell her to look for him if she came to town. Of course, he might well have married and moved away. There was no telling unless she asked, but who might know? A small sigh escaped her. She was still confused about why the Lord had brought her here. Never had she imagined she might end up in Minnesota, getting to know her grandfather.

"Lord, what is my purpose here?"

Before writing her letter, she felt compelled to open her Bible. She had been taught to seek wisdom and direction from the Word of God.

"Show me what you want me to know, Lord."

Psalm 116 was the place she turned to and read aloud, "'I

love the Lord, because he hath heard my voice and my supplications. Because he hath inclined his ear unto me, therefore will I call upon him as long as I live. The sorrows of death compassed me, and the pains of hell gat hold upon me: I found trouble and sorrow. Then called I upon the name of the Lord; O Lord, I beseech thee, deliver my soul. Gracious is the Lord, and righteous; yea, our God is merciful. The Lord preserveth the simple: I was brought low, and he helped me. Return unto thy rest, O my soul; for the Lord hath dealt bountifully with thee.'"

She leaned back as a sense of peace washed over her. How precious were the Scriptures. They would help to get her through this challenge with her grandfather, and comfort her heart during those lonely hours when she questioned her choice to remain single.

God alone knew what He had in store for her, and for Judith, that was enough.

Judith immediately loved the Episcopal church. The right Reverend Knickerbacker was a grand spokesman who commanded attention. He seemed to be in his late thirties yet led his congregation with the wisdom and appeal of a much older man. His sermon not only held their attention but seemed to touch their hearts as well.

Today he spoke on the good Samaritan, teaching in such a manner that Judith felt as if she were right there watching the event unfold. Her grandfather seemed interested enough, but who could tell what he was thinking?

"In our reading today of Luke, chapter ten, we come to the story of a man seeking Jesus to understand what he must do to have eternal life. Jesus asks him, What is written in the law? In verse twenty-seven, we see the man's answer. 'Thou shalt love the Lord thy God with all thy heart, and with all thy soul, and with all thy strength, and with all thy mind; and thy neighbour as thyself. And He said unto him, Thou hast answered right: this do, and thou shalt live.' But the man was confused, at least we must assume this from his next question. Verse twenty-nine has him asking Jesus, 'Who is my neighbour?'"

The reverend looked at his congregation. "Who is your neighbor? Who are you called upon to love as yourself? Or as John later relates in his Gospel when Jesus says, 'love one another as I have loved you.'"

Judith had often heard the story of the good Samaritan. Her mother and father had told it to her as a child, and Judith had tried to imagine playing the part of each stranger who encountered the beaten man who lay bleeding on the side of the road.

Reverend Knickerbacker continued reading from the Bible. "'And Jesus answering said, A certain man went down from Jerusalem to Jericho, and fell among thieves, which stripped him of his raiment, and wounded him, and departed, leaving him half dead. And by chance there came down a certain priest that way: and when he saw him, he passed by on the other side.'"

Judith remembered arranging the scene to act out. She had placed her doll on the ground beside the road. Then with regal strides, she walked past the doll, thinking of how the priest had passed by on the other side, not wanting to get too close.

The reverend continued, "'And likewise a Levite, when he was at the place, came and looked on him, and passed by on the other side.'"

Again, Judith remembered pretending to be the next man to walk by and do nothing. Even as a child, she'd felt a sense of confusion. How could they just leave an injured person bleeding on the side of the road? It had pierced her heart.

"'But a certain Samaritan, as he journeyed, came where he was: and when he saw him, he had compassion on him,'" Reverend Knickerbacker read. "'And went to him, and bound up his wounds, pouring in oil and wine, and set him on his own beast, and brought him to an inn, and took care of him.'"

In Judith's playacting, she had gone to her doll and gathered her in her arms. She had taken a cloth to wipe away the blood that she imagined there, then wrapped the doll's legs and arms and placed her in her doll carriage. The sense of love had been overwhelming to her. Judith could feel it even now.

Reverend Knickerbacker continued with great gusto. "'And on the morrow when he departed, he took out two pence, and gave them to the host, and said unto him, Take care of him; and whatsoever thou spendest more, when I come again, I will repay thee. Which now of these three, thinkest thou, was neighbour unto him that fell among the thieves?'"

The minister closed the Bible and looked at his congregation. "'And he said, He that shewed mercy on him. Then said Jesus unto him, Go, and do thou likewise.'" He paused for a moment. "It is such a simple matter to love another as you love yourself. You give yourself drink and food. Give unto others. You bathe and clothe yourself. Provide the same for others. You shelter yourself in safety and warmth. Do so for those who have not such provisions."

Judith felt tears come to her eyes and hurriedly took out her handkerchief to stem the flow. She couldn't help but feel the need to serve others as this story encouraged. She wanted only to see the needy receive what might help them to survive and thrive. When she thought of the orphanages back in Philadelphia and all of the little ones who had no home, no loved one to care for them, it was heartbreaking. How could good people ignore such things? It made her even more certain that staying with her grandfather in order to receive money for her charities had been the right decision. Whether or not he would make her his heir remained to be seen, but with what he had already shared, Judith was determined to show the deepest love possible.

She put her handkerchief back in her purse, and she noticed a man watching her. He had an odd scowl on his face, and his eyes were narrowed as if in anger. It was then that she realized he wasn't really looking at her at all, but rather her grandfather.

She looked at the older man at her side. He didn't seem to notice much of anything as he stared straight ahead. Judith glanced back at the younger man, but he was now looking at the reverend. There was something so familiar about him. Then Judith noticed Mrs. Deeters was seated several people away from the man. Perhaps she knew him.

The reverend concluded his sermon by encouraging the congregation to give generously to the various charities sponsored by the church and elsewhere. He also suggested folks consider volunteering their time to worthy causes.

"A person can tithe not only money, but time," he said before leading them in the benediction. "If you have interest in this, please come and speak to me."

When the service was over, Judith helped her grandfather to his feet and walked at his side as they exited the church.

"Wait for me in the carriage," the older man suddenly instructed. "I have someone I need to speak to."

His exit surprised her, but she supposed he knew most of the people in attendance. Mrs. Deeters had told her this was the church where most of the wealthier people attended.

"I'm Sarah Knickerbacker," a woman said, approaching Judith. "I don't believe we've met."

Judith smiled. "Judith Stanford. I'm here for the summer to be with my grandfather, James Ashton. I very much enjoyed the reverend's sermon. I am highly involved in charities back in Philadelphia and would love to contribute while I'm here in Minneapolis."

"How wonderful. Why don't you allow me to arrange a gathering of like-minded women and introduce you?"

"I'd appreciate that very much," Judith agreed.

"I'll send word to you at your grandfather's home when I have a date and time."

"Thank you. I will look forward to it, Mrs. Knickerbacker."

"Oh, do just call me Sarah."

"And you must call me Judith. I've a feeling we'll become good friends."

The slightly older woman smiled and nodded. She clasped Judith's gloved hands and gave a squeeze before leaving to speak to some other ladies. Judith made her way to the carriage and paused there to glance over at some of the other congregants. Once again, she saw the angry-looking man. He was quite handsome and clean-shaven. His dark-eyed gaze seemed fixed on the back of her grandfather's head. There was definitely something amiss between them. She wondered what it was that had so infuriated the man. She might have gone to ask him, but his gaze began to move in her direction, and Judith realized her grandfather had come to join her.

"Well, do get into the carriage instead of standing about," James Ashton ordered her as he might his staff.

"I was enjoying the fresh air." A rumble of thunder to the south caught her attention. "I suppose, however, it is about to rain." She let the driver help her into the carriage, but as she took her seat, she couldn't help but see the man who was watching them. When their gazes met, he seemed momentarily fixed on her, and then just as quickly, he looked away as if embarrassed.

Judith motioned to her grandfather as he took his seat. "Who is that man over there?"

Her grandfather looked up, but not before the man disappeared into the crowd. "What man?" her grandfather asked, tapping the side of the carriage to signal to the driver.

"He's gone now," she said as the carriage driver urged the horses forward.

Thunder sounded again, and James Ashton glanced upward. "We should have come in the brougham. Get us home before the rain, Charles," he commanded the driver.

"He looked so angry at you," Judith said, unable to stop thinking about the man.

"Probably lost out on some business deal or failed to act when I suggested he do so. There's always someone disgruntled with me. You'll learn soon enough that less successful people despise those who have been prosperous."

"I suppose that is especially true when those prosperous people are less than considerate of the needs of others. Like in the story of the good Samaritan."

Her grandfather gave a harrumph of disapproval but said nothing more. Judith knew he would never agree with her thoughts on the matter.

They barely made it inside the house before the heavens opened and rain poured from the skies. The valet Judith only knew as Winchell stood ready and waiting to receive his employer.

"I'm rather spent from this ordeal," her grandfather said, handing his coat and hat to the man. "I'll take lunch in my room. Have Mrs. Markle prepare a tray."

"Yes, sir," Winchell replied, giving his employer a nod.

When her grandfather headed for the stairs, Judith followed suit and walked behind him. She worried that he might have overdone it and feared he could fall. However, they reached the second floor without another word or issue. The old man turned toward his suite of rooms, and Judith went to hers. She still had so many questions about this man.

Harriet awaited Judith in her sitting room. The room was more than a little chilly, but the redheaded maid had thoughtfully made a fire.

Judith handed Harriet her hat and gloves and moved to warm herself by the fire. "My grandfather plans to take a tray in his room for lunch. Would you ask the cook to arrange one for me as well, please?"

"Mrs. Markle already planned on it. When Mr. Ashton takes his food in his room, she never orders the table set."

"Well, I suppose that makes sense, being as he's the only one who has been around all these years. You might let her know that it's fine with me to continue that way. No sense being formal when it's only me."

Harriet nodded. "Do you need help to change your clothes?"

"No, I'm fine. Thank you."

"I'll go arrange for your lunch, then." She gave a curtsy and left before Judith could reply.

Judith moved to the dressing room, released the buttons on her skirt, and let it drop to the floor. She then unfastened her jacket and slipped out of it before placing both garments across the back of a chair. The dressing room was quite well furnished, and Judith found that even though she'd brought a rather sparing wardrobe, Mrs. Deeters had arranged for other items to be purchased and added to her closet. Apparently, her grandfather didn't want her to find herself in need. The thought crossed her mind that she should probably ask Helen to send an additional trunk of items. She would add the request to the letter she'd started on Friday.

She located a warm blue woolen skirt. After shedding her bustle and pad for a little more comfort, Judith pulled the skirt on over her head and dropped it in place. The white blouse she'd worn to church was a bit nicer than she usually wore to just sit around the house, but she didn't feel like asking Harriet to return and help with the row of back buttons. It would suffice.

Doing up the buttons on her skirt, Judith remembered the face of the strange man. He had dark brown eyes and a straight nose. His brown hair had a bit of wave, much like her own.

She moved to the window and looked out at the rain. Who was he? And why was he so angry? Was it as her grandfather had suggested? Had he been wronged by James Ashton Sr. in a business dealing? Was he plotting to take his revenge?

Judith smiled and shook her head. She was letting her imagination take charge. If she was to ponder anything, it would be more beneficial to think about how she might play her role as a good Samaritan in Minneapolis.

As the family sat down to lunch after Sunday services, Roman was still stunned at the realization that Judith Stanford had been sitting next to James Ashton in church. What was she doing in Minneapolis? No doubt she had been the woman he'd seen earlier in Ashton's carriage, but how could she possibly keep company with such a man?

"Roman?"

He glanced up. His mother, sister, and aunt were all staring at him. He forced a smile. "Sorry. I've got my mind on a dozen things." It was a bit of a lie. He was only thinking about Judith.

"Would you offer grace?" his mother asked.

"Of course." He bowed his head. "Father, we thank You for this meal, and for the hands that prepared it. Bless us in Your will. Amen."

"Amen," the trio of women said in unison.

Roman's mother held out her hand. "Give me your plate, Roman, and I'll dish you up some roast and vegetables."

He did as she instructed and waited until she'd filled everyone's plate before picking up his fork. He stabbed a piece of the roasted beef and then glanced up. He could see that everyone was looking at him.

"I'm sorry. I've just been a bit preoccupied."

"With the young woman you were watching at church?" his mother asked.

"I didn't see that he was watching a young woman," Aunt Mary said, nudging Claudette. "Did you?"

Claudette giggled. "No. Have you finally been pierced with cupid's arrow? Wouldn't it be glorious if Roman fell in love after all these years?"

"My attention was on James Ashton. How that man has the audacity to show up in church is beyond me."

"It is the place for sinners," his mother chided. "Roman, you're going to have to forgive Mr. Ashton one day. There's no sense in carrying around your anger toward him. I've had to give mine over to God in order to keep it from eating me alive. You must do the same."

"Ashton is responsible for killing Father," Roman replied, looking again at his plate. "I've given it to the Lord to deal with, but forgiveness is slow in coming."

"It's been nine years," Aunt Mary joined in. "I understand how Roman feels, even though Andrew wasn't related to me. He was like a brother. So kind and considerate when my own Eustus died. No brother could have been dearer."

"That's just how Andrew was," Roman's mother said, smiling. "He loved you as a sister."

"Papa was kind to everyone," Claudette said, sounding a little sad. "I miss him so much."

"We all do," Roman admitted. "And, had James Ashton not been the heartless deceiver that he is, Father might still be with us today."

"But he's not here, and we must accept that and allow God to heal our pain-filled hearts," Mother declared. "Now let's eat before our food gets cold. Better you should dwell on the beautiful young woman at his side. Or any other single young lady."

Everyone dug in, save Mary. She surprised Roman with her next comment. "What of the woman you weren't watching? The one seated beside Mr. Ashton. Did you notice her?"

Roman wished they'd all just forget the woman. "Of course I did. I believe I met her back east at a fundraiser. Judith Stanford."

"Yes, that's her. She's James Ashton's granddaughter."

"What?" The thought of her being related to that wretch soured Roman's stomach. "I didn't think he had any family."

"He has one granddaughter. He asked her to come here so that he might inspect her."

"Inspect her?" Roman asked. He leaned back in his chair, leaving his meal uneaten. "For what purpose?"

"Becoming his heir. He has no one to inherit his vast fortune. He cut his son off years ago and had nothing to do with his family. Now he's desperate to ensure that his riches won't just go to the government or sit doing nothing for years while it's decided where it should go."

"And Judith, is she just like him? Does money guide her days?" Roman asked, allowing his distaste for anything associated with Ashton to creep into his tone.

"Surprisingly enough, no. She doesn't appear to be anything like him. In fact, she was the reason he was at church today. Apparently, she isn't afraid to stand up to him. Mr. Ashton demanded she remain with him all summer. His doctors have given him only that much time before they believe he'll die."

"Good riddance."

"I agree," Aunt Mary replied. "However, when Mr. Ashton demanded she stay, she said she would pray about it. She's a woman of faith, and I heard from Mr. Ashton's lawyer that she's been working for a variety of charities since the death of her parents. Mr. Black was sent to Philadelphia to bring her to Minneapolis, but she refused to come. She said she didn't want the old man's money."

Roman found himself liking Judith more and more. "So why is she here?"

"Mr. Ashton sent Mr. Black back with a check for ten thousand dollars. I'm told Judith arranged for it to go to her charities, and then she agreed to come for a visit. When Mr. Ashton demanded she stay the summer, he offered her another ten thousand for her charities and then—" She stopped and looked around as if Ashton himself might overhear her. "And then he upped it, at her demand, to thirty thousand. She said she was going to build houses for the war widows. After that, she said she would stay so long as he attended church with her on Sundays. I know I shouldn't be repeating this. God forgive me for my gossip. Still, I was so shocked that he agreed to go. Judith asked me about a good church, and I couldn't help but recommend ours."

"That is quite the tale," Roman's mother admitted. "However, I would just as soon we put it aside. You're quite correct, it is gossip, and our sins are plenty enough."

Roman said nothing, but his mind churned with thoughts of Judith standing up to her grandfather. He didn't even know the old man had a granddaughter, much less that she should be the woman Roman had met in Philadelphia. The woman he couldn't seem to get out of his head.

"I'm sorry that Daniel couldn't join us today," Mother said, drawing Roman out of his thoughts.

Claudette shrugged. "He promised his mother he would take her to the cemetery. It's the first anniversary of his father's death, and it's been quite hard on her. She has his older brother and their family, of course, but Daniel knew it was important to her that he come with them to the grave."

"But of course." Mother reached out and squeezed Claudette's hand. "I could have spared you."

"I know, but I wanted them to have this time as a family. I'll join them soon enough. I just hope they weren't caught out in the rain."

Roman smiled at his sister. She had grown up so fast in the last couple of years. Despite losing their father, she had managed to maintain a hopeful spirit of joy.

He finished eating and then excused himself, knowing his mother would never allow him to help with the dishes. She knew he worked hard, and she always did her best to see that he had free time to himself on Sunday. Once in a while, a patient would show up begging for help, but usually his Sundays were quiet, and he cherished the rest.

He made his way upstairs to his small bedroom. The house was inadequate in many ways, but it was theirs free and clear, and he was very grateful for how God continued to look after them.

Sitting on the edge of his bed, Roman removed his shoes, thinking a nap might well be in order. He rid himself of his coat and tie and then stretched out on the bed with a sigh. But when he closed his eyes, Judith's image appeared once again. He couldn't shake the feeling that she was going to be more than a passing thought in his life. But how could he ever have anything to do with an Ashton?

"Where are you and Claudette off to?" Roman asked, seeing that his mother and sister were readying themselves for an afternoon outing.

"We've been invited to tea at Mrs. Van Cleve's. Mrs. Knickerbacker and some other ladies are going to discuss the needs of the orphans and friendless in Minneapolis and St. Paul."

Roman kissed his mother's forehead. "I wish we had a carriage, and I would happily drive you."

"The walk will do us good. Things have dried out nicely after last Sunday's rain. Goodness, but here it is Friday. Where has the week gone?"

Roman had wondered the same thing himself. He'd been so busy with patients that one day had blended into another. Still, he continued to think about Judith. She consumed his thoughts day and night, and he'd become determined to meet up with her one way or another.

"I'm glad you could come home for lunch," his mother said, taking up her gloves. "I suppose you will rush right back to work now?"

"Yes. Dr. Lester needs me to help him with a rather difficult surgery. One of the flour mill workers mangled his arm in an accident. We thought we could save the arm, but it looks like amputation will be the only solution to saving the man's life. He's finally stable, and it's safe to operate."

"I'm sorry to hear that he'll lose his arm. Poor man will need a lengthy recovery. Does he have family?"

"Yes, actually. And they seem qualified and willing to take care of him. I've already spoken at length to his mother."

"What a relief. I know you and Dr. Lester are already stretched to the breaking point caring for others."

"Yes, but as John is always telling me, times like these are what faith was made for." He smiled and gave a shrug. "God will provide."

"Indeed He will." Mother glanced toward the narrow stairs. "Claudette, are you coming?"

"I'm on my way, Mother." She bounded down the stairs like a young girl rather than a woman of nineteen.

"You might mention to your ladies that there has been an increasing number of children hanging around the river," Roman related. "I'm not sure if they're orphans or just part of the destitute masses. I thought I recognized one as being from a family I called on. They seem to be somewhere in the age of twelve to sixteen. It's a dangerous place for them to be. The potential for accidents as well as run-ins with unsavory characters is high. When I try to talk to them, they just run. The police are aware of them and tell me that so far they haven't caused any trouble that they're aware of. Perhaps if the Ladies' Aid set up some sort of refreshment stand as you did that time last winter, then you could talk to them and encourage them to gather elsewhere, perhaps go to the friendless refuge for a hot meal."

"We can certainly try. I'll mention it at the tea," his mother assured him.

Claudette stretched up and pulled Roman's head downward to place a kiss on his cheek. "Roman, Daniel is hoping you can join us for dinner tonight. He would like a chess game after the meal. He says he's been able to beat everyone but you and wants another chance to win."

"Well, given the fact that I'm the one who taught him to play, that's high praise. I'm sure at this rate, he'll surpass me in no time at all. But, yes, I plan to be here for dinner tonight."

"Thank you, Roman." Claudette turned away to check her bonnet.

"Good. Then on our way home from tea, we'll stop at the grocer's and pick up a few things. Bring the basket, Claudette," Mother instructed. "Roman, we will be praying for the young man and for you and Dr. Lester as you perform the operation."

"Thank you. We'll need all the prayers we can get to pull this poor man through."

Roman was already apprehensive of the surgery given the wound had gone gangrenous. Once such a bad infection entered a person's system, it took a terrible toll on the body. Roman had seen such things many times on the battlefield and could almost recognize on sight those patients who would and wouldn't make it. The way John had described the young man they'd be working on, Roman wasn't at all confident they could save him. Still, all they could do was try.

"What are you all dressed up for?" Judith's grandfather asked as she prepared to leave the house.

"I've been invited to join some of the church ladies for tea this afternoon."

"But I'll be needing the carriage and driver, so you must remain here."

Judith chuckled. "Sir, I walked all about Philadelphia. I'm

certainly not too good to do the same with St. Anthony and Minneapolis."

"It's hardly appropriate for you to walk unescorted. You are from a wealthy family, and there are those who would take advantage of that fact."

"I am not from a wealthy family. Your financial situation is your own. Mine, while comfortable, has never been that of the upper classes of society. A thief has only to glance at me to know I wear no jewelry and my clothes are not fancy."

He studied her for a moment and frowned. "It might do well to order you a new wardrobe."

"My clothes suit me perfectly well. I do not need more clothes."

"I'll be the judge of that. I can hardly have my granddaughter going about in rags."

Judith fumed. "My clothes are not rags. They are handmade by a very gifted seamstress. When I pay calls on the ladies of society in Philadelphia, they always ask who made them and in turn hire the woman for themselves. You needn't concern yourself with me. I'm only staying the summer."

"Yes, but there will be times when we will entertain," he said, shaking his head. "Or be entertained. I will expect you to dress accordingly. I will not have it said that my granddaughter is unkempt."

"I am hardly that. Now, if you'll excuse me, I must be about my business. Mrs. Van Cleve is expecting me."

"Horatio Van Cleve's wife?"

"I have no idea. I can only say that I received an invitation to tea and to discuss things dear to my heart." Judith headed for the door, where Mrs. Deeters stood at the ready. "I will see you at dinner this evening, sir."

With that, she left before her grandfather could say another word. There were times when Judith really questioned her choice in staying. She wanted to know the man better, but he rarely spent time with her. She ate breakfast alone in her room. Sometimes they dined together for lunch, where he would speak about various business transactions that were going well or causing issues for him. Supper was always at seven in formal dress, and very little conversation took place. Afterward they often spent a bit of time together in the sitting room, but otherwise, Judith saw very little of him.

"Mrs. Stanford, how nice to see you."

She looked up to find Bert Black coming up the front steps. She smiled. "You've been away again, Mr. Black."

"Yes, your grandfather had me finalizing some paperwork and closing out some arrangements in Chicago."

"I hope all went well for you." She waited for him to pass her on the steps, but instead he stopped.

"I wonder if I might ask you something?" He smiled.

Judith had an idea that he probably wanted her to go out with him somewhere. She'd been glad for his absence, but now that he was back, she supposed his attention would start up again.

"It might be best to wait until later. I have an appointment, and I'll be late if I don't hurry. Grandfather is waiting for you, I'm sure. He mentioned going out today, and I presume you'll be accompanying him. I'll leave you to that." She headed down the steps before he could recover his surprise.

"Mrs. Van Cleve, it's so nice to meet you," Judith said as Mrs. Knickerbacker introduced her to the hostess. "I've heard great things about you."

The white-haired woman smiled. "It's a pleasure to meet you, Mrs. Stanford. Sarah has told me of your work in Philadelphia. You should fit into our group without any trouble."

"Judith has great interest in helping with our work here in Minneapolis since she'll be with us through the summer,"

Sarah Knickerbacker explained. "I know she'll be of great value to us."

"I'm sure you're right, Sarah." The older woman ushered them into the sitting room, where other women were already gathered. She approached the closest two. "This is Mrs. Martha Turner and her daughter, Claudette. Ladies, this is Mrs. Stanford of Philadelphia. She will be staying with her grandfather this summer and has asked to be involved in our work with the poor."

"Wonderful." Mrs. Turner and her daughter got to their feet. "It's so nice to finally meet you. We saw you at church Sunday but were unable to reach you before you left."

"My grandfather was concerned about the weather and hurried us home. But it is my pleasure to meet you both. Turner is a name familiar to me." She thought of the handsome doctor she'd met, and it dawned on her that the man she'd seen sitting near these women at church might well be related to him. There were similarities in their looks, but the man in church was without beard and much dourer. Perhaps a brother? She started to ask, but Sarah whisked her away for introductions.

"Ladies, please take your seats." Mrs. Van Cleve began the meeting. "As you know, these monthly teas are often fraught with bad news and fearful situations for our community. However, I am happy to report that an anonymous donor has made a generous contribution to our charity, and we will be able to purchase blankets and other supplies for many of our destitute families." She continued with information related to several personal projects she had taken on before concluding and asking if anyone else had news.

Mrs. Turner stood. "Most of you know my son, Dr. Turner." The women nodded, and Judith perked up at this. "He asked me to mention to our group that there has been a growing number of children spending time down by the river. He fears many are living there or nearby without the supervision of adults. The police are aware of them. The children seem to be between the ages of twelve and sixteen or so and scatter rapidly when approached. He thought perhaps we could coordinate to meet nearby and offer refreshment, then encourage them to come for meals at the friendless refuge. We can make ourselves a sort of mothering brigade."

The women chuckled at this, and Mrs. Turner continued, "We could arrange for police to keep watch in case of problems, but since we have done this kind of thing before, I think we'll be all right. The children apparently have no fear of begging. We might be able to set up a station with food and other necessities."

"Are these children orphans?" one of the ladies asked.

"He isn't certain," Mrs. Turner replied. "He's tried several times to approach them, but they run away. Roman did think, however, that he'd seen one of them before. He thought the young man might be a member of one of the families he'd been treating."

Roman Turner, the same doctor she'd met in Philadelphia! And this was his mother and sister. How wonderful! She could easily explain her interest in him to them and perhaps have a chance to meet.

Mrs. Van Cleve again took charge and seemed so at ease. There was nothing shy or withdrawn about this woman. "With those matters settled, we'll have our tea and conversation."

"She grew up in the army," Mrs. Knickerbacker said, as if reading Judith's thoughts.

"Excuse me?" Judith asked.

The reverend's wife laughed. She nodded her head toward Charlotte Van Cleve, who was instructing a young maid with the service of tea and refreshments.

"She grew up as the daughter of a soldier. In fact she was the first white child born in the area that is now Wisconsin. Her middle name is Ouisconsin, the French spelling of the state."

"How fascinating." Judith continued to watch the woman with great interest.

"She met her husband in the army and married at sixteen. They moved around a great deal and had a dozen children."

"A dozen! Oh my."

"Well, with those they adopted along the way, there are even more. The Van Cleves have always followed their words with actions. And you see her white hair?"

Judith nodded. It was quite lovely.

"She's only fifty-one, but her hair went white after the stress of the war. The governor insisted her husband take charge of the Second Minnesota Regiment. I think it was all just too much for her. Her eyesight and hearing have suffered too. But she is stronger than anyone gives her credit for. I believe she will accomplish amazing things for our cause."

Judith held even more admiration for the woman. She was quite the lady, and her compassion for those less fortunate was impressive.

The talk became less formal, and the women mingled with one another, sharing bits and pieces of information regarding their lives. Judith was of great interest to most, and they didn't seem to have any problem in expressing opinions about her grandfather.

"James Ashton has always kept to himself," one woman shared. "My husband has done business with him, but . . . well, I shouldn't speak ill of anyone, but the results were disappointing."

Judith saw her glance at the other women and felt rather self-conscious. She didn't know if it was best to explain her situation or not, but telling them of her father's plight seemed important.

"My father was disowned by him when he decided to marry my mother. They were young, and my grandfather did not approve. He had nothing more to do with my father."

"How terrible," Mrs. Turner murmured.

"How is it that you have come to stay with him?" Mrs. Van Cleve asked.

"It's a rather complicated story. I will say that I have agreed to remain here for the summer. I hope to know him considerably better."

"Perhaps you can persuade him to stop cheating men of their life savings," an older, tired-looking woman said. The anger in her voice was most evident.

"Hazel, that was uncalled for," another chided.

"Hardly. There's not a one of you here who hasn't suffered at James Ashton's hands." Hazel fixed Judith with a hard look. "Your grandfather has a way of dealing in business that keeps him just barely adhering to the laws of the land. He has no heart and has been the ruin of many a family."

Judith frowned and shook her head. "I'm so very sorry to hear this. I really know nothing of the man."

"Well, it's time you did. Your grandfather persuaded my husband to put up property as a guarantee for one of their dealings. I have no understanding of how it all worked together, but in the end, your grandfather was the one who held the purse strings and somehow managed to steal away our holdings. If you don't believe me, just ask him. Better yet, ask Mrs. Turner how he treated their family. It killed her poor husband."

"Hazel Clemmons, you will cease this talk immediately. Judith is hardly to blame for anything her grandfather has done." Mrs. Van Cleve stepped forward, waggling her finger. "Now, let us discuss something that is less volatile in nature."

The women looked embarrassed, though Hazel Clemmons appeared as if she had more rage pent up inside. What had her grandfather done to these families? She had known him to be ruthless with his own people, but now it seemed he was less than honorable among his business partners as well.

"I'll take my leave, lest I say more that I will regret." Hazel moved toward the hall door, and Mrs. Van Cleve followed her.

Judith glanced around. "I don't know what to say, except that I am sorry for whatever my grandfather has done to cause each of you grief."

Mrs. Knickerbacker came to her side. "You aren't to blame. Especially knowing that he had nothing to do with your family. You couldn't know what he was doing." She put her arm around Judith. "Don't let this dissuade you from continuing to participate with us. Hazel will recover her dignity, and I'm sure she'll apologize once she realizes just how she sounded."

"I don't believe she owes me an apology. The woman was obviously hurt. Is she correct in saying that most of you here have suffered because of my grandfather?" Judith looked around the room. The other women had stopped talking and were obviously far more interested in what Sarah Knickerbacker had to say.

"Please. Be honest with me," Judith begged. "I want to know the truth. Is that truly the kind of man my grandfather is?"

They slowly began to nod. One of the women Judith hadn't yet met motioned to the Turners. "Your grandfather did Mr. Turner so wrong that he despaired of life and died."

Judith looked to Mrs. Turner and her daughter for confirmation. Mrs. Turner moved closer and smiled. "It's all in the past. What happened was tragic, but it is behind us. I've forgiven your grandfather."

Judith thought of the angry man in church. "Who was the man who sat beside you in Sunday services?"

Her smile broadened. "That is my son, Dr. Roman Turner. If you offer your services in charitable work, you're bound to run into him outside of church."

"I have already met him, in Philadelphia. It was a pleasurable meeting, although our circumstances were much different. When I saw him at church, I thought he looked familiar, but when I met him, he wore a beard and mustache."

Roman's mother nodded. "He has changed over the years. He works tirelessly with the poor. Given your reputation for working with them as well, it seems only natural that the two of you should have encountered one another."

"But now I fear it will be unpleasant for him to see me again," Judith said, feeling a strange sense of sadness. "He did not know then that I was an Ashton."

She understood now why he had scowled in such a hateful manner. His mother might well have learned to forgive James Ashton Sr., but it was clear that Dr. Turner had not.

That evening, Roman was all ears as his mother described their day with Judith. To hear her mother and sister tell it, Judith was just this side of being a saint.

"She was only getting started with such things when I met her," Roman said, trying to sound disinterested.

"She works with a dozen different charities in Philadelphia," his mother said as they sat down to dinner. "The city fathers there all know her and seek her out for advice regarding areas that are run-down and destitute. She has pushed hard to help get money allotted to folks in the poorer areas for cleanup and repairs so that the inhabitants can live in healthier conditions."

"I suppose she told you all of this." Roman knew his tone was a bit sarcastic.

"No, she said very little. Mrs. Van Cleve had learned about her after Sarah Knickerbacker mentioned she wanted to help locally."

"She works a lot with the orphanages," Claudette added, looking at her husband-to-be. "I think you'd enjoy meeting her, Daniel. She even speaks Italian."

"How'd she come by that?" the young man asked.

"She's college educated, and her father ran a steamboat service. She said there were quite a few Italians who worked for her father. In fact, she said there is a big neighborhood of Italians in Philadelphia." She looked at Roman. "She did tell me that much."

"Probably one of those poorer neighborhoods she works with," Daniel said, shaking his head. "My people aren't always welcomed and so struggle to get work and respect."

"I think she's a charming young woman. She mentioned having met you in Philadelphia," Roman's mother said, casting him a quick glance as she passed a platter of fried chicken. "She said it was a pleasant encounter but fears you'll think otherwise now."

"Now that I know she's an Ashton?"

"Roman, she had no idea of what her grandfather was like."

"But the women at the tea were only too happy to tell her," Claudette added. "I felt sorry for her, but she handled it with grace and kindness."

Roman helped himself to the chicken before passing the platter to his sister. "Why was she at the meeting?"

"She'll be here all summer and wants to work with some of our charities. She doesn't seem afraid to get her hands dirty or work."

"A lot of people say that and then back away when they learn what that really entails." Roman wasn't buying into the idea of Judith's sainthood.

"I think you should meet her again before judging her. She acts nothing like her grandfather," Mother declared.

"I'm not trying to be unkind or judgmental," Roman began, "but after a few weeks in that despicable man's influence, I think you might find her changed."

"She has a strong Christian faith, so I think she'll be fine," his mother countered. "But to ensure she has the support of Christians, your sister and I intend to befriend her."

Roman didn't know what to think about that. He had to admit, he was intrigued by Judith and all the positive things that his mother and sister had said about her. Mother was never one to offer idle praise, nor was she easily duped. The fact that she found this young woman to be of godly principles and faith suggested to him that it was, in fact, the case.

"So have you two set the date for the wedding?" Mother asked Claudette.

"We have. We would like to be married at the church on September eighteenth. We plan to go see Reverend Knickerbacker tomorrow and schedule it." Claudette smiled at Daniel before adding, "If no one else is already getting married on that day."

"It sounds like a perfect date. The heat of summer will be off of us, and it shouldn't yet be overly chilly. Daniel, I'll write your mother a letter for you to take her tomorrow. We should probably start discussing what kind of celebration we want this to be."

"Our celebrations are always full of people and food," he said, laughing. "I see no reason to make this one any different."

Roman listened to them continue to discuss the wedding and reception as he ate. He'd already made up his mind that on Sunday he would again meet Judith Ashton Stanford and judge for himself if she was as sincere and perfect as they described. No one was without their flaws.

"Did you hear me, Roman?"

He looked up and shook his head. "I'm afraid not. What did you say?"

"I asked how the surgery went today. I know you're very tired, so I assume it was difficult." His mother reached out and patted his arm. "I hope it went well. We prayed for you."

"Yes, it went as well as it could. Now we must wait and see what happens. If he makes it through the next forty-eight hours, he'll have a good chance of recovering."

"Then we will pray for him all the more," Mother replied.

After dinner, Roman went to his room to catch up on some medical reading. There was a book he'd just received that covered a variety of new medical techniques, and he was eager to read it. Keeping up with the changes and advances in medicine was critical. Unfortunately, not all his colleagues felt the same way, and many were inadequately trained to begin with.

Prior to the War Between the States there were a mere one hundred thirteen doctors in the entire United States Army. After the war, there were twelve thousand in the Union Army and three thousand in the Confederate. Some were well-trained and educated men who signed up to serve when the war broke out. However, many were men posing as doctors.

Now those so-called doctors had spilled out across civilian life, and most had only their war training to back up their practices. It was of great concern to many of the doctors who had diligently studied at a medical college and then practiced under the observation and training of an experienced doctor.

Roman was eager to support better licensing practices and training for doctors. He'd met many a man who never should have called himself a physician. It would take changes in the law to begin eliminating those unqualified pretenders.

But with the bad came the good. The war had also brought about many changes and improvements in medical procedures. He supposed that was the way with any war. Necessity forced a man's hand and imagination. Breakthroughs often came about because of the urgency in the operating room and on the battlefield. He'd seen that a lot and had even created his own procedures and innovations.

Surgery had already been a focal part of Roman's training, and he was known to be quite good at what he did. Because of this, he was highly regarded and called upon to do some of the more delicate and difficult operations, especially when they involved men of great importance or their sons. More than once, he'd been called away from one battlefield to attend another. It had been dangerous and harrowing at times, but it had made him a better doctor in the long run.

Roman settled into a chair and turned up the lamp to provide better light. He started to read, but his mind quickly took another direction. Judith. It wasn't the first time in the last four years he had thought of her. Most of the time he could busy himself enough to stave off feelings of loneliness, but he was just as vulnerable as the next man. Vulnerable to thoughts of falling in love . . . marriage. The women in his family teased him often enough about it, but he always pretended it wasn't a big concern. But with Judith Stanford back in his life, or at least the possibility, Roman couldn't pretend such thoughts didn't matter. He was ready to fall in love.

"But it can't be her. She's an Ashton." He closed the book and his eyes. "I can't fall in love with an Ashton."

Sunday morning, Judith had breakfast in her room. The poached eggs and toast were perfect, as was the coffee. She'd developed a taste for the nutty brew as a girl in the pilothouse of her father's riverboat. When she'd been young, they had traveled as a family up and down the river. Many a morning she would sneak up to see her father in the wheelhouse. She would take him a cup of coffee just as he liked it, creamed and sugared. He had always welcomed her, and she would sit beside him while he guided the boat, and they would talk. Sometimes, he'd let her have sips of his coffee. She supposed it was why to this day she drank it with cream and often sugar, as he had. It always served to give her pleasant memories.

She sampled the coffee a second time. They had known such happiness until the day that her little brother Frank fell overboard and drowned. Judith's heart still ached at the memory. Her mother and father had been devastated, and she'd tried so hard to be brave for them. Judith remembered snuggling up next to her mother and infant brother, Jonathan, on the sofa to offer consolation. She'd done the exact same thing years later when Jonathan had died in the war. He'd barely been eighteen.

Mother had never quite recovered from losing Frank. She left the river for a great many years, determined to never again return. In time, though, she had missed the life she'd grown up with. Missed her husband too. When Judith headed off to college, Mama had reluctantly packed her bags and returned to life on the river. Sadly, it was that existence that took both Judith's parents.

At their funeral, one of the older church women reminded her that as children of God, they were never out of His care. Judith had struggled with thoughts that perhaps somehow Satan had taken advantage of the moment, but her friend assured her that Satan could never have the upper hand with God.

"It might seem he gets away with things," the older woman had said, "but there will come a reckoning, and he knows it well. His time is short, and so he does what he can to draw the children of God away from their faith and trust. Don't give Satan a chance to lead you away, Judith. Think not on the things of this world, for we are but a vapor."

The words were strangely comforting. God would not be bested, and while it was hard to lose her parents this way, she knew they were safe and one day they would all be reunited.

But now she was here in a place far from home, getting to know a man who had offered her father nothing but pain. How could she allow herself to love a man who had so clearly cast love aside? The entire matter was painful to even consider.

Upon finishing her breakfast, Judith put aside her questions and got to her feet. She began dressing for church, doing her best to focus on the Sabbath rather than her memories.

Harriet and Beth appeared just as Judith had finished donning her undergarments. Beth set out her hairbrush and pins, along with two ebony combs that Judith sometimes used when arranging her hair. Harriet, meanwhile, helped Judith into her dressing gown.

"It looks to be a beautiful day. Hot too," Harriet said. She went to where several gowns hung pressed and ready. "Would you like to wear the lightweight blue gown? I don't think you'll regret it. Pity a woman has to wear so many layers of clothes just to make herself fashionable."

"The blue dress sounds fine," Judith told her. She sat down to the dressing table while Harriet went to fetch the gown. Judith finished securing her stockings, then Beth untied the ribbon from her braid and began to brush out her hair.

Judith was still not used to people waiting on her hand and foot. In Philadelphia, Helen sometimes assisted her if a chore proved to be too demanding, but normally Judith did everything for herself. That was the way she'd been brought up, and she was glad for that simple upbringing. In time, her charity work consumed more and more of her days, so she had given in to hire a cook and cleaning lady, but they only came in three times a week. The remaining days Judith and Helen did for themselves. Now Helen was managing it all alone.

Judith had to admit, Harriet and Beth did a good job, especially with her hair. Beth seemed to have a knack for arranging the thick mass of waves. Today she parted Judith's hair in the middle and then worked with each side individually, rolling and curling and pinning it all in place. When this was complete, she studied Judith's arrangement for just a moment and then decided against using the combs.

"I think you should wear one of the new hats," Beth suggested. She disappeared to retrieve one.

Judith hadn't even known her grandfather had arranged for new hats until Harriet told her last night. Apparently after their discussion on Friday, James Ashton had sent Mrs. Deeters out to arrange several new accessories and gowns. Judith had thought to tell him he could just send them all back, but she had read that verse in the book of Romans on Friday evening that said, "As much as it lieth with you, live peaceably with all men." She supposed that included her grandfather and said nothing. Surely she could be peaceful about a few hats and gowns.

Beth returned with the straw hat and held it up. It was rather pretty with its mushroom cap shape and blue-ribbon trim. Mrs. Deeters had seemed to understand Judith's simple tastes and had done what she could to bring her styles that would meet with her approval.

"It looks quite nice. I'm sure it will be perfect."

"Winchell told me that your grandfather is too ill to attend services with you," Harriet said almost as if it were an afterthought. "Apparently Mr. Ashton had a bad spell in the night, and the doctor was called."

"Why was I not told of this when it happened?"

"Your grandfather forbade it. He said to let you sleep," the maid replied.

Judith waved the twosome out of her way and, without even bothering to put on her shoes, padded off down the long hall to where her grandfather's suite was situated.

She knocked on the door instead of flinging it open as she felt like doing. Winchell appeared almost instantly, however, so no flinging was needed.

"I want to see my grandfather. I was just told he's suffered some sort of attack."

"Yes, miss. He was overcome with chest pains in the night. The doctor came and issued something stronger for him to take. He seems calmer this morning."

Judith drew a deep breath and forced herself to relax. "Is he awake?"

"Oh, yes. Wait here. I'll see if he's up to speaking with you."

Judith did as instructed. Winchell returned almost immediately. "He said he will see you."

The valet led the way. Judith was impressed with her grandfather's suite of rooms. It was clearly designed with a man in mind. He had chosen dark colors and large pieces of furniture. Over the fireplace hung the head of a grand stag, and rifles lined the walls. There must have been fifty guns displayed.

Judith continued following Winchell into the massive bedchamber, where a large mahogany four-poster bed was positioned at one end of the room between equally impressive floor-to-ceiling windows that looked out in the direction of the distant river. In the bed, looking quite small and frail, James Ashton Sr. had been propped up with a breakfast tray over his lap.

"I heard you weren't feeling well."

"Just a minor spell in the night. The doctor insisted I remain in bed for a few days. I won't be able to attend services with you today."

"I can stay home and help care for you." Judith didn't know why she offered such a thing. It was far too intimate a task to volunteer for. She didn't even really know this man.

"I have Winchell. I have no need for anyone else. I've instructed Charles to drive you to church and wait for you there."

Judith moved closer to the bed. "Thank you, I appreciate that. Is there anything I can do for you before I go?"

"No, nothing. However, there is something that I have in mind for you to begin on tomorrow."

"What is that?"

"I'd like you to familiarize yourself with my various business dealings. I have a great many holdings, and my investments are quite diverse. Since you have extended yourself to a higher education, I believe you'll be able to comprehend these things. Plus, Bert tells me you head up several of the charities you work with. It would seem you are no stranger to running a business.

"In the morning, Winchell will have ledgers and paperwork related to some of the basic holdings brought to your room. Read through those and get an understanding of them. Write down any questions you have. Then you and I will discuss at length the purposes for each one and what I had in mind when pursuing each investment or project."

Judith couldn't hide her surprise. "You want to involve me in your personal business?"

"Last night reminded me that my time is very limited." He fixed her with a frown. "I have no choice but to educate you on the matter. There is no one else I can trust to manage things after I'm gone."

"But your lawyer surely has an understanding of all of this and could continue managing it for you."

"No. Mr. Black has been useful to me, but there is a great deal of which he has no knowledge. In time . . . in the weeks we have left . . . I will confide it all only in you."

It was only then that Judith realized just how serious the attack must have been. James Ashton Sr. was afraid. She could see the fear in his eyes. He had finally accepted that his death was near. And he desperately needed to know that his heir could manage his holdings.

"Very well." Judith squared her shoulders and nodded. "I'll devote myself to it, starting tomorrow."

She thought about her pledge all the way to church. She could barely pay attention to the sermon for trying to figure out how this was all going to work. Not only that, but the temperature inside the church was climbing, and Judith had to admit to feeling a bit overwhelmed.

Her grandfather's plans for her were even more consuming than the heat. What if she learned all about his dealings and saw for herself the deception? The thievery? The swindles that were just barely legal? What could she do then? How could she face these people, the new friends she was making? She worked her fan vigorously.

The pastor was praying the benediction before Judith even realized what was happening. All she knew for certain was she needed fresh air. Several people came to her side almost immediately to ask her how she was doing. A couple even asked where her grandfather was. Judith didn't feel like speaking to anyone. It was as if her collar had tightened around her neck. She tried to move toward the door but found the crowds of people slow, and her steps halted.

"Judith, can you wait a moment?"

Judith turned around and found Martha Turner. Beside her was Dr. Roman Turner. He watched her with such an intensity that Judith found she had to look away as her cheeks warmed.

"Judith, I believe you've met my son, Dr. Roman Turner."

Judith had no choice but to look up; however, the effect was not at all what she'd expected. The room began to swirl around her as darkness closed in. She reached for Roman's shoulder and felt his arms go around her. It would seem once again she had made a spectacle of herself in front of Roman Turner.

"Judith. Judith, open your eyes."

She heard the male voice from far away. It was pleasant and gentle. It was the voice of someone who cared about her. She struggled to open her eyes and found the dark-headed, angry man staring down at her. He didn't look angry anymore. Instead, his face held an expression of grave concern.

A smile touched her lips, and her eyes closed again. She was no doubt dreaming. Surely that's what happened.

"Judith, open your eyes. Come on. Take a deep breath."

She obeyed the order. Things began to clear a bit more. She suddenly realized that she wasn't alone. Mrs. Turner and her daughter were on the other side of Roman, and all of them looked quite concerned. She sat up after realizing she was lying on the pew. Roman was squatted down beside her.

"Easy does it. Take it slow," he commanded.

"What in the world happened?" She put her hand to her head.

"I think you overheated," he said, still watching her as if she might faint again.

"It seems I've done it once again. I do not bear the heat well." She straightened and leaned back against the pew.

"It's no wonder. You do not perspire, I've noticed." Roman felt her forehead. "I'm wet with sweat, and even Mother is damp, but you're dry, and your skin is hot to touch."

"And quite red," his mother added.

Reverend Knickerbacker and his wife soon joined them. "How's our patient, doctor?" the reverend asked.

"Much better."

"I've never had my sermons cause someone to faint," Reverend Knickerbacker said smiling. "I hope that won't be a regular thing for you."

Judith tried to hide her embarrassment and got to her feet. "I was just apologizing. I have trouble with the heat." Roman jumped up to stand beside her. His nearness made things all the worse.

"Yes, it's terrible," Sarah Knickerbacker declared. "I felt a little overcome myself. Let's get her outside. The fresh air will help a great deal." She handed Roman a wet handkerchief. "This might help."

"Yes, thank you." Roman reached out and dabbed the damp cloth against Judith's forehead. "Did you come in your grandfather's carriage?"

She looked up, feeling acutely aware of the man and his past with her grandfather. "Yes." She barely whispered the word.

Roman put his arm around her waist and all but carried her

out of the church. The others followed. Roman didn't seem to notice them, however. He got her to the carriage, and the driver immediately opened the door.

"I'm going to ride home with her and make sure she doesn't faint again," Roman announced, climbing inside. At least he had the good sense to take the opposite seat.

"I'll stop by tomorrow and see how you're feeling and also speak to your grandfather," Reverend Knickerbacker announced.

Judith eased back and closed her eyes. "That would be fine, I'm sure."

"Driver, let's get her home. She's overheated and needs to rest."

Almost immediately the carriage was in motion, and Judith knew she'd have to face the fact that she was alone with Roman Turner.

"Thank you for helping me." She forced herself to look at him. His eyes were narrowed as if fearing she was growing sicker. "I feel quite fine now. Just a little shaken up."

He handed her the handkerchief. "I didn't mean to embarrass you in speaking about the lack of perspiration. It's likely a physical condition you may have had all your life. Do you recall ever perspiring?"

"No. I never really thought about it, but I've never been one to sweat."

"That's most likely the reason you suffer with the heat. Your body has no means of cooling as it might normally do. I don't know a lot about such conditions, but I'll try to learn more and advise you."

"I hadn't ever really thought about it being a problem."

"When you get home, it would help if you could take a cool bath," he said.

Normally such a topic would seem out of place and embarrassing, but Judith only nodded. He was, after all, a doctor and would know the importance of such things.

"I will." She held his gaze and then said the only thing that kept coming to mind. "I'm sorry."

"You don't need to apologize. I'm glad I was there to catch you . . . again. If you'd hit your head on the pew, it could have resulted in the need for stitches."

"It's not that." Judith leaned forward just a bit. "I'm sorry for what my grandfather did to your father . . . your family . . . you."

His expression was stoic. "You owe me no apology for that. I'm surprised you even believe wrong was done."

"I realize that I had nothing to do with it, but after hearing a great many people speak of him doing similar things, I've no doubt he's guilty. My only question is how it can be made right."

"Made right? It can hardly be made right. You can't bring my father back to life."

"I know." She studied him for a moment and then looked away as they reached the other side of the river.

They rode in silence after that. Judith couldn't seem to put her thoughts into words, and Roman seemed unwilling to broach the subject further. This wasn't at all how she had planned to come together with the man who had haunted her dreams these last four years. But she was a firm believer that things happened for a reason. In time, no doubt God would reveal those reasons, but for now it seemed best to remain silent.

10

Judith read her grandfather's ledgers and financial contracts until lunchtime, then went downstairs. She needed to get away from business dealings and focus on something else.

"Are you ready for lunch?" Mrs. Deeters asked.

Judith was more thirsty than hungry but nodded. "I think I'd like to eat outside under the shade trees. I just feel the need to do something different."

"I can arrange that for you. It's much cooler than the stuffiness of this house."

"Perhaps if we opened up the windows it might help," Judith suggested.

Mrs. Deeters nodded. "It would, but your . . . Mr. Ashton won't allow it. He worries that being this close to the river might bring about the ague."

"Is that possible?"

"I really have no idea, ma'am. You go on out, and I'll bring a tray. There's a small table and some chairs arranged for just such a situation."

Judith made her way through the sitting room's French

doors, which opened out to a lovely stone-paved area with a dozen or more chairs. Beyond that, the gardener had created a walkway with flower beds lining either side. An abundance of tulips bloomed along the walk. They were a riot of colors swaying gently in the breeze. Beyond them were rows of rose bushes, just leafing out with a hint of blossoms to come. Judith could imagine the wonderful scent that would come once they were in full bloom.

The air seemed much cooler in the garden, and Judith thanked God silently for the blessing. She had dressed casually for the day, wearing a simple white blouse and linen skirt. Taking a seat beneath the trees, Judith thought of her grandfather's business dealings. From the sound of things, they would soon be her responsibility. How had she gotten herself into this?

Just a few weeks ago, she hadn't even known the man, and now here she was studying his finances in order to take over for him when he died.

Lord, I have no idea why You've brought me here, but given what everyone has to say about this man, and my own observations, it would seem there is a lot of pain and misery associated with the house of Ashton.

Just then Mrs. Deeters appeared, carrying a large silver tray. "I hope I didn't take too long. Mrs. Markle had your luncheon ready, but I had to stop a moment to instruct one of the downstairs maids."

Judith spied the glass of iced lemonade and reached for it first. "You were very quick, Mrs. Deeters." She took a long, cooling drink.

"Please call me Mary," the woman replied. "At least when we're alone."

"I'd like that, Mary." Judith placed the glass against her cheek and sighed. "I'd like for us to be friends."

Mary smiled. "I'd like that too. Especially now that I've gotten to know you."

"I'm sure I caused quite the concern showing up and being so unknown. You probably feared I would be just like my grandfather."

The housekeeper's cheeks flushed, and she looked away as if embarrassed. Judith felt sorry for her.

"I didn't say that to cause distress. It's just something I've felt when I've been in the company of people my grandfather has wronged. Working for him must surely be a challenge."

"I hardly think it's appropriate to respond, but it's always of concern when anyone new arrives. Your grandfather was quite firm on the fact that we were to make your stay perfect," Mary replied.

"And it has been. I have no complaints, though I know that so many other people do. My grandfather does not have the reputation of being a kind or fair man. In fact, from what I see, he's ruthless and harsh. A man who cares little about what anyone else wants or needs."

"Then I suppose there's no sense in me denying it. His business associates have a strong respect for him."

"More like a strong fear of him, I would say. The household staff no doubt feel that way too. I've watched the way you all tiptoe around him."

Mary bowed her head slightly. "If I'm perfectly honest, I would say that as well."

Judith nodded. "Mary, would you sit with me a moment?"

The housekeeper took the chair at Judith's right. "I can spare a few minutes."

"I want to thank you for the things you purchased on my behalf. I appreciate that you took the effort to buy what you thought would please me rather than my grandfather."

The woman glanced up, looking rather relieved at the topic. "Of course. You are a pleasure to buy for. Such a trim shape, and your skin tone goes well with most every color."

"Thank you." Judith glanced toward the house. "There, now if anyone asks, we were discussing my wardrobe."

Mary gave her a momentary look of panic. Judith shook her head. "Don't be afraid of me, Mary. I want to be perfectly honest with you. I didn't come here out of any great love for my grandfather. I came here only because he gave me money for my charities back east. Now I'm hearing about horrible things he's done to others here in Minneapolis and elsewhere. He wants me to take over his investments once he's gone, but I can only agree to do that, to become his heir, on one condition."

Mary still looked fearful. "And what would that be?"

"That I can somehow right the wrongs he has made."

A whisper of hope framed Mary's next question. "Are you speaking truthfully?"

"I am. I would and do say the same before God Himself. He is, after all, my witness. Having learned who my grandfather really is, I'm more determined than ever to find a way to help those he's harmed, starting with your sister Martha and her family."

"Oh, if only you could. You don't know the half of what Mr. Ashton did to my sister's poor husband, Andrew. He was a dear man with a kind and gentle spirit. He was like a true brother to me."

"I know there are those who blame my grandfather for your brother-in-law's death. I would like to know more about that."

"I will tell you what happened, and you can judge for yourself. Mr. Ashton was cruel and, indeed, did cause Andrew's death, after a manner. It all began—"

"Miss Ashton, you have a visitor," Harriet said, appearing on the path.

Bert Black drew alongside her and smiled. "I am delighted to have found you. May I join you?"

Mary looked at Judith and gave her a nod. "I'm glad to know you were pleased with my selections. There will be two gowns coming this week. I gave the seamstress your measurements and had her make adjustments to them first. They should arrive by Thursday."

"Thank you, Mrs. Deeters. And thank you for bringing me lunch. Perhaps you could bring something for Mr. Black?"

"No, I've already had lunch, but I don't mind sitting here with you while you enjoy yours." He claimed the chair Mrs. Deeters had just deserted.

Mrs. Deeters followed Harriet toward the house. Judith had no desire to share her time with Bert Black, but there was no way to dismiss him without being rude.

"What brings you here today?"

"Business, as usual. I've been speaking with your grandfather and understand he is trying to teach you about his holdings. It's all quite complicated, and I'm certain it must be vexing to you. I wanted to come and offer my help. You see, I've worked with him for so very long that I'm sure I know it as well as he does." He chuckled at this and shrugged. "I even might know it better."

"You are kind to make such an offer, but currently I find that I understand it quite thoroughly. My grandfather and I will be discussing any questions I have this afternoon."

"Good, good. That makes my other purpose in seeing you even easier."

"And what is that purpose?"

"To ask that you allow me the pleasure of taking you out to dinner on Friday evening."

Judith had feared this might be his approach. "I'm sorry, but no. I cannot leave my grandfather for an evening of pleasure. He has just suffered a serious attack, and his condition warrants his remaining in bed. I will be here at his side until I feel it's acceptable to leave. Church will most likely be the only outing I allow myself."

Bert frowned. "I am sorry that he is growing worse. Of

course, the doctor did make it clear that he only has a few weeks, perhaps months."

"Yes, and that makes it even more important that I stay close. Besides, and I want to be perfectly honest with you because you deserve that much . . ." Judith tried to soften her tone. "I have no interest in courtship at this time. I've acquired new responsibilities, as you know, and feel I must devote myself to them, as well as my grandfather."

"I certainly cannot fault you for your kindness, especially given you hardly know the man and he wasn't exactly generous to your family."

"No, but perhaps in dying he will come to see his need for the Lord and repent of his ways." Judith picked up her lemonade again and sipped it slowly. She hoped Bert would tire of asking for her company.

"You know, I can tell you quite a bit about your grandfather. I've shared a great deal of time with him and learned a lot under his tutelage."

Judith uncovered her lunch and found salmon mousse atop slices of cucumber and tiny dill and chicken sandwiches. There was also a plate with cheese and strawberries. "Are you sure you've had enough lunch? I could have another tray brought."

Bert held out his hands. "No, I'm just fine. But please consider my offer of help. There's a lot you don't know."

Judith arranged a couple of sandwiches onto the plate with the salmon. "I'm sure that is true. It would seem I learn things every day. If I have need of your assistance, I will call upon you. For now, however, I want to allow my grandfather the time he desires. It is his hope to teach me the things he wants me to know, and I am eager to give him that opportunity. There is much we can accomplish together."

She saw a shadow of displeasure in Bert's expression but said nothing. She knew he was doing everything in his power to get her to spend time with him. He was just unwilling to be refused.

Taking up her plate and adding a few strawberries, Judith found herself wishing she'd not allowed Mary to slip away. She would have much preferred asking Bert to leave them to their discussion rather than to continue with his.

"I'm sure you're probably curious about life here in Minneapolis. You might even wonder why I chose to live here when I hail from Boston."

Judith eased back against the cushions. "I remember you saying on the train that when my grandfather came west because of business opportunities, your father sent you along to serve the legal firm as my grandfather's personal attorney."

"You have a good memory."

Judith smiled. "Yes, I do. It's something I've always been known for. Just as you are known for your quick understanding of legal matters. It was one of the reasons you graduated at the top of your class."

He chuckled. "Well, it's affirming to know you listened so closely to the things I shared. That shows a degree of caring that most people lack."

Judith had been trapped with him for hours on end while traveling west, and the man had talked of nothing but himself for most of the trip. It had nothing to do with caring.

The food was especially refreshing, and Judith found herself hungrier than she'd thought. She continued eating as a light breeze rustled through the trees. It would have all been quite pleasant if not for Bert.

"What do you think of Minneapolis?"

Shifting her weight a bit, Judith glanced around. "I've mostly seen St. Anthony, but grandfather did drive me around a bit on the other side of the river. I believe in a few years there will most likely be a vast expansion of the city and its people."

"You are correct in thinking that. I've seen it start up from next to nothing and now this. There are plans for additional bridges across the river, expansion of the railroad, and, of course, incorporating St. Anthony into Minneapolis. That will happen in the next few years if the powers that be have anything to say about it. Oh, that reminds me, have you had an opportunity to see the falls?"

"Not well. I have caught glimpses."

"I would love to show them to you. More industry is being built along the riverbanks, which makes it difficult to see them as well as you once could, but there are still a couple of lovely places from which you may observe them. We could go there most any time."

"You forget, I am focusing on my grandfather for the time. The falls will still be there when he is gone."

"Do you know the falls have been altered greatly over the years? The water is wearing down the rock."

"As water will do," Judith offered as she continued to enjoy her lunch.

"Mr. Black, Mr. Ashton is asking for you," Mrs. Deeters announced. She had slipped into their company so quietly that Judith almost did a double take to reassure herself that the woman was really there.

"Thank you, Mrs. Deeters. You may also take the tray." Judith got to her feet. "It was quite an enjoyable meal. Please thank Mrs. Markle. It was light and perfect for a day like today."

Bert stood and offered Judith his arm. "Might I escort you to the house?"

"Thank you, no. I have some things to discuss with Mrs. Deeters before I return." She fixed him with a dismissive look and waited for him to leave. After several painfully long moments, he realized the situation and gave a nod.

Once he was gone, Mary smiled, and Judith did as well. "What is it you needed to discuss?" Mary asked.

"Apparently the St. Anthony Falls have been greatly altered

over the years. The water is wearing down the rock, Mr. Black informed me."

Mary looked at her as if she'd lost her mind. Judith just shrugged. "It was something to discuss and allowed me not to have to be escorted back to the house by Mr. Black. He seems determined to court me."

The housekeeper burst into laughter and picked up the tray. "Oh, you do my heart good, Mrs. Stanford."

"Call me Judith."

"Miss Judith is familiar enough," Mary replied. "That is more appropriate for our present situation."

Bert wasn't happy to fail at starting a courtship with Judith Ashton. She seemed abnormally unconcerned with marriage and having a family of her own. The few times he'd tried to bring up the topic, she easily changed the subject as though it meant nothing to her. Good grief, she was an old maid with limited choices. His research had shown her to be thirty years old. And while she was comely, even beautiful, many a man would surely cast her aside for fear of her being unable to bear children.

What was it she wanted? She had shown no interest in her grandfather nor his wealth on the trip to Minneapolis. At first Bert had thought it was all an act, but the woman truly seemed unconcerned. Perhaps she had a great deal more wealth of her own than she let on. She was, after all, the owner of a steamboat service.

He made his way to Mr. Ashton's room, still quite perplexed. He'd never had any difficulty wooing young ladies. In fact, he had nearly allowed himself to get engaged on more than one occasion. It wasn't until he realized that he might be able to work his way into James Ashton's good graces and be appointed his heir that Bert put serious thoughts of courtship aside so he could give the man the focus he required. Despite the granddaughter's arrival, he could still have the entire inheritance if he could just convince Judith Ashton to marry him.

Winchell met him at the door to the old man's suite. "He's waiting for you."

Bert nodded and headed into the bedroom. Ashton looked particularly frail, perhaps even more so than when Bert had been with him an hour earlier.

"You called for me?"

"Yes, Bert. I want to go over the changes in the Iverson contract. Some ideas came to mind, and I believe we should look into the legalities."

Bert nodded and retrieved the papers in question. The old man was a thorn in his side at times, but he had promised to mention Bert in his will. If Bert could just hold out until the end, he would be rich. He would have a good part of the Ashton fortune, and maybe even have it all. It would work out. He was certain of this. He just had to endure for a little while longer.

Then a thought came to mind. When he'd asked Judith to join him for the evening, she had said something about being unable to leave her grandfather for an evening of pleasure.

So she does see an evening with me as being pleasurable.

He perked up a bit. Perhaps she really did care for him more than he realized.

By Friday, Judith could see a pattern to some of her grandfather's dealings. He was always the moneyed partner. His associates usually had some form of collateral to offer, and generally speaking it came in the form of land.

Noting this, she couldn't help but wish there were older records to consider. Her grandfather had released additional materials for her to study, but everything was written up in the last five years.

Catching sight of the time, Judith closed the ledger she'd been reading and prepared to go to her grandfather. Every afternoon at two, he had requested she come to his room to discuss what she was learning. It was rather fascinating to hear his reasonings behind certain projects and his projections of what he felt he could accomplish in the days to come. He was determined to leave a legacy in his Ashton Block in downtown Minneapolis. Unfortunately, Judith knew the legacy he was really leaving behind made him much despised instead of respected and admired as he hoped.

She made her way to his room and encountered Mary on

the way. "I wonder if after I visit with my grandfather, you and I might have a talk. Perhaps in the garden again."

"It looks like it might storm this afternoon, but we can surely find somewhere to speak without being overheard." Mary walked with Judith and paused when they stood at the door to her grandfather's room. "You know the doctor just left."

"No, I didn't realize." Judith frowned. "Is the news bad?"

"I don't know. I showed the doctor out and figured I'd come up and confer with Winchell. He'll be able to tell us everything."

As if speaking his name had summoned him, Winchell opened the bedroom door and looked in surprise at the two women.

"May I help you?"

Judith nodded. "I was coming to speak with grandfather per his instructions. However, Mrs. Deeters just mentioned the doctor was here. I wondered what he had to say."

Winchell stepped into the hall and pulled the door closed. "The news is not good. He has ordered your grandfather to remain bedfast. He said that Mr. Ashton is not strong enough to be up on his own without overtaxing his heart. He may sit for fifteen to twenty minutes each morning and afternoon, but otherwise should rest in bed."

"I see." Judith hadn't expected things to happen quite this fast. "Did he say . . . well . . . did he speak of when . . ." She fell silent. It was harder than she'd expected to ask about when the doctor thought her grandfather might die.

"He felt confident that your grandfather's death would come sooner than he originally thought."

Judith looked up at the older man. Winchell was probably ten years her grandfather's junior, but time with the man had clearly aged him. How she wished he felt comfortable enough with her to talk about her grandfather and their history together.

"Well, I suppose we must simply forge ahead and do whatever we can to make him comfortable."

"Yes, miss," Winchell said with a heaviness in his tone that left Judith feeling sorry for him. He had spent his entire life caring for her grandfather. No doubt he was worried at his own advanced age regarding what he would do once the man died.

She put her hand on his arm. "Winchell, you are a faithful and loyal friend to my grandfather. I know he appreciates all that you do, but I want you to know that I do as well. If I am chosen as heir and decide to remain in Minneapolis, you will always have a place here. I hope you also know that you can come to me with anything you need."

His stoic expression softened. "Thank you, miss." He stepped back and reopened the door. "I'm sure he is eagerly awaiting your visit."

Judith moved past Winchell and headed into the room. It was the first time Winchell hadn't gone ahead of her to announce the visit.

James Ashton sat propped in his bed, reading the newspaper, as Judith often found him when she came for their business discussions. He looked over the top of the paper, then folded it closed.

"I wondered if you were ever coming."

"How are you feeling today? I know the doctor saw you earlier."

"Yes, yes. The man is all doom and nonsense. He has no means of helping me, but ever so much confidence in my demise."

Judith pulled up a chair and sat down. "Well, we all must die sooner or later. Perhaps if you had more confidence in what lay beyond, you would be less disgruntled."

"Are you going to preach at me?" He frowned but didn't forbid it.

"Preach? No. But I am always happy to share with you the

simplicity of accepting Jesus as Savior and Lord. The Bible makes it quite clear that Jesus is the only way to God and the reconciliation that we so desperately need. Jesus died once for all, so you might as well accept what has been freely given."

He looked at her oddly. "You speak with such certainty that I wonder if there were ever any doubts for you."

"Doubts? About Jesus?" She shook her head. "Never. I know many people speak of difficulty in believing. Sometimes even preachers talk about how hard it was to come to a place of faith and acceptance, but that is not the case for me. My father made it clear that God is a reliable source of love and trust. He is faithfully the same yesterday, today, and forever. To be certain, God alone is the only constant in my life. How could I doubt Him when He has proven Himself over and over?"

"And what proof has He offered?"

Judith was surprised that her grandfather continued to pursue the discussion. "He has always answered my prayers. He has shown me His nature in the Bible. I see His handiwork in all of creation and find comfort in His promises."

"You say He has always given you everything you prayed for. How can that be?"

"I didn't say that He always gave me everything I prayed for. I said He always answered my prayers. To be certain, there have been times when God has refused my requests, like when my parents died even though I had prayed for them to return home safely. But even in that, He answered. I have learned from my father's example that praying for God's will in all matters is better than seeking my own."

"Your parents died during the war, did they not?"

"Yes, in 1864, but it wasn't due to any fighting. The boiler on the riverboat was faulty and blew up. It was such a powerful explosion that the boat was quickly engulfed in flames. The doctor felt certain that the blast itself killed my parents instantly. He believed they did not suffer.

"They were the most important people in my life. Still, God allowed them to die. It was His will, and I can accept that. It doesn't mean I like it, but I trust that God had a purpose even in that. And His love for them, taking them instantly—well, that blessed me too."

"Why?" Her grandfather's tone was demanding.

"Well, if anyone can account for my thoughts behind that, you surely can. Many die from disease and sickness, as you well know. Lingering day after day, suffering pain and fear of what is yet to come is hardly a comforting way to pass from this earth. However, I believe firmly that God can be a comfort to those who have Him as Lord, though I am rather puzzled at what others like you do for peace of mind during such a time."

Her grandfather's eyes narrowed. "I need no comfort or peace. I am a man of action and have been so all my life. I neither fear nor welcome death. It simply is a part of each man's life. I accept it for what it is."

"And in your mind, what is it? You see, for me I know death is but a door to eternal life with my heavenly Father. When I received Jesus as my Savior, my sins were washed clean, and I became God's own child. I can assure you that life on this earth is not the end but merely the beginning."

"You should have been born a male. Your confidence and conviction would suggest that you could make a great revivalist or perhaps politician. You are strong-willed and outspoken. In a man, those things are rewarded. Not so much in a woman."

Judith laughed. "And well I know that."

Her grandfather studied her for a moment, then shook his head. "But perhaps it serves you well enough to be a woman, for such nature is unexpected. I have come to realize that you are full of surprises."

"I am an Ashton, after all." She waited for him to challenge her.

"Indeed, you are that."

She smiled at this new acceptance. "Good. Now, are you ready to discuss business?"

"Mary, I've poured over all of the books and contracts in my grandfather's office," Judith began, "but I'm wondering where I might lay my hands on his older dealings."

"There is a room on the third floor where his oldest records are stored. He's always said that no one is to have access, but I have a key. I go in from time to time to dust and make sure things are still in order."

"I want to go there. I need to read through the old contracts and see for myself how he cheated people in the early days. It seems to me that I have a great deal of work to accomplish once he's gone."

"What do you mean?"

Judith got up from behind her grandfather's desk. "I mean, James Ashton Sr. wasn't as good at hiding his manipulations and schemes as he might have thought he was. Perhaps God has given me the ability to read between the lines, but I can easily see what my grandfather has done. And, while he might have managed to conduct business in a legal manner, it certainly wasn't done in an ethical one."

Mary Deeters nodded and produced a ring of keys. "I'll show you up there at once. You'll need a lamp."

Judith grabbed one of the lamps from the hall table and followed Mary up to the third floor. Mary pointed out the rooms of various staff, including her own, as she moved to the far end of the hall. "Mr. Winchell is the only staff member to have a room on the second floor. It's attached to the back of your grandfather's suite. He wanted to have the man close at all times."

"It's no wonder Winchell is so devoted."

"It would be best if no one knew you were working up here," Mary said as she unlocked the door.

Judith could well understand her concern. "Do you suppose it would be better if I were to take some of the records to my room? Perhaps you could help me."

"Yes, we should just take a few at a time so there's no sign that someone has moved things around. I doubt your grandfather will have the energy to come up here and check, but it's best we not give anyone a reason to suggest it."

An hour later, Judith was set up in her sitting room with a handful of business ledgers and stacks of correspondence. All were dated from as early as 1855. Judith began reading and found herself completely immersed in the founding days of the area. The civic leaders from both sides of the river came together to make plans for a suspension bridge that would span the Mississippi. It would be the very first, and James Ashton did his best to impose himself in the planning. He noted the importance of this being a toll bridge. There would be plenty of people who would want to cross the river without having to make a lengthy ferry ride. A toll would help to pay not only for the bridge but for its upkeep as well. Judith noted he recommended fifteen cents per horse, ten cents per cow, and two cents for each sheep. People were to be charged depending on their ages, anywhere from three to five cents. He wrote down that these recommended prices were later accepted.

She continued poring through the papers and her grandfather's notes. There were several situations where he acquired a great deal of land. The dealings were a mix of failed loans and prearranged agreements. By the time Harriet came with her supper tray, Judith was more than ready to put her work aside.

"It's funny that Mr. Ashton would have you reading all those business reports," Harriet declared, uncovering Judith's dinner.

Mrs. Markle had outdone herself. A filet of beef smothered in a burgundy sauce with braised garlic and rosemary potatoes awaited her sampling. There was also coffee, to which Judith immediately began to add sugar and cream.

"I suppose my grandfather sees the sense of utilizing people he knows to be trustworthy," Judith replied.

"I don't know how you do it. I can barely read through a letter. I can't imagine reading all those papers and ledgers. I was never good with numbers."

"We all have our gifts. You do an amazing job of ironing and mending. I'm not as good at that."

Harriet straightened after uncovering Judith's dessert of bread pudding with vanilla sauce. "I've never been praised for my work. I suppose it is a sort of talent. God gave us each our abilities."

"Exactly," Judith said, smiling. "And our responsibilities. For example, I'm the only remaining relative of James Ashton. It has left me with a critical job to do. Since I believe nothing happens by chance or without God's knowledge, I will accept this as His will for me and do my best."

"Oh, miss, I do love the way you talk about God. It reminds me of my mother. She's gone now, but she was always encouraging me to put my trust in God's goodness."

"I would encourage you to do the same, Harriet. He's never failed me yet."

Harriet nodded. "I'm sure that's true for myself as well." She paused at the door. "May I ask you a question?"

"Of course, Harriet. What is it?" Judith stopped stirring her coffee and met the girl's concerned expression.

"Well, the servants here know that Mr. Ashton isn't long for the world. God bless him." She paused, looking to see if Judith was willing for her to continue.

"Go on." Judith put the spoon down and gave the girl her full attention.

"Well, it's just that we're . . . well, we're kind of worried."

"About what?"

"Our situations . . . our positions. If Mr. Ashton does die, will you retain us?"

Judith thought of Winchell's look of worry earlier. She hadn't considered how the others must be just as concerned about their employment.

"If my grandfather chooses me as his heir, and I choose to stay, you will all have a place here for as long as you continue to give good service. I wish I could offer you something more permanent at this moment, but decisions haven't been made. However, should you choose to take positions elsewhere, I will give good recommendations for each."

The look of relief on Harriet's face was instantaneous. "Thank you, miss. It's good to know."

"You may tell the others if the subject comes up. However, don't give yourselves over to lengthy deliberations. We don't know what the future holds for any of us. God alone will guide us. Trust in Him."

"Yes, miss."

Judith waited until the girl had exited the room to pray her thanks for the meal. She also prayed for wisdom to know how to deal with the information she was taking in. Her grandfather had cheated most of the early settlers of Minneapolis and St. Anthony. But there were also legitimate dealings that had merited him gain simply because he was a smart businessman. He had made a fortune for himself through those things, which was what puzzled Judith. Why should he stoop to questionable arrangements when he was able to make plenty of money through ethical means?

When Mary checked on her later that evening, Judith was ready for a new set of books and papers. Mary took the old books and returned them to the storage room, then brought Judith additional ones before bidding her good night.

"Do you have everything you need, Judith?" She held a hand to her stomach as if in pain.

"I do, but I'm concerned about you. Did you overdo it carrying those things upstairs? It was thoughtless of me not to help."

Mary shook her head and grimaced. "No, it's an old complaint. I have pain from time to time. The doctor says it has to do with something in my body called a gallbladder. Some kind of stone has formed, perhaps more than one. It's quite difficult to remove it. It's all right, though. It should pass in time, and I'm sure to feel better. Please don't worry yourself."

"You will let me know if you need something, won't you?"

"Of course, but as I said, please don't worry about it." The mantel clock chimed. "Will there be anything else?"

"No, I'm fine. Please get some rest."

Mary nodded and hurried from the room as if uncomfortable that anyone should know of her situation.

Judith had never heard of such a thing as a gallbladder. She prayed silently that Mary might find healing and that there would be no further trouble from these stones that were causing such pain. At times like these, Judith marveled at the intricacy of the human body.

"We truly are fearfully and wonderfully made."

In the morning after breakfast, Judith began again sorting through the papers and ledgers. She had to say this much for her grandfather: He was meticulous at keeping records. He wrote down the details of each transaction, as well as his thoughts on the matter. It was rather like being able to go back in time and know what the man's motivations were. None of them were good, and yet he noted them all. It was almost as if he were proud of his decisions. Perhaps he was.

James Ashton Sr. was focused solely on greed and accomplishment. The person he admired most in the world was himself. He spoke of previous dealings that had taken place in Boston, leaving Judith to wonder about his deceptions and underhanded operations prior to coming to Minneapolis. No doubt there were other records elsewhere regarding those situations.

I have offended Governor Sibley. Ridiculous man. Sibley learned of my plan to purchase public school land for pennies on the dollar. It would have been a simple matter, but he had to get involved and vetoed it for no better reason than his dislike of me, Judith read from a book marked *1858*. It seemed her grandfather was happy to steal from the state as well.

By noon, she was ready for additional materials, but Mary hadn't yet come to see her. It concerned Judith enough that she carried the ledgers to the third floor and stopped at Mary's room on the way.

She gave a light knock. Mary responded in a weak voice, and Judith hurried to open the door, despite the load she carried. She came into the room and placed the books on a nearby chair.

"Mary, are you all right?" She went to the woman's bedside. "What can I do?"

"Nothing. The doctor was already here. Winchell brought him after he saw your grandfather. The doctor thinks the worst of it has passed. The pain in the night was so severe I could barely breathe. Now it's but a minor discomfort."

"There must be something that can be done."

Mary closed her eyes. "He says there is nothing."

"Have you asked your nephew, Dr. Turner?"

"No. I didn't want to worry the family. I haven't even told my sister. Usually, the nausea and pain pass within a day or so. I was just planning to get up and get to work."

"You need to let your nephew know. As I understand from Sarah Knickerbacker, he is an exceptional surgeon. Perhaps he could remove this stone that is causing you so much trouble. He might have some new information that my grandfather's doctor is lacking."

"Mr. Ashton's money pays for the best doctor. I'm sure he would know if there were more that could be done."

Judith wasn't convinced of that. Her grandfather would not

be likely to encourage his own physician to give his attention to a mere servant. Judith wondered if he even knew that the doctor had looked in on Mary.

"How goes your research?" Mary asked, changing the subject.

"It's quite alarming. I see how my grandfather has been responsible for harming so many people, and his own personal feelings are ones of selfish ambition and pride at what he's accomplished. It's no wonder my father walked away. He was nothing like my grandfather." Judith sat down on the edge of the bed and felt Mary's forehead. She had a slight fever. "Who is taking care of you, Mary?"

"The girls check in on me. They're good help. Don't worry about me."

"Of course I shall worry. But better still, I shall pray and endeavor to do whatever I can to aid you. Is there anything in particular that you need?"

"No, I'm all right. Even now, the pain is subsiding, and I need to get to my duties. This is the way of my condition. In a few hours, I'll be right as rain." She smiled, but Judith could see she was still hurting.

"Look, I'm taking charge. I want you to stay in bed today. You have tomorrow off anyway. Remain in bed and rest. If anyone asks, I will tell them that I ordered you to do so. I'll speak to Harriet and Beth and see that they check on you hourly. I'll also arrange with Mrs. Markle to make you some chicken broth. That should sit easy in your stomach."

Mary reached for Judith's hand. "I appreciate that you are so kindhearted, but please don't worry about me. Just do what you can to help my sister. Now that you can see the truth of your grandfather, you needn't doubt that he was the cause of her husband's death."

"Do you feel good enough to finish telling me what happened?"

"Yes. It was just before the war when Andrew first started working with your grandfather. Andrew held a great deal of land. Most of it was located in much sought-after areas. In one particular location, Andrew intended to build a row of homes for newcomers who couldn't afford to buy land and build. He had figured he would rent out these places at a reasonable price and provide a steady income for the future. He planned that there would be twenty houses all connected to the other.

"He went to your grandfather to arrange financial help. He needed a loan, despite having a good amount of money saved up. He felt certain that because of the number of people who were moving into the area, he could rent them out quickly and pay back your grandfather in no time at all."

"So what happened?"

"Andrew misread the contract and the arrangements. The money was due back in full far sooner than he originally had thought. The entire thing collapsed like a house of cards, and Andrew lost his money and the land, which he'd had to put up as collateral. Your grandfather refused to extend the time of repayment, and Andrew realized he'd been duped, although it was his own fault for not having read the contract more carefully, or better still, seeking legal counsel. Your grandfather had legal right to do as he chose. Andrew lost everything. He had no choice but to sell the lovely house he'd built for his family and find one that was of lesser cost to rent. He did what he could to try to regain his financial foundation, but nothing seemed to work out for him. He saw his dream realized for another man when Mr. Ashton built the houses elsewhere. It killed something inside of him. Little by little, Andrew despaired of life. He stopped eating and eventually took to his bed. He died there not long after."

"How awful. I am so sorry." Judith hadn't yet read the information from her grandfather's point of view, but no doubt he celebrated the land acquisition as a great victory.

"Judith, whatever happens to me, please promise you will try to make things right for my sister. Roman doesn't make a large salary, although he could. His heart is to work with the poor, to extend the healing of Jesus. The charities pay him, but they can't give him much money. My sister and niece do what they can to add to the finances, and I give them money as well, but they deserve so much more. They had great comfort and lovely things and lost them all. My sister and I were from a well-off household. Our father was a banker, and we wanted for nothing. Still, Martha has never complained about losing any of it, save her beloved husband."

The sorrow in Mary's eyes was enough to renew Judith's desires for truth and justice. "I promise you, I will do whatever I can to make it right. I'm ashamed to know that my grandfather would act in such a deceptive way, but if he makes me his heir, I will set things right in St. Anthony and Minneapolis. You have my word."

"I think he'll be fine eventually," Roman said as he administered some burn salve to the toddler's arm. The little boy cried and did his best to wriggle away from the nun who held him.

Work at the makeshift orphans' home was difficult at best due to a lack of funding. Some of the area ministers had been working to see a better facility put together, but charitable works were completely reliant on churches and generous people. There seemed to be fewer and fewer funds available from either, and as of late, the churches seemed less interested in community projects. Some even refused to work alongside those from other denominations.

Added to this, Roman had heard it whispered that a financial crisis was not far in the future. There were problems with inflation that seemed to suggest it could be a nationwide issue, perhaps even extending to Europe.

With tender care, he wrapped the boy's arm. "I'm glad the law thought to remove him from his father's abuse." The nun had told him this had been no accident. Others witnessed the child's father fling a pot of boiling water at the crying toddler. Thankfully, most of it missed the boy.

Roman couldn't understand what would prompt an adult to lose their wits with a child. It wasn't as if a two-year-old could understand his father's despair at losing his job.

When he completed his task, Roman ruffled the boy's golden curls and smiled at him. "I know it hurts, partner, but in time hopefully you won't even remember."

Still, what was this child's future? It was possible a judge might hear the case, but most likely the toddler would be returned home once a promise of safety was given. The boy's mother was off tending to her sick father. Perhaps once she returned, the child's life would be safe once again. It was even possible his father would find work. Things might improve, and the incident would be forgotten.

But Roman couldn't forget it. He knew the burns would blister and ooze. They would hurt and cause the boy to suffer, and there was little he could do to remove the pain. The little ones were always suffering. Hunger, pain, and often a lack of a home and family. These weren't uncommon issues. No matter how much Roman did, the poor kept coming. Their misery spilled over into his own.

He headed down the street, hoping to make it home for lunch. He was nearly to the bridge when Reverend Knickerbacker hailed him from his buggy.

"Dr. Turner, might I drive you somewhere?"

"I was headed home, so that's rather out of your way." Roman smiled and held up his bag. "I was just tending to some of the children. Any word on when we might get a better facility for them?"

"Climb up here, and I'll tell you what I know. The drive isn't that far, and you know they refuse to charge me a toll since I am on God's work."

Roman laughed and climbed into the buggy. "Very well, then. You'll save me a charge to cross the bridge."

The tollman waved the reverend on as they approached the bridge. Roman eased back against the leather upholstery and relaxed.

"I was sorry to hear that your aunt is under the weather."

"I didn't know she was." Roman looked at the man for further explanation. "What's wrong?"

"I visited James Ashton earlier. He has become quite ill, and since he visited our church with his granddaughter, I thought it my obligation to check in. The doctor was there and told me his days are numbered. While we were speaking, he also mentioned seeing your aunt. She's suffering biliary colic and was in quite a bit of pain through the night. She seemed to be better, however. When I spoke to her, she was resting and told me the pain was greatly diminished."

Roman frowned. "I didn't realize she was ill. She's not good about telling the family, for fear my mother will worry. I would go and check on her myself, if not for Ashton. I would not want to have to speak to him."

"He's bedbound so there's little worry of that."

"Then I'll go to see her immediately. Might you drop me at the Ashton estate, instead of taking me home?"

The reverend nodded. "Certainly. I'm glad she'll have you to check up on her, but honestly, Roman, you should let go of your anger toward Mr. Ashton. The past is laid to rest, and soon Mr. Ashton will be as well. Your anger hurts only you and does nothing to bring about justice for the wrongs done to your family."

It was true, and Roman knew it full well. He had struggled for nearly ten years with this burden. "I know the Bible tells us to forgive, but that man has done such evil."

"You aren't his judge, Roman. The Lord will deal with him. We live in an evil time, and the devil seeks to destroy all that he can. He is at present destroying your peace of mind, and dare I say your joy?"

"I suppose you might as well. Thoughts of Ashton and all that he did to my family do cause great distress. I know that God is in control of my heart, but James Ashton seems to control the world around me."

"But you know that isn't true. It is but a façade. The devil finds great satisfaction in deceiving people into believing he can give them the power to thwart God's plans. He has certain powers, that much is true, but as Christians, we need not fear his abilities."

"We are told to resist him."

"We are told first to submit ourselves to God," the reverend corrected. "Submit first, then resist with God's strength and power. The devil will then have no choice but to flee. We cannot defeat him on our own, however."

"It would seem no man could defeat James Ashton."

"No, but perhaps a woman shall."

Roman shook his head. "I don't understand."

Knickerbacker shifted on the seat as they exited the bridge. He glanced at Roman a moment. "Judith Stanford is a woman of God. Her grandfather has made her his heir. He told me as much as we spoke about his great fortune and all that he's accomplished. He intends to see her go forward with all his ambitious plans, but I have a feeling that God's plans are quite different."

"I'm sure he'll make provisions that won't allow her to do much good."

"I believe we should be praying for that young woman. My Sarah says that she is determined to see the poor helped and the lonely comforted. I believe God's influence over Judith is stronger than that of her grandfather. Remember, the wrong he did you and yours was not the only wrong he did. He rejected his own son and cast him aside, leaving him to make his own way. Which he apparently did, just as you and your family have done."

"But the devil has a way of taking hold of a person before they even realize what has happened."

Knickerback looked back at the road. "Do you mean to offer yourself as an example?"

"Why would you say that?" Roman was beginning to feel a bit chastised.

"I only point out the obvious truth. Do you suppose it to be the will of our Lord that you have carried hatred for almost a decade? It's certainly not beneficial to sharing the Gospel or offering encouragement to others. Hate destroys as nothing else can. And perhaps it causes the most damage to the person who offers it up."

Roman couldn't deny that his anger and hate had taken its toll. He heaved a sigh as the reverend directed his horse to turn onto the Ashton drive. The palatial estate spread out before him as a reminder of all his family had lost. James Ashton had built his home on the wealth he'd taken away from his partners. He had set himself up as a financial king over all, not even caring about the people he'd hurt.

"You're right, of course. I have given the devil a foothold. It wasn't my desire to do so."

"Of course not, Roman. The pain you experienced at losing your father and seeing such harm come to your mother and sister left you devastated. It is when we are at our most vulnerable that the devil whispers in our ear. I know from the experience of losing my children. I might well have lost my very mind, but God in His righteous mercy sent me protection as I prayed. Remember the Bible speaks in Ephesians of how we wrestle not against flesh and blood but against principalities, powers, the rulers of the darkness of this world, and spiritual wickedness in high places." He brought the horse to a stop and gave Roman a smile. "He doesn't leave us as orphans. He has given us spiritual armor and the help of heaven. Let go of the darkness that would destroy you, Roman. Embrace the love of God. Forgive this man of his wrongdoings, knowing full well that God is master of all."

Roman heaved a sigh. "I've never said this before, but I will try." He climbed down from the buggy. "Thank you for the ride and for the sermon."

The reverend smiled. "I'll be praying for you. You are called to a higher purpose, Roman. A purpose you cannot reach with fetters on your ankles."

"I appreciate the prayers." He gave a wave as Knickerbacker put his horse in motion and left the Ashton estate.

Turning, Roman stared up at the massive house. His father's losses no doubt helped to build the place. Anger caused him to tense. In the past, Roman would have accepted it and let it take him into dark brooding, but not this time. The reverend was right. It was time to put such things aside.

"Set me free, Lord," he whispered. "I give it to You."

Roman squared his shoulders and went to knock on the door. To his surprise, it opened quickly, and Judith Stanford greeted him.

She smiled. "It's good to see you again, Dr. Turner. I was wondering how I might get you here, but I wasn't supposed to say anything." She paused and laughed. "Here I am rambling. Do come in."

It was the first time Roman had ever been inside the Ashton house. And even though his aunt Mary had described the wealthy furnishings, Roman was momentarily taken aback.

"It is a bit much," Judith commented as she followed his gaze.

"Indeed." Roman looked at her. "I don't mean to intrude and frankly wouldn't have come if the Reverend Knickerbacker hadn't assured me your grandfather is bedbound."

"Yes, he is. The doctor says his heart is failing him fast."

"He also told me my aunt is ill. She's the reason I've come. I'd like to see her."

"Of course. Mary didn't want me to say anything to you, but she's suffering with gallbladder difficulties. Apparently, it's been ongoing for some time now. She said the doctor implied there was nothing to be done, but I thought perhaps you would have a different opinion."

"I very well may. I'll have to speak to her first, however."

Judith smiled. It was such a pretty smile. Her entire face seemed to light up. Why did she have to be an Ashton? He drew in a deep breath and pushed aside the negative thought. He was truly determined to rid himself of this hatred.

"Come along, I'll take you to her. I commanded her to stay in bed today and tomorrow. I don't even think she should exert herself to attend church. I have the cook making her chicken broth and milk toast. It seemed the right thing to do, but if you have other suggestions, I can definitely instruct Mrs. Markle to do otherwise."

"It sounds as though you made good choices."

Judith headed up the stairs. "She's on the third floor, so just follow me."

Roman did exactly that, watching her trim figure move quickly up the stairs. She waited until they were on the third floor to speak again.

"It's considerably warmer up here. I've opened some of the windows to let in the breeze. I hope that wasn't the wrong thing to do. I was told my grandfather worried about the river air causing the ague."

"Airing out the place is a good idea. How are you managing the heat?"

"I'm dressing in lighter-weight clothes," she said, holding her arms out. "As you can see."

"I haven't yet been able to find much information on conditions that cause a person to be unable to sweat. Make certain you drink plenty of fluids and keep a cloth and water available. You should be able to lower your temperature in such a manner. And tepid baths are also quite good."

"Thank you, I will keep all of that in mind. For now, I've also enjoyed sitting beneath the shade trees in the garden. The air there always seems cooler." She smiled, and Roman momentarily forgot about why he'd come.

"I'll leave you to visit Mary. I do hope you can help her to feel better," Judith said, stopping in front of one of the many doors. Roman had to force himself to keep from reaching out to push back an errant strand of her hair.

"She's just inside. Would you like me to announce you?"

He regained his senses and cleared his throat. "No, that's all right. Thank you for taking care of her."

Their gazes locked for a long moment. Roman couldn't help but remember the feel of her in his arms when she'd fainted. He wanted very much to hold her again. Why couldn't he just talk to her about his feelings? Did it really have to matter that she was related to James Ashton? It wasn't as if she had done the harm.

"There's something I want to say."

Judith cocked her head slightly to the right. "What is it?"

She sounded just as caught up in the moment as he felt. He started to reach for her, then stopped. This really wasn't the time or place. Yet how could he let even another moment go by without telling her how he felt?

"I—well, that is—you are—" He stopped and shook his head. "I think the heat is getting to me. I just want to tell you that I have great admiration . . . for you."

Her eyes widened. "I feel the same about you."

He swallowed the lump in his throat. Why couldn't he just speak in a coherent manner? He felt like a schoolboy caught doing something wrong.

"I wish . . . that is, I hope we might . . . well, get better acquainted."

"Ah . . . yes." She seemed rather breathless. Was she getting sick? "I'd like that."

"I suppose I should see Aunt Mary."

She nodded and stepped away. "I'll, uh, leave you to visit." She appeared flustered.

"Wait!" Roman's gaze narrowed. "You sound . . . well, you sound uneasy. Is the heat causing you distress?"

Judith stared blankly for a moment. She shook her head. "No. I'm fine. You should see Mary." With that she hurried away.

Well, you made a mess of that, he chided silently. Roman watched her until she disappeared down the stairs. He pulled himself together and reached for the door. His hands were shaking slightly. What was this power she had over him?

He drew a deep breath and gave a light knock. There'd be time to assess the matter later.

"Come in," his aunt's voice called.

He stepped into the room and glanced down at the woman who was propped up in bed. "I heard you were unwell."

"Judith shouldn't have sent for you."

"She didn't. Reverend Knickerbacker told me you were ill." He pulled up the chair to her bedside. "But seriously, you should have sent for me."

"I knew you didn't want to come here."

"But I would have, and now I have. Reverend Knickerbacker said you are having gallbladder trouble. Judith confirmed this."

"Mr. Ashton's doctor said there's nothing to be done."

"Mr. Ashton's doctor doesn't know everything. How long have you struggled with this?"

"Several months now. It comes and goes."

Roman nodded. "And is it a little worse each time?"

"Yes. I usually have great nausea with the pain. Sometimes fever too. This spell was the worst yet. I was in severe pain all last night."

"It might sound frightening, but there is a surgery to remove the stones. It seems to give instant relief to the patient. It is of course a risk to do surgery on anyone, but you can hardly allow it to continue getting worse."

She frowned. "Can this kill me?"

He let out a deep breath. "Actually, yes."

"Are you able to do this surgery?"

"I've never done it before, but I have read a great deal about it."

"If you think I should, then I would trust you to do it." His aunt smiled. "I believe in your abilities, Roman."

"Better to keep your trust in God and ask Him to bless my abilities. You say you're feeling better. Is the pain gone?"

"Mostly. Judith has taken good care of me."

Roman nodded. "She told me what she's been doing. She's actually done all of the right things."

"She's quite special, Roman. Nothing like her grandfather. I really think you should get to know her for yourself and not judge her so harshly just because she's an Ashton. I think you'd really like her if you did."

He smiled and patted Mary's hand. "I think you're right. I think it's quite possible I would really like her."

"She's really feeling much better, but you are, of course, welcome to come and visit her for yourself," Judith told Martha Turner at church the next morning. "I am to blame for her not being here today. I told her to rest."

"I'm glad you did," Martha Turner replied. "She's not good at taking time for herself."

"Neither are you, Mother," Roman said, joining them.

His mother laughed. "It would seem our family has issues with leisure time."

"Or the lack thereof," Roman added.

Judith felt a little strange anytime Roman came near. She

supposed it was because of their intimate encounter the day before. She couldn't be sure, but she thought perhaps Roman was having feelings for her. If so, it only served to heighten her own for him. There was just something about the man.

"Oh, Dr. Turner, before I forget, I have something for you." She reached into her purse. "I meant to give this to you yesterday, but you left before I could see you again." She handed him five twenty-dollar gold pieces. "I want to contribute this to your charity work. Your mother said you often treat the poor and receive nothing in return. Let this help you with your supplies and personal needs. The worker is worthy of his wages." She met his dark-eyed gaze and felt the air leave her lungs. Why did he have such a powerful effect on her?

"Thank you for the donation. This is a great deal of money." He seemed genuinely surprised.

"There are so many needs. I know from my work in Philadelphia. This won't take you all that far, but my hope is to donate more as time goes on. And I would be happy to help in any way you might need me. I have even done some nursing. I'm not formally trained, mind you, but I worked for a time as a nurse during the war and learned a great deal. We had a great many wounded soldiers brought to the various hospitals in Philadelphia. The need for nurses was great, and since I'm not squeamish, I volunteered after my husband was killed."

He looked at the money again and then smiled at her. "I would be pleased to have your company in my work. There are a great many needs in our city."

His smile and approval warmed her to her toes. Judith felt her cheeks warm. "I should take my seat before the services start." *Or I faint again.*

"Judith, I want you to meet my fiancé," Claudette said, coming to join them. "This is Daniel Moretti."

"I'm pleased to meet you, Daniel."

He was a dashing young man with black hair and a winning

grin. “The pleasure is mine.” Judith was glad for something else to focus on rather than Roman’s nearness.

“Judith, why don’t you sit with us since you’re alone and our Mary is absent?” Mrs. Turner asked, taking hold of her arm.

Claudette and Daniel were already moving to take their section of the pew. Martha followed, pulling Judith with her. Mrs. Turner sat down beside Daniel, and Judith had no choice but to take the seat beside her. It would have been rude to do otherwise.

Roman looked down at her for a moment, then slipped in next to her. The fit was tight, putting Roman’s broad shoulders against her. Judith could feel the warmth of his body. She could smell his cologne and hair tonic. She forced herself to breathe.

Why did he have to be so handsome? How in the world was she supposed to focus on the sermon?

With Mary fully recovered and back to work, Judith could devote her full attention to her grandfather's business records once again. She came to look forward to their afternoon discussions, although his weakening condition was evidenced in his quieter demeanor. Even so, he seemed more than willing to relate stories of past dealings and didn't hesitate to answer when Judith asked questions regarding his transactions. It didn't appear to bother him in the least that he'd taken advantage of others. His mind was still able to recall details with amazing accuracy, and to him, business was simply business. If someone was hurt in the process, well, that was their problem.

"If a man can't look out for himself, he has no business working for himself."

Judith's brow furrowed. "But what about helping your partners to learn so they wouldn't get taken advantage of?"

"It wasn't my place to school them. Nor is it yours."

His attitude was alarming to Judith. He honestly didn't care about duping people. With each improper business deal, Judith wrote down names and suggestions for how she might right the wrong. She was getting quite a long list.

She started to say something, but just then Mr. Black came into the room. He was dressed in a dapper gray suit with a white shirt and red tie. He glanced at Judith with an expression that suggested he knew exactly how good he looked.

Her grandfather struggled to sit up a little better. "I asked Bert to join us to go over the plans for my block downtown."

Judith quickly forgot all about Bert's finery and went to help her grandfather. His skin bore a sickly yellow-gray pallor. His eyes, which always seemed alert, were dull, and his gaze fixed on something across the room. Judith helped him to straighten, then did her best to put his condition from her mind. Even so, she wondered when the end would come.

"I was happy to accommodate," Bert said, smiling at Judith. "Miss Ashton is such a pleasure to work with. I must say that there aren't many women who are as astute and knowledgeable."

"Stop trying to pay court to my granddaughter." Her grandfather eyed the man with contempt. "I didn't ask you here to play the part of suitor. Now give me the figures for my building materials."

Judith listened as Bert read off a list of numbers and their corresponding items. Her grandfather wanted the buildings in his block to be hewn out of marble. He wanted his block to stand out as a shimmering memorial. It was akin to erecting a huge gravestone downtown, at which all could come and worship. But she had other plans. He might well desire to have an Ashton Block downtown, but Judith intended the use for those buildings to be quite different. Wouldn't it be wonderful if one building was a hospital and another an orphanage? Perhaps there could be a place to facilitate the coming together of area churches to coordinate aid and shelter for the destitute. She would still call it the James Ashton Block, but with her father in mind, as well as her grandfather.

"And I believe we can get those items shipped to Duluth and then sent by railroad to Minneapolis," Bert summed up.

"Good. I like the sound of that. When will you place the order?"

"Immediately, if that is your desire."

The older man nodded, and Judith made a mental note to speak to Bert before he left. She didn't want him ordering up marble and brass for buildings that could just as easily be built of brick.

"Judith, I have a great deal of work to do with Bert, so if you'll leave us for the time being, you and I can continue our discussion later."

She nodded and got to her feet. "Just have someone come for me when you're ready to continue."

Outside his door, Judith ran into Mary, who was instructing a new housemaid on the finer details of cleaning.

"Use the linseed-oil mixture. It brings out the sheen of the wood," Mary told the girl. "Polish every piece of wood in the hall with it."

"Yes, ma'am." The girl seemed eager to please.

"How are you feeling, Mrs. Deeters?" Judith refrained from calling her Mary to maintain the façade of employer and employee.

"Better, miss. Thank you." She smiled. "Would you care to have coffee brought to your room?"

"Yes, that would be nice." With that, Judith disappeared down the hall. She would await Mary in her sitting room, where they could speak in private.

About fifteen minutes later, Mary appeared with a tray. "I brought some of Mrs. Markle's berry scones. She is quite gifted in her baking."

"Yes, she is. I'm glad my grandfather was particular in hiring a cook. The woman is extraordinary. I shall be happy to keep her on."

A look of surprise crossed Mary's face. "Does that mean you intend to remain in Minneapolis?"

Judith smiled. "I am considering it. I like it here. It's fresh and exciting. I'm asking God to show me exactly where He wants me."

Mary placed the tray on the small table by the sofa. "Would you like me to serve?"

"No, just sit and let's discuss what's happening. Please help yourself to the refreshments." Judith poured herself a cup of coffee. "I was just listening to my grandfather's plans for his downtown block. The man is thinking to spend hundreds of thousands of dollars. It's quite ridiculous. And for what? A bank, an investment firm, and other financial institutions."

Mary handed her the cream. "I've never understood the way the rich spend their money. But then, I've never been rich." She chuckled as if she'd made a great joke.

Smiling, Judith poured the cream and set it aside. "It just seems that people who have the means to make others happy, or at least taken care of, have little sense in how to do so." She took up the sugar before stirring. "I need to speak to Mr. Black before he leaves. Would you direct him to the front parlor when he is ready to leave? Then just let me know, and I will join him there."

"Of course." Mary adjusted the front of her apron. "Do you need anything else?"

"No, but stress with Mr. Black that it will take only a moment. I don't want him thinking I want to sit and bask in his company."

Mary nodded and smiled. "It won't be any trouble. I'll see to it that he waits." She stood. "You know, my sister is quite fond of you. She said you volunteered to go with some of the women to serve refreshments to the homeless down by the river."

"I did." Judith frowned. "I'm very troubled that there are so many children who seem to be without homes or guidance. Philadelphia has many great institutions that help with these matters. I keep thinking perhaps my help here would be better needed than back east."

"Yet another reason to favor Minneapolis. I'm sure that some of these children have run away from bad situations."

"No doubt. I hate that such a life only serves to worsen their lot. If they don't get a strong foundation with a basic education, then it's harder for them to find jobs with decent wages as they grow older. It's like a stone rolling out of control. I know we do what we can to lend aid, but they need so much." Judith shook her head. "I feel so inadequate to help."

"But you've a good heart, Judith. God has given you the desire to serve, and you do it beautifully. I'm praying that He'll show you exactly what you need to do. And you know, it wouldn't hurt to have a good man at your side. Someone like my nephew." Mary smiled. "I think you two would make a fine couple."

"I've admired him since I first met him, but your nephew hates my grandfather. I'm not sure he could look past that for long."

"He's learning to forgive and let go of the past. He confided to us that he wants to let go his anger toward Mr. Ashton. With the right woman, he would find it much easier to look forward than behind."

"Especially if that woman could help make amends." Judith sampled the coffee and shook her head. "Oh, Mary, there's just so much to do."

◇◇◇

"Will there be anything else?" Bert asked James Ashton. The man was completely worn out, so Bert presumed he would need to rest.

"Just this. Don't think you can change my will."

Bert's eyes narrowed. "Sir?"

"I know you've an eye on my money. I know you've tried to woo my granddaughter, thinking that if I don't leave you enough, you'll get my money by marrying her."

"Sir, that's hardly the reason I've taken an interest in your granddaughter. She's a beautiful woman, and I found her charming from the moment we first met. It was love at first sight for me, and her feelings for me are growing each day."

"Bah! She's too sensible for that. As for you, you're in love all right, but it's with my money. If you manage yourself properly, there will be something for you. However, if you continue to annoy me, I will have you cut out."

Bert knew he would need to tread lightly. "I apologize if I've offended you, but I truly have fallen in love with your granddaughter. And I believe she's starting to return my affections. I do hope to win her heart."

"She's not for the likes of you. She's smarter than you, and her faith will never allow her to settle for anyone who doesn't feel as she does about God. But that's beside the point. I forbid it. I don't want you thinking you can marry her."

Bert had to bite his tongue to keep from blurting out that the old man would soon be dead and have no ability to interfere. He knew Judith's feelings for him were growing. She smiled at him all the time. She even complimented him on his clothes from time to time. He thought perhaps he would tell Mr. Ashton about those incidents, but they were so tender and special to him. Why let the old man ruin his moments? Instead, Bert remained silent and figured James Ashton could think he'd won this round.

"You might as well know, I nullified the will that you drew up for me. I've had two other lawyers take charge of it. They each have a copy of the new will, and upon my death, they will handle the matter of disbursing my estate. I've left most everything to Judith, but there are still provisions for you and Winchell."

Provisions? At one time, Ashton had talked about leaving him half of his wealth since he had no other heir. This was not the news Bert wanted to hear. It felt as if an iron band had tightened around his chest. How dare the old man try to ruin his plans.

"I can see this does not meet with your approval; however, in the long run it will prevent any confusion or suggestions of impropriety. It would be rather questionable if you were to manage it and inherit at the same time. I've simply saved you any conflict."

Bert didn't really believe that was Ashton's intention, but he forced a smile. "I trust that all is as it should be." He got to his feet. "Will there be anything more?"

"No." Mr. Ashton reached over and pulled the cord that would signal Winchell. "You're free to go."

Bert did so immediately. He feared if he stayed even another minute, he might say things that would see him completely disinherited. The old man had taken away some of his power, but Bert still felt confident he could convince Judith of his sincerity. She really was starting to have feelings for him. Of this, Bert was certain. Once the concern about her grandfather faded and the man was dead, she'd need a friend, and he intended to be there for her.

He'd just reached the top of the steps when Mrs. Deeters appeared. "Oh, Mr. Black, Miss Ashton asked that you meet her in the front sitting room. She only needs a moment of your time and will be down shortly."

The news was exactly what he needed. She wanted to see him. This was better than he could have hoped for. He all but flew down the stairs and made his way to the appointed place. He tried to think of where he might sit that would encourage her to draw close. He studied the room and finally chose the sofa by the front windows.

He considered what he might say to her when they were alone. For now, he would let her set the pace. She was a woman above reproach, so of course she couldn't speak of courtship with her grandfather so ill. Still, there were things that she might mention to encourage him, and things that he could say that would stimulate such conversations.

Judith appeared promptly and swept into the room like a regal princess. She didn't even consider sitting beside him, however, and claimed a throne chair to the right of where he sat. He was disappointed but said nothing.

"I'm glad you could wait a moment," she said.

"I would wait forever if you asked. You know how I feel about you."

She frowned. "Yes, well, I asked you to wait so that we might discuss my grandfather's request that you order the building materials for his block."

"Is there something you want to say about it?"

"Yes. My grandfather is dying, and I would prefer you to refrain from ordering those materials. I realize I have no right to ask you to do so, but it seems that putting it off for the time being would be prudent. We need to focus on what comes next. I intend to speak to my grandfather about what kind of funeral he desires. Unless, of course, he's already made arrangements with you."

"No, he hasn't. He's been far too consumed by the details regarding his block of buildings."

"Yes. He sees that as his memorial to society, but we both realize he's left an entirely different legacy through his business practices."

Bert was surprised at her comment but kept it to himself. There was no telling how he might use this to his benefit later.

"I don't believe it will matter if we wait. There is no hope of the materials arriving before he dies."

"Good. Then I will trust you to hold off on any orders of materials." Judith stood.

"Is that all you wished to discuss?" Bert asked, trying not to sound overly eager. "I was hoping perhaps you would allow me to extend an invitation to have dinner with me."

"I thought I made myself clear." Her tone was firm, but her expression softened. "I do not have any interest in being courted by you. Please do not ask me again. I wouldn't want things to become unpleasant between us." She headed to the pocket doors and turned with a smile. "Now, if you'll excuse me, my grandfather will want to see me right away."

Bert wanted to demand she return and agree to his request but knew that was hardly acceptable behavior. And, after all, it was perfectly in keeping with proper etiquette that she should refuse him while dealing with such an overwhelming family situation. He smiled. She cared for him. He knew she did.

Roman finished his examination of the man's leg and smiled. "It's healing nicely, Eb. You've kept it clean, and that was the best thing you could do for the wound."

"Never held much store by washin' up and such. Spent the first forty years of my life living in the wilderness. Not a lot of soap to be had." The old man chuckled and lowered his trouser leg. "Seems I've always got a bar of the stuff in my hands these days."

"Well, it's probably saved you from amputation this time. Keep doing what you're doing, and I believe you'll be just fine."

"What do I owe ya, Doc?"

Roman looked at him. "Have you been able to work this week?"

"Yes, sir. Been down at the rail yard loading."

"Then ten cents will cover the new bandage and ointment." Roman knew better than to suggest the service was free. Eb was very proud and would never take charity.

The man pulled some coins out of his pocket and found a dime. "Here ya are. Do I need to come back?"

"No, not if you keep it clean and dry. This should continue healing and scab over. If it doesn't, or if it swells and becomes painful, come back and see me. You'll be able to tell if it gets worse."

The man nodded. "I know what proud flesh looks like. I'll watch it close." He headed for the door. "Thanks, Doc. Got to get back to work now."

Eb was his last railroad worker for the day, and Roman was glad to be done. He collected his medical supplies and stuffed them back into his bag. Things had gone well today, despite his thoughts being constantly distracted by Judith Stanford.

He had considered her as he'd fallen asleep the night before. She was also the first thing on his mind when he'd awaken. The fact of the matter was that she was constantly at the forefront of his thoughts. Even his mother had noted that he was awfully deep in contemplation that morning at breakfast.

It wasn't going to fix itself or go away. That much he knew. Other things in life had bothered him in the same manner, and until he was willing to deal with them, they caused him no end of trouble. Judith wasn't exactly trouble, but she was something, or rather someone, that he needed to deal with.

He thought of that moment outside his aunt's bedroom. He had never wanted to kiss anyone as much as he'd wanted to kiss Judith. He found himself wanting to speak to her of love and a future. In all honesty, there had never been any woman in his life that made him feel the way she did. Judith Ashton Stanford had completely captivated his heart.

"See you next week, Doc?" one of the men asked as Roman made his way from the building.

"Of course. I'll be here then and hopefully not sooner. Try to keep the men out of trouble."

The man laughed. "We do our best, but sometimes accidents just find their way to us."

"I understand that." Roman gave the man a wave and put on his hat in one sweep of his arm.

He glanced skyward. The cloudless canopy reminded him of a crystal-blue lake he'd learned to swim in. Oh, for the carefree days of youth. When he'd been a boy, he might have asked his father what to do about his feelings for Judith.

"*Take it to prayer, Roman. You can never go wrong by taking a matter to prayer,*" he remembered his father telling him more than once.

Since allowing bitter hatred toward James Ashton to grow, Roman's prayers had been limited. It was hard to pray when he knew the anger he held. Now that he was working to let that go, Roman found he considered prayer and Scripture more often.

"Well, Lord," he murmured as he walked toward the toll bridge, "You know I'm trying to change my heart." He glanced around, hoping no one heard him. The rest of his prayer was silent.

I need to know what to do. I've fallen in love with my enemy's granddaughter. I know there isn't another woman in the world for me. Judith is the woman I believe You would have me marry.

That realization nearly stopped him in midstep. This was where all of his thoughts had brought him. He wanted to marry Judith Stanford. And he wanted to do it soon. Now he just hoped she wanted the same thing.

Judith found her grandfather asleep when she returned and decided against waking him. He was sleeping more and more these days. A part of her was saddened at the thought of his passing. She couldn't honestly say that she was all that close to him, but he was her grandfather. She had always known about him. Known about his anger toward her father and unwillingness to accept her mother. However, she wished she could know him better. Everything about him. Understand his reasons for the choices he had made. Know the heart of a man who could turn his back on his only son and desert him.

She glanced back at the door to his suite. Perhaps if given time, she could find something to love about him. God knew there were probably more than enough people who hated him.

Including Roman Turner.

She sighed. After sitting so close to him in church and hearing his rich baritone voice join in singing, she had felt a strange connection to him. His desires to aid society matched her own.

Since losing Alden in the war, Judith had put a wall around her heart that she swore would remain in place until she died. A solid rock wall, imperviable to love and romance. Roman had somehow chiseled a hole in that wall, and where that would lead them was completely unknown.

Returning downstairs, Judith went in search of Mary. She needed to exchange records and papers once again. She found the housekeeper overseeing a couple of the footmen as they polished the silver.

"Mrs. Deeters, I was just wondering if I might speak to you."

"Of course, miss." She followed Judith into her grandfather's office. "What can I do for you?"

"I need to change out the ledgers again. They're in my bedroom. There's no rush. I won't begin again until after dinner. Right now, I believe I'll take a little walk in the garden."

"This came for you earlier," Mary said, pulling a card from her pocket.

Judith took it and looked at the information. "Seems there's to be a charity event on the eighth of July. It's to be held at the Wagners'."

"Then it will be a gathering of the finest of Minneapolis

families. The cream of our society. You'll need a very nice dress. Something much more elaborate than what you have."

"I don't need to attend. Surely with my grandfather dying, I can be excused from such an event."

"Yes, but you speak so eloquently regarding the plight of the poor. Perhaps the Wagners heard about this and extended the invitation to you because of that. They didn't include your grandfather on the invitation, did they?"

"No, it's addressed to me alone." Judith frowned. "Perhaps I can find out something more about it before I decide."

"Even so, we should arrange a gown."

"I can send home for something. If I wire Helen, she can put a trunk on the train tomorrow. It should get here in plenty of time. Could you arrange for someone to send a telegram?" She opened the drawer of her grandfather's desk.

"Of course. What should it say?"

Judith jotted down the information, instructing Helen to pack her two finest evening gowns. As an afterthought, she requested her mourning dresses as well. When grandfather passed, she'd definitely have need of them again.

"Here you are. I've put the address information on the opposite side."

Mary took the paper and looked it over for a moment. "I'll have it sent today."

A knock sounded at the front door. Judith wondered who had come calling. She followed Mary to the foyer and waited to see who it was.

"Why, Roman, what brings you here?" Mary embraced her nephew and stood back.

"Actually, I came to see Mrs. Stanford. I wonder," he said, looking past Mary to Judith, "would you take a short walk with me?"

"I was just planning to do something like that anyway." Judith smiled and looked at Mary. "I doubt we'll be long."

"Take as much time as you like. I'll get those papers for you."

Judith felt her heart skip a beat as Roman offered her his arm. She hesitated, then gave a nod and took hold of him. He moved slowly down the outside stairs, giving her time to gather her skirt. At the bottom, he looked around.

"I'm not sure which way to go."

"We have a lovely garden walk. Take the path here and go around the house." Judith motioned with the tilt of her head.

They strolled in the direction of the south lawn. Judith felt out of place. She didn't know why Dr. Turner had come, but there was discomfort in the awkward silence.

"I'm sorry, but I must ask why you came today. We hardly know each other, and walking the garden is usually reserved for . . . well . . ."

"Courtship?" he asked.

"Yes. Or family and close friends. We're neither."

"I wouldn't mind being close friends. Which is why I'm here." They reached the garden path, and Roman paused. "I know there's been trouble between our families."

"I know that as well. I've read the documents and ledgers my grandfather kept at the time." She was surprised to hear herself confess this to Roman.

"Aunt Mary told me she explained things to you as well."

Judith couldn't look away from his intense gaze. "Yes. She did. I'm so very sorry to hear what happened. My grandfather was quite ruthless with people. Not just your father, although perhaps he wronged him more than most. I'm deeply ashamed of what he did."

Roman looked at her oddly. "I wanted to hate you as much as I hated him. When I learned he had a granddaughter, I suspected you must be just like him, despite having met you years ago. But you, Judith Stanford, are nothing like him. You're a woman of God, and generous to a fault. You care deeply about people and put action to your words. I cannot hate you."

"Well, thank the good Lord for that grace," she said, giving a nervous laugh.

He grinned, and it seemed to light up his eyes. "When I first met you, I must say I was rather captivated. I've thought a lot about you over the years."

She swallowed the lump in her throat. "I've thought about you as well."

His eyes narrowed just a bit, and his expression grew quite serious. "I believe God orchestrated that meeting."

She nodded. "I do, too, and for so many reasons."

"Tell me."

His voice sent a tingle up Judith's spine. "I don't think I can, at least not all at once. But . . . well, I don't know if your aunt told you or not, but I intend to make amends for my grandfather. Not just with your family, but all the others as well. If my grandfather makes me his heir as he's said he means to do, then I will use his wealth to at least set things in motion to make financial amends. Obviously, I cannot turn back time and change what happened, but I will do my best to rectify the wrongs he's done others."

"That would take a great deal of money. You'd probably be left with nothing."

"It's not my money anyway. I live quite well on what my father left me. I've been praying for God's direction on this, and I know He will show me what is to be done. My grandfather is having me study his business arrangements so that we might discuss his desires and plans. He just doesn't realize that I've taken it to a deeper level, and I'm doing what I can to keep track of the people he swindled. In time, I will return what I can to them."

"You are beyond all expectations. I have never met anyone like you." His expression betrayed honest admiration.

Judith felt her cheeks warm at his praise. She looked to the ground. "I desire only to do God's will. I see so much wrong in what my grandfather did, not only to the people here," she said, looking up again, "but in how he treated my father and mother. I know it hurt my father terribly that my grandfather cast him out. Still, my father never spoke against him. He taught me that to hate him would only eat away at my heart."

"As it did mine. I'm determined, however, that it is time to allow the Great Physician to heal me of my wounds. I'm resolved to forgive James Ashton."

"As am I. For years I was determined to have nothing to do with my grandfather, even after my folks passed on. Now, I see that God has brought me here for a purpose, and that purpose is to set things right. And perhaps be an example of Christian charity to the one man who needs it most."

"If your grandfather finds out that you want to right his wrongs, he might well disinherit you."

She smiled. "I know. That's why I've said nothing to anyone save Mary, and now you. I'm not even sure why I told you, except that there is something about you." She studied him. "I know this will sound odd, but in some ways, I feel as if I've known you a very long time. Not just because we met four years ago. It's something deeper."

"Does that mean we can be friends? Perhaps even more?"

For a moment, Judith thought her heart might have stopped beating. She forced breath into her lungs. "Yes." She barely whispered the word, but it was enough.

"May I call you Judith?" he asked, and she gave the slightest nod. "And you will call me Roman?"

She nodded again, uncertain she could even form words. She had felt something similar when Alden had come into her life. Similar, but not at all the same. Roman Turner had just demolished the wall she'd kept so closely guarded around her heart. What in the world was she to do now?

Roman wasn't at all sure what had come over him. He wasn't sorry for having said the things he'd said. Nor was he sorry for implying that he wanted more than friendship. Still, he knew how very forward he'd been and could see by the look on Judith's face that she was uncertain of what had just happened.

"I must apologize," he said, looking around rather than at her.

"Would you like to sit?"

"Yes, let's sit for a moment. I'd like to collect my thoughts."

She smiled and led the way. "I find this to be a rather nice spot."

The place she chose was under the trees. There was a gathering of cushioned metal chairs and a small table. It seemed quite restful, but Roman didn't believe he could rest. Not given the way he'd just made a fool of himself.

"I'm sorry I got a little carried away. There's something about you, that . . . well, never mind. I'm sorry that I didn't even stop to ask you how your grandfather was doing. You must think me terribly rude."

"Not at all. He's not doing well. His heart is failing. The doctor had once believed he might live until the end of the summer but now says it will be perhaps a couple of weeks at most. Apparently, it can come in one big attack or his heart will simply cease to function." She held up her hand to his surprise. "You don't need to tell me you're sorry. I know that a great many people will be happy when he breathes his last. I don't even know him well enough to truly understand what I feel about the situation. I am praying that he will make his peace with God. I know Reverend Knickerbacker has visited him twice, although I have no idea what they have discussed."

"The reverend is a good man. He cares deeply about people, and I doubt your grandfather has had cause to alienate him."

"If he has, the reverend is good at hiding his feelings. Still, I'd feel better if I knew my grandfather understood the simplicity of salvation in Christ. I suppose I won't rest until I share that with him myself. Then I'll know for sure he's heard the good news. I know it would please my father and mother to know I'd done such a thing."

"You must miss them." Roman wasn't sure what else he might say. He glanced at Judith's profile and found himself once again lost for the moment. He was completely smitten. It was as if he were a schoolboy. He silently chided himself to remember he was nearly forty years old.

"They were good people. You would have liked them, especially my mother. She was the one who taught me about the importance of giving and helping those less fortunate, although my father felt the same way. I've managed to make it a focal duty. I plan to be a part of charity work for the rest of my life."

"As do I."

She turned to him. "Mary said you were in the war when your father died."

"Yes. I immediately enlisted as a doctor with the Union Army."

"I'm sure it must have been terrible for you, especially being separated from your family."

"It was harder than anything I'd ever been up against."

Judith surprised him by touching his arm. "I'm so sorry."

"I've always associated it all with that man." He glanced back at the house. "I've kept a lot of hate inside, and until now, I wasn't sure I could ever let it go."

"What's changed?"

He looked back at her. "You came into my life, for one thing. I wasn't expecting anything good from James Ashton." He gave her a sheepish grin. "Sorry if that was rather forward. My mother has been a big influence on me. She is faithful to pray and encourage me. She's been after me to forgive, always pressed me saying that hating James Ashton wasn't going to change the past, but that it could certainly alter the future. She was right."

His expression turned serious. "I've been so angry and frustrated by the past that I'm miserable in the present. I could never see that a decent future was even possible. Now I do. I don't know how easy it will be to forgive your grandfather, but I intend to do just that."

Judith offered an encouraging smile. "I know it will benefit you greatly. After all, how can you be friends with the granddaughter of the man you hate?"

Or get her to fall in love with you. The thought made Roman smile. He shrugged. "Exactly."

"Sometimes we just need proper motivation," Judith said. "Whether it's needing to right wrongs, to help those in desperate need, or to forgive. We need to remember that the love and grace of God has blessed us, and we need to extend that to others."

In that moment, Roman had what he could only describe as

a vision of the future. He could see himself and Judith sitting just like this, years down the road, talking about something else that was important to them. They would make this spot a special place. Their place.

After Roman left for home, Judith didn't have words for her feelings. Roman Turner had taken her by surprise with his appearance and honest explanation of his emotions, but she was very glad it had happened. For reasons beyond her understanding, she knew that something life-changing had just taken place in her grandfather's garden.

She made her way upstairs to see how her grandfather was doing. It was nearly six, and soon dinner would be served. Perhaps she should ask for her tray to be brought to his room so that they could share the time together.

Knocking at his door, Judith waited until Winchell appeared. "Good evening. Is he awake?"

"Yes, miss. He told me you were welcome to see him if you came."

"How is he feeling?"

"The rest seemed to help a great deal. He's sitting up, and I believe he'll be able to eat a little dinner."

She nodded and made her way inside. The older man was propped up in the bed with his newspaper.

"Good evening, sir," she said, sweeping into the room as if they were meeting in the office rather than his sickroom.

"France wants our wheat, which means England will start bellowing for it as well," her grandfather said as he folded the paper. "Should be good for our prices, and we'll make plenty over the deal." He put the paper on the bed beside him. "We have a strong investment in wheat."

Judith smiled. "I'm sure that pleases you."

"Making money always pleases me. It should please you

as well since you're the one who will ultimately benefit from this." Judith let his words sink in but said nothing.

"So what did you do with the rest of the day?" he asked, looking at her as if he knew she'd spent part of it with Roman Turner.

"I received an invitation to a charity fundraiser at the Wagners'. It's to be held July eighth. Mrs. Deeters told me it would be quite formal. I'm not sure I will attend—"

"But you must. The Wagners are quite rich. You should attend the party to be seen, if nothing else. You need to consider taking a husband and doing it soon. It would probably be better if folks didn't know that you're my heir. There are those who would take advantage of that, but on the other hand, it will present you with optimal bargaining power. You should be able to marry my wealth to another even greater fortune if you play this right."

"That's hardly why I would marry again." She frowned and took a seat in the chair by his bed. "Honestly, there are better reasons to choose a mate."

"I suppose you're one of those who believes in love and romance. All the flowery notions that addlepated females are known for."

"After losing my husband at Gettysburg, I've really had no desire to seek another romance."

His expression altered to one more stoic. "He served honorably."

"Yes. He was a wonderful man. You would have never approved of him, but my mother and father adored him. He taught at the local university, and he was brilliant and quite eloquent. He was always being asked by powerful men to run for political office because of his way with words, but Alden had no interest in such things. He loved teaching."

"You're right. I wouldn't have approved."

To her surprise, this amused rather than angered her. She smiled. "I'm getting very good at figuring you out."

"Hardly. That's a matter of being sensible. No great guesswork needed." He stretched a bit, grimacing. As he settled back into the same spot, Judith felt the overwhelming urgency of the situation.

"Do you fear death?"

He stilled at that and looked her in the eye. "Every man fears death to some degree. If they say otherwise, they're liars. Death is the end of all they've worked for. You want to be able to look back and see that you actually accomplished something, but even when you can, there are questions. A man always wonders if he did enough. Did he leave his mark on the world? Will people remember him?"

"And that's important to you? That people remember you?"

"Of course. That's our purpose here. To do whatever we can to make ourselves known, so that people will remember you when you're gone."

"To what end?"

"It's the only way to achieve immortality."

"But that's not true. You must believe that there is a God. I know you haven't desired to answer to any man, but you must agree that you will answer for what you've done when you stand before the Almighty."

"I believe there is a God, of course. I just don't believe He cares about me as an individual."

Judith leaned forward. "But of course He cares for us as individuals. He's our Creator. He cares very much what happens to us. Why should you create things and care for them, and believe God incapable of the same? He has provided for us and watched over us. The Bible says He knew us in the womb."

"Hardly the kind of talk I'd expect from my granddaughter."

"Well, I believe it's talk that must be had. You stand on the brink of death. I must tell you that the only way to have eternal life is to put your trust in Jesus as your Savior."

"Why are you so convinced I need saving?" For once there was no contempt in his tone.

Judith prayed for guidance and continued. "Because we're all sinners. Romans three tells us we've all sinned and come short of God's glory. Because of that, we have a price to pay—death. Romans chapter six, verse twenty-three tells us, 'For the wages of sin is death; but the gift of God is eternal life through Jesus Christ our Lord.' Jesus is the only way to reach the Father because Jesus cleanses us of our sins. When He died on the cross, He took our sins on Himself."

"Then it's already been taken care of. Why must I do anything? You see, I believe that God gives us life and then waits for us to live it out. He will reward us for what we accomplish as we go along our way. Then we grow old and die."

"And you believe there is nothing beyond the grave?"

"Why should there be? All things must come to an end." He put a hand to his chest. "My heart will stop, and that will be the end of me."

"No! No, Grandfather that isn't the end."

He looked at her for a long moment. "You called me Grandfather. Have I truly earned the right?"

She sighed. "Yes. I believe you have, and I'm sorry that I ever said what I did. It was rude, and I wasn't at all considerate. I need your forgiveness for how I acted."

"Nonsense. I prefer that people speak honestly."

Winchell arrived at that moment with her grandfather's tray. "Dinner, sir." He brought the tray in and placed it on the table beside the bed.

"Just set it here with me." He patted the area beside him. "I have no energy for a lot of fuss. I'm really not hungry, but with it close at hand, I can sample it if I feel up to it."

"I could help you," Judith offered.

The old man shook his head. "Just go now. It's getting late, and I don't wish to discuss business. I'll speak with you tomorrow."

"Very well." Judith got to her feet, wishing she could know if her words about Jesus had made any difference. Had he understood? Had she said the right thing? It wasn't like she was a preacher who knew all the proper words to speak.

Oh, heavenly Father, please help him to understand the truth.

James Ashton sampled a piece of dinner roll. It was tasteless. Food held less and less appeal. The things that he had once loved to dine on were now ashes in his mouth. And on the occasion that something did taste acceptable, it generally soured in his stomach. He supposed it was all just a part of his dying.

He thought of Judith. She was so compelled to preach to him. She believed so completely that the Bible spoke the truth, that there was more to God than the simple fact that He had created the world and all that was in it. She saw Him as having an active part in her life. She believed He was present in the details of her day-to-day living. He could even say that she was passionate about her beliefs. He'd heard the way her voice had taken on notes of urgency.

Could she know what she was talking about?

Winchell returned with a glass of port. James generally had a single glass each night before bed. It helped him to sleep. The valet placed the port on the bedside table and straightened.

"Will there be anything else, sir?"

"Winchell, do you believe in God?"

"But of course, sir."

"Do you consider yourself a Christian?"

The man stared at him for a moment. James looked at him as if seeing him for the first time in a long while. Winchell had aged considerably in the last few years. The man was what?

Sixty? No, sixty-five. Ten years his junior. His graying hair and wrinkled face bore witness to the years. He had spent his entire life in service.

"I do, sir," Winchell finally answered.

"So you are of the opinion that there is something beyond the grave? Some form of life that carries on into an endless span of years? Eternity?"

"Yes . . . sir."

He could see the questioning in Winchell's eyes, but of course the man would never actually ask what was on his mind. He had learned early on to speak when spoken to and offer opinion only when requested to do so.

"And what do you believe is required to become a Christian?"

The valet straightened. "Accepting Jesus Christ as our Lord and Savior."

"And how does one do that, exactly?"

"Ask, sir. God is willing that none should be lost, the Bible tells us."

"Do you read the Bible, Winchell?"

"I do indeed, sir."

"And you believe that if I die without Jesus Christ as my Savior, I will perish to eternal damnation without God?"

"The Bible does say that Jesus is the only way to the Father."

James thought about his servant's answers for a moment, then nodded. "That will be all, Winchell. Take the tray. I've no appetite."

"I'm so glad you could join us," Martha Turner declared as Roman helped Judith into the back of an old buckboard. If her grandfather saw this, Judith knew he'd be absolutely appalled. That the granddaughter of James Ashton Sr. should ride around in the back of a wagon like freight would have caused him great displeasure.

"Sit here by me, Judith," Claudette said, patting the wooden seat. Someone had thoughtfully built a bench behind the driver's seat, and it was to there that Judith made her way.

Judith noted the barrels and crates all around them. "What is all this?" she asked, looking to Claudette.

"Supplies. These are some of the things Roman was able to buy with the money you donated. We'll use it all at the orphans' home. It seems like a lot, but it really isn't. Not when it comes to helping so many children."

Judith nodded. Yesterday after church, Martha had invited her to come along on a trip to lend a hand with the children. It seemed there was an outbreak of scarlet fever, and the two Sisters who ran the place were quite desperate. Judith had eagerly agreed to help, assuring Roman that she'd had the disease as a youngster and knew it was rare to catch it a second time.

Roman paid the toll and drove the buckboard across the river while his mother explained what they might be up against. "It's not a formal orphanage, but rather something that's been cobbled together by a few well-meaning folks. Roman attends to the medical needs along with his good friend Dr. Lester."

"And how many children are being cared for?" Judith asked, glancing over her shoulder.

"At present, there are ten," Roman replied. "They range in age from infants to twelve years old. A farm family is about to adopt the twelve-year-old. His parents were killed in the Dakota War. He was just four years old, and his mother managed to hide him during the attack. He still sometimes has nightmares."

"I can't imagine being so young and watching your parents be killed." Judith offered a silent prayer for the boy.

"The people who are adopting him were friends of his folks. They managed to leave the area when the war started. They didn't return until just last year. When they learned about Samuel's plight, they came forward with the request to have him become a part of their family. I think it will be healing for all."

"That's wonderful. He will have people around who knew his family and can share stories and keep their memory alive."

Judith couldn't help but feel sorry for the child, however. It had been hard enough to lose her parents as an adult. How terrible for a young one to have his family taken from him in such a violent manner.

When they finally arrived at the house, Judith wasn't impressed. It was just a little two-story wood house. It hardly seemed big enough to house the two nuns, much less an additional ten children. The barn in back of the house was bigger.

Roman parked the wagon near the back door, then led the way to the front. He knocked and waited until one of the Sisters came to answer. The older woman who appeared walked with a limp but gave Roman a radiant smile. "It was good of you to come, Dr. Turner. I'm afraid some of the children are gravely ill, but blessed be the name of the Lord."

"I've brought a great many supplies. We'll start unloading them in a moment, but first I'd like you to meet someone. You of course know my mother and sister." The women nodded and smiled at one another. "This is our friend, Mrs. Stanford. She's quite active with a variety of charities in Philadelphia and wanted to join us in helping here today."

"We're grateful for all the help we can get," the woman explained. "I'm Sister Agnes. I work here with Sister Ann."

"I'm pleased to meet you." Judith took hold of Sister Agnes's hand and just held it a moment. "And I'm very glad to help you in any way I can."

"We have a great deal of need. Some of the children have grown quite ill. I fear they simply haven't the strength to endure."

Judith fought to keep from frowning. The idea of children dying was always difficult to consider. She looked to Roman, hoping he might have something to say.

"We will see what we can do to get them back on the road to recovery," Roman offered. "Is Mr. Brannon here to help with unloading?"

"He is in the barn. I'd be surprised if he hasn't already started unloading."

"Wonderful. Now, I want you and Sister Ann to go and rest. We will be here for a couple of hours, and during that time, you both should nap."

"Oh dear, no. We couldn't do that."

"I'm the doctor, and it's what I believe you need to do in order to remain healthy." He gave her a smile. "A short rest will do you good. I'm guessing you and Sister Ann have been getting nothing more than the briefest of sleep."

"God provides the strength we need. We trust Him for our rest." She had a perfect expression of peace on her face.

"All right, let's get the wagon unloaded. Show us where you want the supplies." Roman looked at Judith and winked. "While I unload things, I'll pray that God convinces you that rest is in your best interest. Mother, why don't you go with Sister Agnes and see that we have plenty of hot water and towels available. Claudette, you come with Judith and me."

Judith hid her smile as they moved out to return to the wagon. She liked the way Roman managed things. He treated people with great respect but was firm in the way he thought things ought to be done.

"Mr. Brannon," Roman said as they reached the wagon. "I'm certainly glad you're here to help. We had a generous donor provide all of this, and I knew I'd need your help with unloading it."

The older man straightened and dusted off his pant legs. "I'm glad to lend a hand with this. I've been digging a root cellar all morning, and it'll be good to do something different." He reached up to grab a large crate and hoisted it to his shoulder. "Just follow me."

Judith, Claudette, and Roman made several trips along with Mr. Brannon. They brought the supplies into a small room that had been added to the back of the house. There were numerous shelves, some rather bare. Judith noted there were stacks of towels and washcloths on one, rolled bandages and other medical supplies on another. What looked to be homemade soap was stacked on another shelf, along with jars of what she figured was soft soap.

The sisters had everything neatly organized, including one entire wall of various food goods. These were some of the shelves that looked rather empty.

"We've enough flour, sugar, and oats to keep you for a month or more," Roman said when Sister Agnes appeared again. "There's also an order of pork to be delivered tomorrow and a dozen laying hens."

"Oh, wonderful. We will certainly appreciate that. Some of the older hens have stopped laying, and I'm afraid they're headed to the soup pot," the sister said, smiling.

"Now we will go and check on the children. These things can be unpacked by my mother and sister." He looked to Claudette, who nodded with enthusiasm.

"We'll have it all put away in no time," his sister replied as their mother joined them.

"There's plenty of hot water on the stove, Roman. And Sister Agnes has a stack of towels on the table. Washcloths too."

"I've also put a basin of washing-up water in each room and a bar of soap. I know you said it was important to wash our hands."

"Wonderful. I'll grab my things, and we'll go visit the children." He went to where he'd left the large black bag.

Judith took that moment to retrieve her apron from the wagon. She drew it on over her head and tied a big bow in back. She wasn't really all that sure what to expect. She knew how things were ordered in Philadelphia at the state-owned children's home, but here with this private institution it might be completely different.

"We should start here with the infants," Sister Agnes said, taking them down the hall. "There are four, and they're all very sick. I fear one or two might not make it through the night."

She opened the door to a simple but adequate room. There were cribs against the far and side walls. A single rocking chair was situated in the middle of the room, and a changing table and two dressers were against the wall to the right of the door.

Judith felt her heart go out to these little ones who had no way of explaining how bad they felt. Nor could they understand what was wrong with them.

Roman started with the first infant. The head of the crib had a card that read *Baby Boy 1.* With practiced precision, Roman unwrapped the blanket that had been used to swaddle him and drew him out. The poor child was wearing just a diaper, making it easy for Judith to see he was covered in a red rash. The infant whimpered but seemed to have little energy to do more.

The examination was quick but thorough. Roman's expression showed he wasn't at all happy with the state of the baby. "We need to bring the fever down. He's quite warm. Sister Agnes, I see you aren't resting. Would you bring the little wash basin you use for the babies? Fill it with tepid water."

The nun immediately left. Judith looked to Roman. "What can I do?"

"Bring the lamp." Roman took a tongue depressor and forced the baby's mouth open. "Shine it here so I can better see his throat."

Judith did as he asked, but the affect wasn't all that helpful. She remembered a story she'd heard from one of the doctors in Philadelphia. He told of a time when he'd had to perform surgery in the home of one of his patients. "A mirror. We need a mirror."

"Why?"

"So I can reflect a pinpoint of light to where you need it. I saw it done in Philadelphia."

"Claudette has a mirror. It's in a little case Daniel gave her. She keeps it in her purse."

Judith put the lamp on the table, then went to the back room where she'd left Roman's sister. "Claudette, can I borrow your mirror? Roman says Daniel gave you one."

"Of course." She reached down to the reticule that she'd attached to her waistband. She pulled the drawstrings apart and quickly produced the case, opening it to reveal the mirror. "Daniel got this for my birthday. He says Queen Victoria has one very similar. At least, that's what the store owner in Chicago told him."

Judith smiled. "That's a beautiful gift."

"Whatever are you going to use it for?"

"To reflect light from the lamp. Roman's trying to see into the baby's mouth."

"How marvelous." Claudette shook her head. "I would never have thought of that."

Judith took the case and hurried back to where Roman was. She picked up the lamp and angled the mirror to reflect the light into the child's mouth.

"Perfect. That's very useful," Roman said as he moved the tongue depressor to better see. "Poor baby. His throat is red and no doubt very sore."

Sister Agnes returned with the basin of water. Roman's mother followed close behind with a couple of towels.

"Sister, is he eating at all?" Roman asked.

"He's taken very little sustenance. He won't suckle. We've used an eyedropper to force it, but even so, he's taken very little." She put the water on the dressing table, and Roman's mother did likewise with the towels.

"I've also brought my journal for their care." Sister Agnes produced a small book from her pocket. "You can see for yourself what each baby has taken. I'll put it here atop the chest of drawers."

Roman removed the baby's diaper. "Mother, we need to get his temperature down immediately and get some fluids into him. Otherwise, I fear he won't be long for this world. We may already be too late. He was very small to begin with."

His mother took the baby. Her expression betrayed her concern. Judith watched as she gently placed the infant in the water. He didn't even respond.

Judith fought back tears. She had been in sad situations with babies before this. They were so weak and often couldn't fight against illness. Recovery was completely up to God.

Roman washed his hands while Judith awaited instructions. They moved on to the next baby, who wasn't quite as sick. He gave the child a thorough examination, then went to the next. By the time all four were tended, Roman's mother was taking the baby from the bath.

Judith followed Roman in silence. She gave one last glance at Baby Boy 1 as Roman's mother rediapered him. He didn't even have a name. Not a real name. She whispered a prayer for God's mercy and healing and swallowed the lump in her throat.

Upstairs, they found four more children in the first room. They ranged in age from three to five. All were girls and well enough that they began to cry when they saw people enter the room. They held up their arms from their beds, in hopes of being held.

Judith's heart nearly broke. It wasn't easy to see them in such a state of need.

Roman was certain that Baby Boy 1 would be dead before nightfall. There was nothing he could do to save the child, and it put him in a foul mood. For the benefit of the children, however, he knew he couldn't let that be the attitude he revealed to them. They were sick and hurting. They needed attention and love.

He checked each child as gently as possible, speaking softly and giving lots of smiles. He was amazed at the work Judith was doing. She didn't complain about anything but jumped right in and did what she could to ease the suffering. At one point she held two toddlers at once, doing her best to calm their tears. She seemed a natural at mothering.

Not needing her for the older children, Roman continued

his rounds while Judith made her way back to the baby room. He wondered if she knew how sick Baby Boy 1 really was. He would tell Sister Agnes prior to leaving, but probably not say anything to Judith until later. Perhaps on the ride home.

He glanced at his pocket watch. It was nearly noon. He checked over Samuel, who was on the mend but still feeling poorly.

"Your fever seems to be gone. You'll be feeling better soon."

"I don't like being sick," the boy grumbled.

"If it had come during the school year, you wouldn't have minded. I've heard you say before that you like getting out of school."

Samuel gave him a big grin. "I do like getting out of school. But being sick now is wasting a good summer."

Roman laughed. "You'll soon be able to have fun again. Didn't Sister Agnes tell me last time that you've been taking care of the three milk cows?"

"Yup," the boy said proudly. "I get them milked in the morning and then again just before supper. Mr. Brannon has to do it while I'm sick. And probably after I'm gone. Did you know that I'm getting adopted?"

"I heard about that. Are you happy?"

The boy nodded. "I'll have a real family, and that's good. And the Haglunds are good people. They were friends with my ma and pa before the Indians attacked. I don't remember them very much, but they came to visit me here. They told me stories about when I was little, and a couple of those I could remember. I like knowing that they can tell me about my folks."

"That is a blessing," Roman said, repacking his bag. "When are they coming for you?"

"After I get well. Sister Agnes said there was no sense in sending me to them sick."

"I think Sister Agnes is very wise."

Roman extended his hand, and Samuel did likewise. They

shook, and then Roman gave the boy one last smile. "Make your folks proud."

"That's what Sister Ann told me to do. She said I was a reflection of all they'd taught me when I was little. But I've been staying with so many other people since then that I don't know that I can be a reflection of them at all."

"Then reflect Jesus. That's what we're all supposed to do." With that, Roman left Samuel and made his way back through the house. He found his mother and Claudette in the kitchen, helping put together lunch for the children.

"I'm glad that some of them are actually telling me how hungry they are," Sister Ann was saying. "I'll never again complain about the work associated with meals."

"Where's Judith?" Roman asked, placing his bag by the back door.

"She's with the babies," Sister Agnes said. "She said she wanted to give them a little extra love."

Roman wasn't surprised. In his short time of knowing Judith, he could easily tell her heart was quite tender. He went to the infant room and opened the door as quietly as possible. Inside, Judith sat in the middle of the room, humming and rocking Baby Boy 1.

He smiled at the sweet picture of motherly love. Judith looked up and met his gaze. It was only then that he noticed the tears on her cheeks.

"What's wrong?" He moved closer.

Her expression was one of resignation. "He drew his last breath a few minutes ago. He's safely in the arms of Jesus now."

"The death of a child . . . a baby is never easy to experience," Roman said as he and Judith sat in the garden that evening.

"No, that is for certain."

She'd been so quiet after the Sisters had taken the baby away to prepare him for burial. Roman had thought she might say something on the ride back to the Ashton house, but instead she had withdrawn into her thoughts, and even Claudette couldn't seem to bring her around.

Roman had taken his mother and sister home and cleaned up after leaving Judith at her grandfather's house, but he couldn't stop thinking about her. That was why he returned. He no longer cared that she was an Ashton, nor that she lived in a house probably built with profits from his father's financial ruin.

As they sat in the growing twilight, Roman wanted only to offer her comfort and reassurance. "The poor little guy was just too weak. I think he was most likely born before his full term. He started life with a great disadvantage."

"What happened to his mother?" Judith asked, her voice barely audible.

"Died giving him life. She was unmarried and had no family."

"Forced, no doubt, to work at unpleasant tasks," Judith said, shaking her head. "Roman, it must stop. These poor girls who have no one get caught up in the trap of being used in such horrific ways. We must create help for them, even if society is against them in their moral outrage. Mrs. Van Cleve made a comment asking, 'Where are the men who have created these circumstances?' They pay no penalty, suffer no shunning, and endure very little trouble for their deeds. But the girls involved . . ." Her voice faded.

Roman reached over to take her hand. He knew it was more intimacy than was called for, but he couldn't help himself. "We will find ways to help them. I promise you that much."

For several long minutes, Judith said nothing. She clung to his hand as if Roman were offering her a lifeline.

"There's just so much wrong in this world," she finally said. "I've seen so much of it firsthand. Death and sorrow, misery and suffering. How can anyone just walk by and leave the wounded on the side of the road? Why do we lack a heart of compassion when we are all so in need of love and understanding?"

Roman couldn't have loved her more than he did in that moment. She truly was the only woman he could imagine having at his side. For the rest of his life.

"I know that God has the world in His hands," Judith continued. "I know that He sees each sparrow fall. But why, Roman, why must the children suffer so much?"

He met her gaze and saw the tears that had formed. He let go of her hand and reached up to touch her cheek. "I could tell you how this is a fallen world and that sin cares not for whom it harms. That the devil seeks to destroy all that God loves, but that God will have His way in the end. But I know that would not offer you comfort now.

"The only choice given to us is that we do what we can to be God's servants and do His work. You are a most persuasive woman, Judith Stanford. You have convinced many to help, and you aren't afraid to get your hands dirty and do some of the hard labor that is required. You have such a tenderness toward the less fortunate, and your actions have helped so many."

"But it's not enough, Roman. A handful here and few dozen there. It's not nearly enough. There are orphans and destitute families all over this country. Good people who are trying their best and still failing. Then others come in to take advantage of them, and they suffer all the more." She sniffed back tears. "What is to be done?"

Roman reached into his coat and pulled out his handkerchief. He smiled, and instead of handing her the cloth, he dabbed her wet cheeks. "We keep praying. We keep working to right wrongs and better those who cannot better themselves. We look for the needs instead of ignoring them, and we expose them to the world so that all might know the truth. Jesus told us to love one another as He loved us. Somehow we need to convince our fellow man that this command is just as relevant today as it was when Jesus said it."

"Sometimes it just seems that it's so little. Those children today were struggling with sickness, but even more so they long for love. They need to be cared for by a mother and a father. They need families around them so that in their sickness they can be watched over in tenderness. Not that the Sisters weren't wonderful with them, but they are only two older women with limited resources and strength."

"But that's how it starts," Roman said, giving her a smile. "Someone cares and then another and another. Together they form a group and begin to help. Others join in, and soon truly amazing things start to happen. God calls each of us to do our part, Judith. You cannot do everyone's job. Keep focusing on your calling, and God will bless your obedience."

She nodded and eased back against the cushioned chair. "I know you're right. There's just so much to do."

Roman chuckled. "Just remember, you don't have to do it alone."

"Again, you're right."

"Since you're in a mood to think positively toward me, I'd like to ask you to accompany me to the Wagners' party. I don't feel I can avoid it, and having you there with me would make the evening so much more bearable."

She met his gaze, and Roman lost his heart. "I would really enjoy that. Grandfather wants me to attend, but I was dreading it."

He wanted nothing more than to kiss her but refrained. "Then I will pick you up just before eight."

Perhaps that evening could end in a kiss.

Bert finished checking his appearance one last time. He needed to be perfect. His gray suit had been tailored to show his wealth and attention to detail. His hair was neatly trimmed and his shoes shined. Gazing into the mirror and seeing his reflection, Bert was quite satisfied. There was nothing that should be unwelcomed by Judith Stanford.

He was considered a great catch. At least, he was considered that by a good number of people in Minneapolis. He had always had plenty of interested women, but none of them could offer him what he really wanted—power and money. Judith Stanford could give him both, as well as connections. Not only that, but she was beautiful. What man wouldn't be pleased to have her on his arm?

Smiling, Bert picked up his hat and then headed for the door. He had good feelings about the day. It was the Fourth of July. American Independence was being celebrated across the country, and Minneapolis was certainly no different. Bert had been invited to a grand celebration that evening, and this was the perfect excuse to see Judith. He would convince her to join him no matter what it took. If he could just get her alone, Bert knew he could woo her and entice her to see him as more than her grandfather's lawyer.

He reached the Ashton house nearly fifteen minutes later and checked his watch. It was nearly ten. Tucking the piece back into his pocket, Bert climbed the steps with a sense of satisfaction. He wasn't scheduled to meet with the old man until ten thirty. That would give him some thirty minutes to convince Judith to accompany him.

Bert lifted the knocker and tapped it against the door several times. It was only a matter of minutes before Mrs. Deeters opened to him.

"Good morning, Mr. Black." She stepped back to admit him. "You're rather early."

"I know. I apologize. I thought perhaps I could see Judith before making my way upstairs." He handed her his hat.

Mrs. Deeters shook her head. "Mrs. Stanford isn't home."

This wasn't at all what Bert had expected. "Where is she?" He knew that was none of his business and the height of impropriety to ask, but it came out of his mouth before he could think.

"She had an appointment this morning."

"When are you expecting her home?" He hoped she wouldn't question his eagerness.

"Mr. Black, I hardly see how Mrs. Stanford's schedule is any of your concern."

She hadn't yet closed the door, but Bert feared she might well ask him to leave, especially since she still held his hat. He offered her an apologetic smile. "I'm sorry. I didn't mean to be forward. I wanted to extend an invitation to Judith for a party tonight. I know it's rather short notice, but I hoped she might be free to join me."

"It is very short notice. I have no idea of her plans."

"Well, I suppose my invitation will have to wait. Since I'm

here, would you mind checking with Mr. Ashton and inquiring as to whether we might start our meeting early?"

"Of course. Why don't you wait in the sitting room?" She placed his hat on the table, then opened the pocket doors. "I'll be right back."

Bert entered the room but didn't sit. Instead, he took inventory of the opulent furnishings and dreamed that they might one day be his. The time he'd given this man surely merited something more than whatever insignificant amount Ashton planned to leave him. Of course, he was paid well enough, and Ashton had even set him up in a nice apartment with quality furnishings. But that wasn't the same as endowing Bert with his millions.

Touching the edge of the gilded framed landscape, Bert contemplated what it might be like to have the means to do whatever he wanted to do. He could stop working and simply enjoy the benefits of wealth. He could manage the Ashton fortune and holdings and receive the respect of all. Even his father would be impressed, and that wasn't an easy task to accomplish.

"Mr. Black, Mr. Ashton said you may come up," Mrs. Deeters announced.

He smiled and nodded. "Thank you."

The house was quiet as Bert made his way upstairs. Ashton preferred silence and demanded it from his staff. That was another reminder of the man's power. People might not like him, but they did respect him. Bert would be happy enough with that for himself. He often imagined being asked to the most important parties and social events. His family was well-respected back in Boston, and he made sure that word got around Minneapolis of their social standing. People knew he'd come from money and quality. It was just a matter of time before they put him at the top of Minneapolis society.

Winchell met him at the bedroom door. "Good morning, sir."

"Good morning, Winchell. How's Mr. Ashton feeling today?" He hoped the man was a little closer to his demise. This lingering on was difficult for everyone, or at least it was for Bert.

"He's faring as well as possible."

Winchell led the way into the grand Ashton sanctuary. Bert thought of how he would remake the room and put everything in the furniture styles of Charles Eastlake. The British designer was becoming quite popular as he moved the current trends away from excessive embellishments.

"Mr. Black is here, sir," Winchell announced.

"Yes. Yes. Leave us to work."

Ashton was propped up in bed but looked worse than he had on Friday when Bert had last seen him. Bert knew better than to comment on the man's condition, however. He pulled up a chair next to a small desk that Ashton had put in for him.

"I have the contracts you asked for. I finished preparing them late Friday. The terms are exactly as you dictated." He took the papers to the old man's bed.

Ashton reached up to take them, and Bert could see that his hands were barely able to grasp the pages. Bert returned to his seat and took up his pen. Ashton was prone to suddenly dictating instructions and even letters without warning.

"Did you buy those additional stocks I asked you to purchase?"

"I did. This morning before coming here."

"Good." Ashton appeared to consider the papers, then placed them on the bed at his side. "I'll have Judith look these over when she comes this afternoon."

Bert said nothing. Ashton had no interest in him courting his granddaughter. He'd made that quite clear. There was no sense stirring up an argument.

"The time is coming when you'll handle all these things

with Judith. I'm not pleased at the prospect, knowing you will no doubt torment the poor woman with words of love and nonsense. However, she is strong and capable." He closed his eyes and fell silent.

Bert wondered for the moment if the great man had passed away but knew soon enough that he was still drawing breath.

"Have you ordered the building supplies for my block?"

Bert lied. "Of course. It's all been taken care of. It will take some time to get the marble, of course, but the lumber will come from your own mills. The steel will be shipped into Duluth and brought down by train. I've arranged to warehouse it on site."

"Good. I think that's all I care to discuss for now. Come back this afternoon when I speak with Judith. You may go."

Bert frowned. It wasn't even ten thirty yet. "Are you certain? I can stay on and be here should you think of something additional that needs our attention."

"Just go." Ashton's voice was barely audible. The man was weak and tired. It was a good sign that the end would come soon.

Bert put away the pen. He was in no hurry to go and took his time putting things back in his satchel. "I'll be back at one."

Ashton said nothing.

Making his way back downstairs, Bert contemplated how to remain at the house until Judith came home. Thankfully, she had just returned and was busy in conversation with Mrs. Deeters.

When he appeared in the foyer, they stopped and turned to look at him. He wasn't sure, but there seemed a hint of annoyance in Mrs. Deeters's expression.

"Hello, Bert," Judith said in greeting. "Mrs. Deeters was just telling me that you wished to see me. Have you time now, or has Grandfather sent you on some errand?"

"I have time. Mr. Ashton is far too tired to work. He told me to return this afternoon when you and he will discuss business. I left a contract that he intends for you to go over. If you like, I can remain and explain it to you."

"No, that's quite all right. I'm sure I can manage with the contract, and I'm busy at the moment. We're taking small cakes and cookies over to the orphans' home. I'll look at the contracts this afternoon and discuss them then."

Bert didn't know what to say. He needed to get her alone.

She seemed to sense this and looked at Mrs. Deeters. "Would you mind asking Charles to help load everything? Tell him that I'll be ready to leave shortly. He can bring the carriage around."

"Of course," Mrs. Deeters said, glancing at him.

"I'll speak with Bert for a moment." Mrs. Deeters nodded and took off down the hall. Judith turned to him. "What is it I can do for you?"

"Why don't we sit for a moment?"

She shook her head. "I don't have the time, Bert. Now what is it?"

"I was hoping you might accompany me this evening to a Fourth of July party. It's going to be a beautiful night and a grand affair. I know you would have a wonderful time, and with you at my side, I would as well. I want very much to court you, Judith. I'm most serious about a future with you. I'm sure until now you've been trying to judge my sincerity, but I believe you can see given our time together that I've come to care very deeply for you."

She sighed. "Bert, I have spoken plainly on the matter. I'm not interested in being with you. I feel I've been clear about this, but apparently not clear enough. I don't want to hurt your feelings, but my attentions lie elsewhere."

"You have another suitor?" His stomach instantly soured.

"If I did, it wouldn't be your concern. For the moment, however, I'm consumed with my grandfather. I've given some attention to the area charities, but even with this, I've limited myself because of the situation here. My grandfather needs me, and I am obligated to him. Now, I must go. I promised him I would be gone only a short while this morning. You know very well he won't be with us long, and I want to spend as much time with him as possible."

She went to the door and opened it for him. "I'll be sure and read through the contract when I return home."

Bert knew she was waiting for him to leave, but he felt desperate to convince her to give him a chance. Still, there was hardly anything he could do about it at the moment. She wouldn't even listen, given her rush to see to her affairs. He walked slowly to the door and paused.

"I will wait for you," Bert promised. "You'll see, I'm worth giving a chance to." He smiled. "We would be perfect together. Just think of all we could accomplish."

She shook her head. "I am not interested in accomplishing anything with you, Bert. I'm sorry, but you must find another. Please do not attempt this again. I will not court you. This is my final answer."

He frowned and stopped just outside the door. "Don't say that. I know there is a chance for us. Just give me time, Judith. Once these other things are behind you, you'll be happy for a friend, and I will be here for you. I promise I'll be here."

She didn't respond. It was then that the real problem came to his mind. James Ashton. He was the problem. Poor Judith had to refuse thoughts of courtship because she was obligated to attend him night and day. Until he died.

Judith didn't know how much clearer she could make it to the man. She had told him in no uncertain terms that she would not court him. What more could she say or do? She couldn't very well forbid him to come to the house, because he was her grandfather's lawyer. Once her grandfather died, she was definitely going to seek new counsel.

She sighed and marched past him to where Charles had just brought the carriage. She had thought of offering Mr. Black a ride back to wherever he was going, but she decided against it. He would just spend the time trying to woo her. She settled into the carriage, leaving him standing on the walk to gaze after her. Another sigh escaped. It wasn't like she'd never had men seeking her hand her before, but none had been quite so persistent and annoying.

The warm July sun beat down on her. Bert's visit made her forget her parasol, but thankfully her straw bonnet had a broad brim. Judith did her best to forget about the annoying man and instead put her mind on the duties at hand—the orphans.

She had heard from Mrs. Turner just yesterday that the children were doing much better. Several had recovered in full, including Samuel, whose adoptive parents had come to claim him. She tried not to think about Baby Boy 1, whom she had secretly named Isaac. She thought of that name as she'd rocked him, thinking how in another time and place he might have brought laughter instead of tears. Sister Agnes had told her the Episcopal church would arrange for his burial but that there would be no services. The baby had come unwanted into the world. Unnamed and unloved. No, that wasn't true. She had loved him, even for a few moments, and no doubt the sisters had too.

Sadness washed over her despite her determination to be happy. He was in a better place. A place where he would never be sick again. A place of love and kindness. Judith couldn't help but want that for her grandfather as well. She had spoken again to him last night, sharing elements of her own faith and what she hoped were encouragements from the Bible. He neither stopped her from speaking nor ignored her. In fact, he had asked her a question or two. Still, he didn't express an interest in giving himself over to God.

Please, Father, please save him.

James Ashton awoke with a start. He felt as if a weight sat upon his chest, and it caused his breathing to be quite labored. Was this it? Was this the moment he would die?

He glanced around the room. There was no one with him. Never had he felt so alone. He thought of Judith and her words about salvation. He had never considered himself one who needed saving. All his life, he'd made his own way. His father had taught him to rely on no one but himself. To trust no one no matter how convincing they were.

His beliefs were that life ended with a man's final breath. Then nothing. That was why he had been determined to pursue his own happiness with great gusto. He had made a name for himself apart from his father. He had earned the respect of his peers and the fear of his enemies. He had enough wealth to buy whatever he wanted and to live in opulence befitting a king.

So why did he feel so empty and alone?

Was Judith right? Were all those haughty Christians correct in believing that there was more to life than what this existence gave? Did one pass from this earth and approach another world . . . another lifetime?

He stared at the ceiling and tried to remember all that Judith had said about God and her belief that Jesus was the only way to be reconciled. It wasn't that he hadn't heard such things before his granddaughter came to be with him. His own dear wife had believed those things and insisted he be at her side each Sunday for services. Of course, he hadn't bothered to really listen, but he knew the general tenets of the faith. Man was hopelessly depraved and, without Christ, condemned to hell. He had only ever seen it as religious nonsense, a means of controlling people with guilt and fear. Neither of which was he susceptible to.

Now, however, lingering in the shadow of death, James found himself so very alone. It was a terrible feeling. He hadn't been the most honest of men. He'd duped more than one poor fool in his life. There had been great satisfaction in winning the lion's share, but now that satisfaction seemed unimportant.

In fact, nothing that he'd done seemed of any great importance. He had married and had a son. That had been important. That was his legacy as much as the money he would leave behind. Many would say it was the most significant thing he'd done. Judith was his granddaughter and heir, and he couldn't have asked for better. She was smart and capable. She would be able to take his wealth and do great things. So why did he feel so void of value?

He remembered telling Judith that his heart would stop and that it would be the end of his life on earth, but she had been adamant that it wouldn't be the end of his soul.

And she had called him Grandfather for the first time. Her passion for her beliefs had brought her to intimacy with him. So, again, why did he feel so empty?

Judith had told him he needed to be saved. That his sins had separated him from God. It was all things that he'd heard before and tossed aside as he might a children's fairy tale. A mythology of gods and goddesses and their interaction with mankind. After all, why should the Christian beliefs be truer than those of the Romans and Greeks?

But even as he thought this, James knew from somewhere deep inside that the Christian beliefs were true. He'd just refused to accept them as his own.

He struggled for breath. "Is it too late? May I still find forgiveness?"

The silence was deafening around him. It seemed even the ticking of the clock had muffled, perhaps stopped.

Forgiveness was a word he'd not given much consideration to in life, but in death it seemed vital. Could he be forgiven? Had Christ died for his sins as well as those of others who more readily accepted him?

"If it might be so," he said, glancing again at the ceiling, "I . . . I want it. I want this salvation."

“My niece Claudette is here. She'd like to see you, if you have a moment,” Mary told Judith.

“What a pleasant surprise,” Judith said, getting up from behind her grandfather's desk. “Where is she?”

“I put her in the sitting room. Would you prefer I bring her back here?”

Judith considered it. “No. I'll take her to the garden. It's such a beautiful day, and in the shade, it's quite pleasant.”

“I agree. It has turned out to be a perfect Fourth of July.” Mary Deeters headed for the door. “Would you like me to serve refreshments?”

“That would be lovely, and you should join us.”

Mary left to go to the kitchen while Judith made her way to where Claudette waited. “This is a grand surprise. Why don't we go out to the gardens. The flowers are quite beautiful, and under those wonderful shade trees, you'll find the temperatures considerably cooler.”

Claudette stood. “That sounds divine. It's been such a warm summer.”

The two women made their way out to Judith's favorite place and took seats. Mary appeared just moments later with glasses of lemonade and slices of Mrs. Markle's famed ginger cake.

"Mary, please sit and join us," Judith said, scooting over on the settee.

"Oh, do," Claudette encouraged.

"I wish I could, but you caught me in the middle of something. Perhaps next time." Mary kissed her niece's cheek and made a hasty exit.

Claudette sampled her drink. "This is delicious. Lemonade is something I've not had in a very long time."

Judith knew lemons were quite expensive and no doubt not on the list of affordable luxuries for the Turner family.

"Now, what has brought you here today?"

"The day itself," Claudette replied, then tasted her drink again. She looked so delighted. "We're having a little picnic this evening at the lake. Everyone goes there to celebrate, so there will be hundreds of people. We'll have lots of food. Everyone shares what they've brought, and there will be fireworks. We thought since you'd not been here before to celebrate the Fourth, you might like to join us."

"That does sound like a wonderful time, but I really can't leave my grandfather. He's taken a turn for the worse, and the doctor feels his death will be very soon."

"I'm so sorry, Judith. I thought Roman said he had a month or two."

Judith glanced up toward the house. Winchell had kept her informed regarding her grandfather's condition. "He's progressively gotten worse. It seems each time the doctor comes, he declares the time to be shorter and shorter. I don't think I can leave him."

"Of course not. We understand. It's so hard to watch someone die. I remember my father . . ." She fell silent.

"Do go on. I'd be honored to hear your story."

Claudette looked up with tears in her eyes. "I've said very little about it. Mother was always so devastated and sad that I didn't want to add to it. And with Roman—well, he blames himself for not being here. I still struggle with Papa's passing, though."

"But you suffer in silence because you care so much for others." Judith smiled. "Let me be your confidant and bear your burden as the Bible encourages us to do."

"Papa was my entire world. He was the kindest, gentlest man. He was such a good father, and I always knew I was so special to him. He loved Roman, of course, and was so very proud of him. But Papa said I was his precious gift from God—an unexpected gift. I came long after Mama thought she was unable to have more children. Papa was so happy, she told me. He had always wanted a daughter. We were very close, he and I, and when he was ruined financially, I did my best to cheer him, but I was just ten years old."

"I'm sure in many ways, you were the only one who could offer cheering. You must have given him great consolation."

"I like to think so, but even I can understand that it wasn't enough. He felt the fool for having allowed Mr. Ashton to ruin him. He lost his will to live. Mama said he died from a broken heart. Oh, how I wished I could have mended it for him." Tears slipped down her cheek. "But I wasn't enough."

"Oh, darling girl, it's so much more complicated than that. You mustn't blame yourself. Men are focused on providing for their families. It's the way God has made them. They are to protect and provide, and when those things are stripped away from them, they are left feeling helpless and even worthless. You could have done nothing more than love him."

"I certainly did that. Even as he took to his bed, having completely given up hope, I curled up next to him and read him stories and shared memories. I so hoped they would revive him."

Judith reached over and took hold of Claudette's hand. "How you must have suffered his loss. I am so sorry for all that you endured. And then to find your welfare threatened the next year when the Sioux made war."

"It was a terrible time. My poor mother . . . She suffered so much but did so in silence. I could see the fear in her eyes, but she tried so hard to be encouraging. Friends would relate information, assuring us the Indians would never attack St. Anthony and Minneapolis because of Fort Snelling being so close. But we went to sleep each night wondering what would happen. We worried we might be murdered in our sleep. Mama did her best to keep to our routine. She told me God would see us through, and no matter the outcome, we would remain in His care."

"How awful. I'm so sorry you had to go through that."

"I sometimes still have nightmares, but please don't tell Roman. He already feels guilty for not having been around to save Papa. Then when he heard about the attack in Minnesota, well, Mama said he nearly left the army to come to us. She doesn't ever want him to know how afraid we really were." She bit her lip and wiped at her tears.

"My guess is that he already knows. Your brother is quite tenderhearted. He wouldn't work with the people he's chosen to care for if not for that. He's also smart. Otherwise, he wouldn't have become such a renowned surgeon."

"It's almost as if you've known him for a long time."

Judith gave a nervous laugh. "There are times when it seems that way to me as well. But I believe it's probably more that I'm good at deducing situations. It's what has helped me to help others."

"I think Roman likes you," Claudette said and quickly covered her mouth.

Judith couldn't hide her surprise for a moment, then burst out laughing. "I like him too. I like all of you." She sobered as

Claudette lowered her hands. "I'm only sorry that my grandfather was the cause of so much trouble and pain. However, I intend to do what I can to make up for his cruelty. I don't know yet what exactly can be done, but I will endeavor to see that your family reclaims some of its losses."

"Oh, that would be wonderful. I hate seeing Roman and Mama work so hard. Mama says she loves to sew, but I know she gets very tired. I sometimes worry about her."

It troubled Judith to hear these things. She knew it wasn't her responsibility that such things had happened, but it was her responsibility to see that they were made right.

"I should be going. I promised Mama I'd deliver the message and come right back."

"You haven't finished your cake," Judith said, holding up her own plate. "Mrs. Markle makes a very nice ginger cake." She sampled the small piece and smiled.

Claudette did likewise, taking a much larger bite. "Mmm." Her eyes lit up in approval. "Delicious."

They ate their cake in silence and then drank the last of their lemonade. Judith dabbed her napkin to her lips. "There, now you can return home fully refreshed."

Claudette laughed. "Given all the food that I know will be at the party tonight, I'm certain to be refreshed all evening."

Laughing, they got to their feet and began the stroll to the front of the house. Judith liked the younger woman very much.

"I know that there are quite a few years between our ages," Judith told her as they reached the front walk, "but I'd like to be your friend."

"I want that as well," Claudette replied. "And perhaps we can be even more."

Judith wasn't at all sure exactly what she meant by that but smiled and nodded. Just then Mr. Black arrived in a buggy. He had driven himself, which somewhat surprised Judith.

"Farewell, Claudette. I'm sure we'll see each other soon." She gave the girl a wave as Claudette headed down the drive.

It was only moments before Bert Black had dismounted. To Judith's relief, one of the stableboys appeared to take control of the horse. Bert bounded up the walk and gave Judith a huge smile.

"I'm back, just as I said I'd be. Isn't the weather lovely?"

"It is. Hopefully you can convince Grandfather to limit his work today. After all, it is a celebration day."

"You know your grandfather. He doesn't know the meaning of the word *holiday*. I doubt he'll have much to do, however, since many others have agreed to put aside work today."

"I doubt he'll have much to do because he's taken another bad turn. The doctor was here earlier and said my grandfather is nearing his time."

"I am sorry to hear that. I know it grieves you. I would save you from this pain, if I could."

"Thank you." Judith hoped that would be the end of it.

"Who, might I ask, was the young lady?" Bert glanced down the street at Claudette's retreating figure.

"Just a friend. Someone from church," Judith replied. She had no desire for Bert to share information regarding Claudette's visit with her grandfather. "Feel free to go on up, but don't be surprised if Grandfather is less than concerned with business. He's sleeping more and more these days."

Bert nodded, but then gave Judith a long look. She didn't like the way he studied her and turned to go back to the gardens. At least this way she wouldn't have to make conversation with him as they entered the house.

"Where are you going?"

She didn't even pause but glanced over her shoulder. "About my business. You should do likewise."

Her steps quickened but not enough. Bert was soon at her side. "Please give me a moment of time."

With great reluctance, Judith stopped and turned. "What is it, Bert?"

He smiled. "I just want to be near you."

"Bert, please. We've already discussed this."

"I know." His brow furrowed. "Mr. Ashton is your first concern. I do agree that he should be exactly that, but the man is soon to die, and you'll need me."

Judith couldn't imagine any situation in which she'd need Bert Black. Still, she didn't wish to hurt his feelings. He was quite sweet in his own way.

"I assure you, Bert, if I need you, I will send for you. Right now, I have more than enough to do on my own, and besides, I'll be following you up shortly so we can all go over that contract together."

Disappointment was evident in his expression, but he gave a nod, and Judith let that be their farewell.

She reached the garden area to find Mary cleaning up the last of their refreshments. "Bert's here again," she told the older woman. "Apparently Grandfather isn't of a mind to observe the celebratory spirit of Fourth of July."

"He doesn't even see Christmas as a reason for commerce to halt," Mary said, putting the last of the dishes on her tray. She straightened and gave a shrug. "I suppose each man must make his own decisions regarding such things. No doubt in dying, he feels it necessary to utilize each day and moment."

Judith nodded. "Claudette invited me to come celebrate with the family this evening, but I told her I didn't feel I should leave Grandfather. Still, I was deeply touched that they invited me to come."

"It will be quite the celebration. I plan to be there myself. Once my work is done, of course."

Judith laughed. "Oh, Mary, I think you should leave as soon as possible. It's a glorious day, and the revelry will be exceptional, I'm sure."

"There are fireworks planned, although individuals are not to be shooting them off themselves. The sheriff posted a large notice in the paper. I'm sure he means to arrest those who disregard his instructions."

"Just be sure to mind yourself, then." Judith chuckled. "Why don't you get going? I can return this tray to the kitchen."

"Oh no, that definitely wouldn't be proper."

"Since when do we care about that?"

Mary laughed but picked up the tray. "It will only take a moment, and then I will be on my way."

"God bless you and your family, Mary."

Judith thought of Roman and hoped he would be able to enjoy the evening. Hopefully accidents would be at a minimum, and he wouldn't find himself caught up in medical repairs all evening. She supposed, however, that was the routine of a doctor.

"Judith! Judith! Come quickly!"

It was Bert again. He was running from around the front of the house and coming at full steam. "It's your grandfather! Hurry. He's not breathing!"

Judith had known this moment would come but even so felt completely unprepared.

"I'll send for the doctor," Mary declared and hurried toward the back of the house.

Judith froze. What was she supposed to do? What could she do?

"Why don't you come and sit down," Bert suggested, reaching out to take hold of her arm.

She pulled away almost angrily. "No, Bert! I need to be at his side."

Racing into the house, Judith gave little thought to having offended the man. She was tired of dealing with him.

Winchell was standing at the foot of the bed. His face revealed the truth of the situation. Judith stepped to her grandfather's bedside and took hold of his hand. It was still warm, so his death must have not come more than a few moments ago.

"Were you with him?" she asked, looking to his valet.

"No, ma'am. I had checked on him earlier, and he was sleeping deeply. I had stepped out to tend to his suits, and then Mr. Black called out for help a short time later."

"It must have come fast," Mary said, having joined them. "He didn't ring for any of us."

Judith sat down on the bed beside her grandfather. He looked to be at peace, but how could she know? She had shared the Gospel with him, but he'd never so much as indicated that he saw the value of making peace with God.

She continued to hold his hand and didn't attempt to hold back the tears that came. She wanted so much to believe he had accepted the truth about God, but now she would never know. At least not until making her own way into eternity.

"Oh, Grandfather." She sighed the words and sniffed back tears. "If only I knew."

A funeral was held on Friday for James Ashton Sr. It was poorly attended, as Judith had presumed it would be. There were a handful of suit-clad strangers, men who she figured had done business with her grandfather or felt obligated enough to pay their respects. Otherwise, the household staff was on hand and, to her great surprise, the entire Turner family.

Reverend Knickerbacker gave the eulogy, admitting he didn't know James Ashton all that well but believed that every man was deserving of decent burial. The service was quite short, relating the usual information about Grandfather's birth and marriage. Judith had shared what information she could, relying on Winchell to fill in many of the details she wouldn't have otherwise known. For herself, she could offer very little. The man had simply not allowed himself to be intimately known by family or foe, and the things she had learned through his business records were not the kind one would want shared.

When the services were over, the reverend and his wife

came and gave their consolation. "We're here for you in any way you need," he assured her.

"Yes, Judith. Please don't hesitate to let us know if we can do anything," Sarah added.

"I do hope you'll give my excuses tonight at the party." Judith had only just now remembered the fundraiser. "I do intend to give you a large donation for the hospital, Reverend. As soon as I know for sure how the financial situation stands with my grandfather's estate."

"You are very kind, and I will look forward to discussing this another time. For now, please don't worry about a thing. We will of course explain your absence," the reverend said, patting her gloved hand.

Judith took up her black fan and began to wave it. The warmth of the day was growing, and she didn't want another fainting incident. Thankfully a breeze blew across the open cemetery, giving immediate relief.

Winchell came to her side as if uncertain as to what should be done next. She had asked him to ride with her in the Ashton carriage and was grateful for his company. Dressed in black livery with a mourning band on his arm, he looked quite properly outfitted for the funeral. It was his expression that suggested he was completely displaced.

"I'm so glad you're with me, Winchell." She was just about to suggest they head to the carriage when Bert approached, hat in hand.

"I am very sorry for your loss. Mr. Ashton was a great man."

She looked at Bert for a moment, then nodded and continued to fan herself. She knew Bert would see her grandfather's demise as the perfect opportunity to continue pursuing her. She had thought a great deal about the future, and while she wanted very much to continue in her new relationship with Roman, she had no desire to keep time with Bert. Not even as her attorney. Of course, she wasn't going to say as much at the funeral, but in the days to come, she would have to call him to the house and dismiss him. That was going to be difficult at best.

"Judith, I believe you should make your way home." She turned to find Roman looking at her with great concern. "The heat may become too much, especially given you're wearing all black."

"I had thought about that," she admitted. "Winchell has been good enough to assist me."

Roman looked to the valet and nodded. "Mrs. Stanford has difficulty in the heat. You should take her home immediately."

"Yes, sir. I will do that." Winchell extended his arm for Judith to take.

"And if I might add, when she gets home you may need to remind her to put on cooler clothing and drink plenty of water or tea. Iced if possible. The heat tends to cloud her thinking, and she might forget."

"I will see to it, sir."

"Thank you, Winchell," Judith said. "And thank you, Dr. Turner. I appreciate your concern. I'm also very sorry that I cannot attend the fundraiser with you this evening. I do hope it's a success."

"As do I. I know the reverend has worked hard for this hospital."

"As I told him, I will be making a large donation once I have my grandfather's affairs in order." Judith noted that Bert looked quite put out. "Good day, Bert. Thank you for coming to Grandfather's funeral."

"I'll be coming by this afternoon to go over things with you."

Grief, but the man was positively officious. "No, please don't. I won't feel up to it, I'm sure. This has all been much too much."

"Would you like me to check on you later?" Roman asked. "I could easily come by on my way to the fundraiser."

Judith smiled. "That would be nice. Given your medical knowledge, you can advise me if I need to do something more to improve my situation."

With that, she let Winchell guide her to the carriage. She noted the look of dismay on Bert's face. He was clearly put out that she had dismissed him. A sigh escaped her lips.

"Are you all right, ma'am?" Winchell asked.

"Yes. I'm completely exhausted, however. I didn't sleep well last night."

"Nor did I," he replied, then immediately apologized. "That was uncalled for. Speaking of my personal well-being is completely out of line."

"Not at all, Winchell," Judith said as he helped her into the Ashton carriage. Once she was seated, she waited for him to join her in the open conveyance. "I want to know that you are doing well. Or that you aren't, for that matter."

"The times are not without difficulties, to be sure."

"Yes, but I want to reiterate that your position is secure." The driver started the carriage for home and hit a rather large dip in the road. Judith bounced hard across the seat, barely righting herself.

Winchell reached out to steady her, then quickly pulled away once she was upright again.

"Goodness, but that was quite the hole we fell into."

"Yes, ma'am." Winchell actually gave a hint of a smile. "The newspaper just carried a story on the poor conditions of some roads. There are plans for improvements."

Judith leaned back against the fine leather upholstery. "That's good to hear." She smiled and shook her head. "But back to what I was saying, Winchell, you are secure in my household."

"Then you have decided to remain in Minneapolis?"

She considered this for a moment. "I have. It seems the right decision. Like it was always meant to be. My assistant back in Philadelphia can manage my affairs there. I also have a businessman who handles the steamboat services my father created. There's really nothing in Philadelphia that beckons me to return. Here, however, there are people I've come to care about. You're one of those.

"I know my grandfather was not easy to work for, and yet you remained with him from the time you were hardly more than a boy. I admire your loyalty and hope you will be frank with me in the days to come, Winchell. I don't need servants; I need friends. I need that same loyalty you gave my grandfather."

"Madam, I am happy to attend you in whatever capacity you request. However, I only have skills and training to perform as a valet. There is also my age to consider."

Judith smiled. "I know. I believe having you around to oversee the men who work in the house will be most beneficial. Also I'll have you close by to offer me advice when needed. I have long missed the advice my father offered, and there's something about you that reminds me of him."

Winchell's left brow raised. He was not one to show emotion, but this clearly betrayed his surprise. Judith shrugged. "I've a feeling we will have a great many difficult days ahead of us. I intend to right the wrongs my grandfather committed. At least, I hope to do as much as possible."

"You should know that Mr. Ashton changed the handling of his will. I'm sure within a few days you'll be notified by the gentlemen who now manage it."

"Gentlemen? There is more than one?"

"Yes. Mr. Ashton feared Mr. Black's attachment to his money and removed the will from his care. Mr. Ashton instead turned the matter over to another law firm. In fact, two law firms. He wanted no opportunity for either to try anything underhanded. He trusted no one."

"Somehow that doesn't surprise me. I suppose when you are

given to underhanded business dealings, you come to expect that from everyone around you."

"Perhaps, ma'am. I do know that he rewrote the will leaving most everything to you. He told me that he had made provision for me, and I believe there was to be a small amount settled on Mr. Black for his faithful service."

"Well, as you know, I've familiarized myself with all of his business records. I know the current projects he has going on, as well as his earliest dealings here in Minnesota. I didn't attempt to go back further than that, but I do intend to try and help those he damaged so badly."

"Like the Turners?"

"Yes, especially them. I feel terrible for what happened."

"As do I. That was a most difficult situation, and not one that was managed well at all."

Judith considered this as they drove. It troubled her more than she could say to know her grandfather had caused the death of Roman's father. How could their love grow with such a horrendous thing between them?

Love?

She knew her thoughts were going toward that possibility more and more. She found Roman quite attractive, and not only that, but his heart was fixed on the same things as her own. She had never expected to fall in love again, much less to do it so quickly, but there was no denying her heart.

But whether or not Roman and his family could completely forgive her was an entirely different matter. While it was true that she had nothing to do with what happened, no doubt she brought them memories of her grandfather's betrayal of trust.

How she wished there'd been more time with the old man. More than just a couple of summer months to be with him and speak to him about God and the Bible. She had no idea if his heart had changed or if he'd even considered the things she'd told him.

She glanced across the carriage as the driver pulled into the Ashton drive. Winchell seemed quite lost in his thoughts.

"Winchell, did you and Grandfather ever speak of spiritual matters?"

"Only once, ma'am. It wasn't long ago. He asked me if I believed in God and considered myself a Christian. He wondered if I thought there was something of life beyond the grave."

"And what did you say?"

The carriage came to a stop, and the driver climbed down to open the door. Winchell waited until they had left the carriage to answer her question. "I told him that I did believe in God and considered myself a Christian. He asked me what I thought was required to become a Christian, and I told him that he must accept Jesus as Lord and Savior."

"And did he reject that idea?" Judith had told him much the same, but it seemed at least a little hopeful that her grandfather asked Winchell his thoughts.

"Not exactly. He asked how one might do that."

Judith felt her spark of hope ignite into a flame. "He did? Oh, that suggests he was considering it, doesn't it?"

"I believe so, ma'am. I told him that he must ask for salvation, that God was willing none should be lost. I also told him that the Bible states clearly that Jesus is the only way to the Father."

Judith couldn't help but reach out to touch Winchell's arm. "And what did he say to that?"

"I believe he was quite . . . well, perhaps disturbed is the best way to put it. He asked me to remove his dinner tray. He said he had no appetite. Later when I spoke to him, he seemed changed, as if he'd taken the words to heart."

"But he never said for certain that he did?" Judith tried to hide her disappointment.

"No, ma'am. But I believe that something did change. From the time the doctor informed him of his impending demise, your grandfather had a certain uneasiness. When I last spoke to him, that seemed to have been replaced. He was at ease. Whether that came from accepting his circumstances or making peace with God, I cannot say for certain. But I believe it was the latter."

"Oh, I hope and pray you're right. I wanted so much to help him see the truth. I know it was my father's dearest wish that Grandfather might know God and put his trust in Him. It would really make everything I've done here worth the trip and the pain."

"Yes, ma'am." He patted her hand as one might a child seeking approval.

Judith was surprised at the comfort she found in his words. She had chided herself the last few days for not having pushed more for her grandfather to make peace with God. She knew it wasn't her place to save him; only God could do that. But she longed to be used by God to see Grandfather find peace and eternal security.

Please, Lord, I pray that You would have mercy on my grandfather and accept him into Your embrace, just as You did the thief on the cross.

Roman knocked on the Ashton front door. He couldn't help himself. He needed to know that Judith was all right, and he'd told her he might come check in on her. It seemed to him that she welcomed the idea. Still, with his aunt Mary given the day off and the household in mourning, it was rather brash for him to come calling. What should he say if she questioned his appearance?

A young woman opened the door. She gave him a questioning look. "Good evening, sir. We are in mourning, and the family is not receiving at this time."

"I'm Dr. Turner. I came to check on the health of Mrs.

Stanford." There, that was the perfect excuse. It would be impossible for the young maid to turn him away.

"Please come in." The young woman didn't hesitate. "Mrs. Stanford is in the garden. I will show you the way."

She led him through the house to double French doors, which led out the back. Normally, Roman might have paid close attention to the details of each room, but at the moment his mind was solely fixed on Judith.

Outside, the air had cooled and made for a most pleasant evening. Roman had enjoyed the walk over, but here in the Ashton garden, it was even more pleasant.

"Mrs. Stanford, excuse me please," the maid called out. "Dr. Turner has come to inquire after your health. Will you receive him?"

Judith was sitting in that place where she had spoken to Roman once before. Their special place. A place that he hoped would be theirs for a long, long time. Her feet were tucked up under her, and her skirts were spread out over the settee to spill onto the ground. It reminded him of a painting he'd once seen.

"Of course I'll receive him," Judith replied. She stood and looked at Roman with a smile. "I'm so glad you came."

The maid took her leave, and Judith waved Roman over. "I was just out here contemplating the day."

"I worried about you overheating. I couldn't bring myself to attend the fundraiser with that on my mind," Roman replied. Judith reclaimed her place on the settee, and he came to sit just opposite her. "I hope you're feeling well."

"I am. I have been considering how to get started on my very important duties."

"And what duties are those?"

"My grandfather was quite concerned about leaving a legacy. He wanted to build a marble block memorial downtown, but I have something else in mind."

Roman frowned. "That man's legacy is already set in stone."

"I know. Sadly, there are those who will never think of him without bitterness. I pray you won't be one of them, but I surely understand if you are. Still, it is my desire to see to a new legacy. That memorial block he wants me to build will be assembled, but not out of marble and not for the benefit of financial institutions. I believe it would be far more beneficial to create hospitals, orphanages, and other more helpful organizations."

"That would be amazing." Roman could see the pleasure such thoughts brought to Judith.

"Not only that, Roman, but I've been long at work going through my grandfather's records since his arrival in Minneapolis. There are a great many people he took advantage of or outright cheated. I intend to see them properly reimbursed."

"That won't be easy."

Judith smiled. "I know, and I'm perfectly fine with that. I will, however, need help. That is why I intend to start with your family. It's my hope that eventually, you might be willing to assist me in seeing these wrongs righted."

"How would I do that?"

"I'm not entirely sure, but you know most everyone in this area due to your duties. I know you can help me locate the people who were cheated. But first I must meet with the lawyers. I haven't yet heard from them. Once I do, I will move ahead with my plans. I intend to return the land Grandfather stole from your father, for a start."

"That property has been fully developed with high rents being reaped."

"I know, and it will be returned to your mother. There will also be a cash settlement. We will discuss what you believe to be fair. Obviously, nothing can make up for the loss of your father's life, but reinstating your financial position is the best I can do."

Roman couldn't help himself. He stood and went to her.

Reaching out for her hands, he pulled her to her feet. "Judith, I don't know what to say. I already came with overwhelming thoughts and feelings for you, but this goes beyond anything I imagined. Kindness and mercy from an Ashton was something I never thought possible. Since I first met you back in Philadelphia, I've known you were to have a special place in my life."

Without thinking, he pulled her close to him and lifted her chin. "I never thought love was possible for me. I presumed God had called me to a life of being single. I thought my purpose was to offer my services and help better the lives of others."

"I thought God had called me to the same," she said, her voice soft and low. "Perhaps, we can answer that call together? Perhaps God no longer wants us to face these duties alone."

Roman nodded and lowered his lips to hers. For the first time in his life, Roman felt as if the chains of the past had truly fallen away. He could forgive James Ashton Sr. He could let go of his anger and hate and replace it with love.

19

After that first kiss, Judith was certain of being in love. Weeks later, as she sat going over her list of things to do, she couldn't help but think of Roman and the passion he had stirred to life in her. She had thought after Alden died that she could never love again. Then she met Roman in Philadelphia, and their encounter had caused her to reconsider. Now, with all that had happened, she could no longer deny her feelings. How happy she was to be wrong. She could love again.

Since the funeral, Roman had stopped by each evening to spend time with her, and it felt as if they'd known each other all their lives. They talked about the things they loved and hated. Both were troubled by the seeming lack of concern society had for those who were destitute. Both longed to find ways to better the lives of the poor, not just by handing them charity but by ensuring educations and proper training for good jobs. They also wanted to see better housing to lower the risk of poverty-related diseases.

There were also other little things that they both shared. Judith talked of her love for the river and steamboat travel.

Roman had suggested she expand her Philadelphia company to include travel on the Mississippi. Judith had to admit that sounded quite promising. Not only for business but for pleasure. The idea of taking a nice long trip on the river with Roman at her side was most appealing.

"Hard at work, I see," Roman announced from the doorway. Mary stood at his side.

"How wonderful to see you." Judith got up and came around the desk. "What brings you here this morning?"

"Aunt Mary, actually. I needed to speak with her, and Mother also sent me to give her a recipe she asked for. I thought it the perfect excuse to see you."

"You know you don't need any excuses." She glanced at Mary and nodded at the paper in her hand. "Is that the recipe we talked about?"

"Yes," Mary replied holding it up. "The best crab cakes in the world. They're Roman's favorites, and Mrs. Markle said she'd prepare them for the evening meal."

"I suppose that means Roman should return this evening for supper. I would hate for you to miss out on your favorite meal."

He smiled and bent to kiss her forehead. "Any meal with you is bound to be my favorite."

"Can you both sit for a moment? I've been going over some of the details of things I want to accomplish. I've spoken to Reverend Knickerbacker and pledged the remaining support he needs for the hospital, but I want to get matters resolved with your family as soon as possible.

"I've retained the lawyers that Grandfather used for the will. I figured perhaps having two men working together would be better than one. They have separate practices but have agreed to put them aside and become my combined legal counsel. I assured them, given all that I needed to accomplish, they would have more than enough work to do. I am, however, having them investigated so that I know their full history."

"And how did the reading of the will go, if I might ask?" Roman asked, his tone cautious.

"You may ask anything." She smiled and shrugged. "I am his heir in everything, but he left a small amount to Winchell and Bert."

"And what about restrictions on things you must do with the money?" They had discussed this prior to the reading. Roman knew that Judith was concerned about such things.

"There weren't any. The matter of his legacy block was stated in such a way to require only that I utilize the land, build a certain number of buildings as already set out, and include an engraving at the top announcing it as the 'Ashton Block.' All of which I can do in my own fashion, and I can utilize the buildings for whatever I choose. None of that was stipulated."

"What an answer to prayer." Roman blew out a short breath. "No marble, eh?"

Judith laughed. "No. No marble."

"What about Mr. Black?" Mary asked. "I know he helped your grandfather plan it all, and I'm sure he is also anxious to know about his inheritance."

"I sent him a letter Monday to come see me. I know he won't be happy at being dismissed, but I cannot work with the man. He has pestered me to court him and doesn't seem to be willing to accept my lack of interest."

"Perhaps I can persuade him," Roman said, smiling. "I can let him know that you are already spoken for."

Judith returned his smile. "I may well need you to discuss that with him, but for now I feel able to manage. Each time he's come to the house, I've had Winchell or Mary let him know that we are in mourning and not conducting business.

"Business, of course, is being managed, but Mr. Black is not a part of it. I know dismissal will come as a shock to him after working faithfully for my grandfather all these years. Now that Grandfather's will has been read, I will have to inform him that he's not reaping the fortune he originally counted on. Although, Grandfather was quite generous with him."

"He must have his disappointment and move on," Mary said, shaking her head.

"I agree." Judith was excited to share the next bit of news. "I had the lawyers prepare the transfer of deeds for the property that was once your father's, Roman. They will have things in order within a week or so. I've also been working with some figures that I want to go over with you and your mother. I want to make certain you feel that they are fair. I've taken several issues into consideration, and if there are additional ones, I want you to speak up and let me know."

"I can hardly believe the way God has answered our prayers." Mary's tone held amazement. "When I came here to work, it was my hope that I might find the evidence necessary to show how the Turners were cheated. This goes beyond my hopes and prayers."

"It's clear to see how God has been in the midst of this since the beginning. I hate to think what might have been had I continued to refuse my grandfather and not come to Minneapolis."

"I do too." Roman met Judith's gaze and grinned. "I can hardly believe I let so much time go by after first meeting you. I must have been crazy not to immediately come back to Philadelphia and seek you out. I thought a great deal about you, to be honest, but my work consumed me."

"I thought a great deal about that as well and, like you, lost myself in my charity work," Judith admitted. "I just convinced myself that our being together wasn't meant to be. I had my work in Philadelphia, and you had yours here. Now I can clearly see that it's possible to continue doing what I was called to do and have you in my life as well. And, Mary, you have been such a dear friend. I'm so glad we were able to work together and accomplish all that we have to set things straight.

Oh, and I keep meaning to speak to you about interviewing a new housekeeper."

"A new one? Have I done something wrong?" Mary looked quite concerned.

"No, Mary. It's just that I would rather have you as a personal assistant than housekeeper." Judith hoped the woman would be happy with this news. "You do an amazing job keeping things running, however. It may be difficult to find someone as good at the job as you are."

"I thank you for the compliment, and I will immediately begin the process of acquiring a new woman to take on my duties. I had thought to discuss the matter with you anyway, because I am hoping to have my dear nephew remove these painful gallbladder stones. So for a time, I won't be able to work."

"Oh, of course." Judith had wondered if Roman was able to help the poor woman.

"It will require a good amount of recovery time." Roman reached over and patted Mary's hand. "But I believe she'll do well. My good friend Dr. John Lester will assist me. He has a very nice operating room, and we will manage quite well."

"She may recover here, of course. In fact, I could set her up a bedroom downstairs. The music room could easily be transformed into a bedroom for you, Mary. We could bring your bed and set up a nice place there for you to recover. And I will hire a nurse to watch over you." Judith looked to Roman for his approval.

"I think that would be perfect. After she recovers a week or so at John's, we could transport her here. She'll need at least a couple months of rest and care."

"Then that's what she shall have." Judith was adamant.

Mary touched her hand to the center of her chest. "I'm so blessed by your concern. Thank you. It gives me great peace of mind to know that God has already provided my needs."

"It's settled, then. Just let me know the dates and I will arrange for the men to bring down your things." Judith was happy that she would be able to take care of the woman. Mary had been such a good friend to her, and it seemed only right that she pay back the woman in some way.

"Well, with that in mind, I hope you'll excuse us," Mary declared. "Roman and I need to discuss the details of when we should accomplish this operation."

"Of course. I have plenty of business to attend to myself." Judith went back to her desk. "I shall see you this evening, Roman."

"I'll be here." He winked.

They were no sooner gone than one of the downstairs maids appeared. "Ma'am, Mr. Black has come to see you."

Judith looked up from her grandfather's desk. Frankly, she was surprised it had taken him this long to come calling since he'd done his level best to see her nearly every day since the funeral. The last few days had been unexpectedly void of his attention.

"Please show him in."

She thought of moving to the chairs situated in front of the cold fireplace, then changed her mind. She didn't want to give him the idea of intimacy. This was a business meeting and nothing more. She whispered a prayer for strength and insight as to how to break the news to Bert. He wasn't going to like being sent away permanently.

Bert came into the room, dressed in his gray suit. He looked as fashionable as always. Judith motioned to the chair opposite the large desk. "Please have a seat, Bert. We have much to discuss."

"I am glad that you finally allowed me to come to you. I must say, I was rather troubled by your unwillingness to see me."

"I've been in mourning for my grandfather, Bert. As you

know. I haven't desired to receive company and am only getting back to a place of tending to business. That is why I sent you the letter. I've met with Grandfather's other attorneys." She pulled a document from the right-hand drawer and pushed it toward him. "This is a copy of Grandfather's will."

Bert immediately began searching through the few pages. Judith knew he wasn't going to be happy.

"As you can see for yourself in the last will and testament of James Ashton Sr., you have been left the sum of five thousand dollars and the deed to your apartment."

"He left his valet one hundred thousand."

"That's hardly your concern, Bert. My grandfather was well within his rights to leave whatever monies or properties he wanted to whomever he wanted. Mr. Winchell had served my grandfather since he was a very young man. I think it was greatly deserved."

"He made certain promises to me. I expected them to be fulfilled." Bert fixed her with a hard look. "I left the comforts of Boston and a good life there to live in this wretched frontier town. He owed me."

"I'm sorry that he disappointed you. I believe you know how my grandfather could be about such things." Judith reached for the will, but Bert snatched it up.

"I will pursue legal challenges, unless of course you and I might reach some agreement." He studied her for a moment, his expression begging her to show compassion.

"Do what you feel you must, Mr. Black." Judith put aside any appearance of friendship or intimacy. "You can see at the bottom of the last page the names of the attorneys who prepared this document. I would suggest you start with them."

"It's just not right. You must see it. You didn't even care about the old man. You spent a lifetime ignoring him and leaving him to the care of others, and now he has left you millions."

"My grandfather hardly required care. At least not until

these last few months. Furthermore, it was his decision to make me his heiress. I was certainly not looking for that position. You might recall that I clearly told you from the moment you first appeared on my doorstep that I had no interest in his fortune. However, now that I have inherited it, I intend to see it used in a way that will right the wrongs my grandfather perpetuated."

"But that's madness. Every man, woman, and child will come knocking on your door once you open that can of worms. They will declare from dawn to dusk that they were wronged by your grandfather. They will demand restitution for things that never happened."

"That's where I'm blessed that my grandfather kept such meticulous records, Mr. Black. I have it all recorded in multiple ledgers and contracts. I feel confident of seeing this through."

"If you don't want his money, why not give it to me? I earned it. I deserve it. I've spent the last ten years of my life with your grandfather. I worked hard for him, even put aside taking a wife and having a family. He was my only family. His fortune is worth millions and I could do great things with it."

"I am fully acquainted with my grandfather's fortune and where it is." She frowned and got to her feet. "The matter is settled, Mr. Black. My lawyers will issue you a check and the deed for your apartment within the week."

She paused and drew a deep breath. "There is one more thing. I suppose this will further your distress, but I will no longer be using your services. Perhaps you can return to Boston, since you hate it here so much."

He looked shocked and jumped to his feet. "You can't dismiss me. I've come to love you. I don't wish to be parted from you."

"Unfortunately, I do not return your feelings, Mr. Black. I've made that clear since you first tried to pursue a courtship with me. As for your services as an attorney, I believe it will be best for me to seek other counsel. These feelings you have for me would serve only as an obstacle."

"That's not true. You do love me. You've merely pushed aside your feelings to care for your grandfather. Now that he's gone, you can love me."

Judith moved from behind the desk and walked toward the door. "I cannot return your feelings." She made the mistake of putting her back to him.

Without warning, he grabbed her and whirled her around to face him. He pulled her into his embrace. "You cannot be serious. I know you feel the same. I can see it in your eyes."

"Let me go." She fought against him, but he only tightened his hold.

"I'll prove it to you." He attempted to kiss her, but Judith turned her head and screamed. She knew Roman would probably hear her, and if not him, then perhaps one of the servants. The house was full of people. Surely someone would hear her distress.

She struggled, doing her best to escape his grasp, but Black was quite strong. He tried again to kiss her, but Judith stomped her heel into the top of his foot. "Help me! Someone help!"

"You must listen to me, Judith. Stop fighting me. Stop fighting the love that I know you feel. I want you to marry me. We can be married immediately."

"That would be rather impossible, Black. Judith is going to marry me," Roman announced from the now open door.

Black was enough surprised by this that he let go of Judith and looked at her. "This can't be true."

Judith glanced at Roman as she took a sidestep. "But it is," she said, nodding.

Roman started to move toward Judith, but Black grabbed her and pulled her back. "No! You will not touch her. She's mine."

Just then Winchell and Mary rushed into the office. Judith

felt such a sense of relief to have them come to her aid that she tried to pull away from Bert. He wasn't having any of that, however.

"You can't leave me. I won't allow it."

Roman took a step forward. "Let her go. She doesn't belong to you."

"But she does. She loves me as I love her. I know she does. We've shared a great many days and evenings in each other's company." He turned Judith toward him. "Remember the train ride here? We shared the private car and many hours of discussion. I know you care for me."

"I don't," Judith protested. "I was merely being polite. Each time you've approached me in this manner, I've rebuffed you. Now release me. I've tried to be nice about this, but you have given me no choice. You need to go now and never return."

But instead of accepting defeat, Black shocked them all by stepping back several feet, dragging Judith with him. When he turned to face Roman and the others, he pulled a revolver from his coat pocket and waved it around before settling it on Judith.

"I didn't want this to become violent, but I can't seem to persuade you otherwise."

Judith could see the fear in Mary's eyes and the anger in Roman's. Winchell stood in his usual stoic manner. It was almost like the setting for a play.

"Mr. Black, this will do you no good." Judith finally spoke. "You need to stop this before you do something that will cause you imprisonment." She looked at the others. She needed to get them to safety. "You should go. Mr. Black and I will discuss this and work through the problem."

"No! They need to stay. I can't have them going for the police."

"This is ridiculous. You can stop it now, and there will be no need for the police."

"I will kill you before I'll let him have you," he replied, fixing his gaze on her face. "You are mine. I won't let him take you away."

Roman took a step toward them, and Black raised the revolver to Judith's head. "I'm quite serious, so you should step back before I feel the need to use this." He cocked the hammer and looked again to Judith. "I love you and cannot live without you."

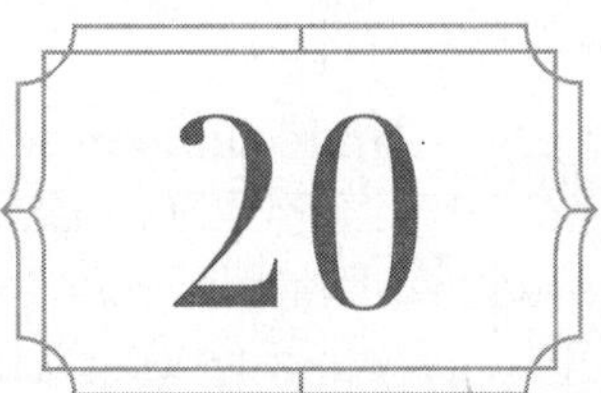

“Whoa, Black. There’s no need for this. I didn’t realize you loved her so much,” Roman said, raising his hands to draw Black’s attention.

“But I do. I love her. It’s not just about the money, but the money should be mine. Ashton promised me a fortune. He told me if I gave up my life in Boston and aided him here, he would make it well worth my troubles. I gave that old man ten years of my life. Years that I might have used to cultivate my own practice, to marry. I could have had my own family, but that old man would not allow for it. He said I had to give him my all.”

“I’m sorry to hear that, Mr. Black. That seems rather harsh.” Roman tried desperately to calm the man. “I doubt that Judith realized how you, too, had been ruined by James Ashton.”

Judith seemed to recognize what Roman was doing and nodded. “I’m so sorry, Bert. I didn’t know.”

Roman might have smiled at her thinking to use his first name, but didn’t want to give away the fact that they were trying to use his imbalance to calm the situation. Playing into his feelings and beliefs of what was due him seemed a simple solution.

"He kept me serving him and him alone." Black lowered the gun but kept it pointed at Judith. "When I met Judith, I knew she was for me. It was the reward that I was always meant to have."

Roman nodded. "I can understand how you feel."

"But she won't marry me and so I must kill her."

"No! You don't need to do that," Roman protested. He could see the fear in Judith's eyes and wished with all his heart he could put an end to this entire situation. "As she said, she didn't know how you really felt."

"It doesn't matter now. I can inherit the money if she's dead. The original will stated as much. Ashton made no provision in the new will, but I will go to the men who created the second will and pay them to add on the provision. I will offer them as much money as I need to, and I know they'll accept. They must be devious in their practices or James Ashton would not have used them."

"Why not simply save yourself the trouble and just marry Judith? Now that she knows how you feel, I'm sure she'll agree to marry you. She didn't realize her grandfather had wronged you, and you know that she is determined to right the wrongs he did."

Black's expression changed to one of momentary confusion. He shook his head as if struggling to make sense of any of it.

Judith took the opportunity to press the matter. "He's right, Bert," she began. "I want to do what is right by all of the people Grandfather wronged. He clearly wronged you. I had no idea, and if my marrying you will make things better, then let us do what must be done."

"See there." Roman tried to inch forward while Black's attention was on Judith. "You don't need to kill her. If you two marry, then as her husband you will have the legal right to control everything. The money will be yours."

"That's right," Black agreed. "It will all be mine. The law states as much. The house, the money, the investments. All of it." He looked at Judith. "And you will be mine. We'll be together."

"That's right, Bert." She smiled. "Why don't we get married right away?"

"Marry her today," Roman suggested. "Mary can go fetch the Reverend Knickerbacker. He would be delighted to do the job."

"Today?" Black looked at each person as if needing reassurance. Each one nodded like the plan was quite reasonable.

"I know exactly where to find the reverend," Mary said, awaiting Black's approval.

"Yes, yes," he finally replied. "Go bring the reverend." Mary nodded and backed out of the room.

Roman was relieved to have her go. It was one less person to worry about, and Mary would know to go straight to the police. Roman glanced at Winchell, who remained stoically silent.

Bert turned to Judith. "You must wear something more fitting. I won't have my bride in black."

Judith looked at her gown and nodded. "I will. I will go to my room and change."

"No. You can't leave me."

"How do you expect her to dress for her wedding day?" Roman asked. He wanted to find any way possible to clear the room of people, especially Judith. Black wouldn't be so inclined to kill the rest of them with his focus on the wedding.

"Perhaps Winchell can bring me a gown from my room. My maids will know where to find a gown appropriate for a wedding. Winchell?"

The man stepped forward and gave a bow. "As you wish, ma'am." He looked up, then looked to Black.

"All right. Go and find a dress." Black nodded and waved the gun. "Go quickly."

With only Black and Judith left, Roman tried to figure out his next move. Black still had the gun. In fact, he once again pointed it at Judith's side.

"Perhaps we should sit to wait for everyone," Roman suggested. There were only single chairs here in the office. If Black approved, he would have to allow Judith to sit on her own. It might be enough separation that Roman could get the drop on Black and rid him of the revolver.

"I'd very much like to sit," Judith said, looking to Black. "I'm feeling a bit overwhelmed by the heat. You know that I don't bear it well."

Roman didn't know if she was making this up or if the growing warmth along with the tension of the moment was causing her distress. Black seemed to consider the matter and finally nodded.

"Sit here," he said, motioning to the chair beside him.

"So what are your plans for the fortune, once you and Judith are married?" Roman asked. "Will you take a wedding trip abroad?"

"A trip? I, uh, I don't know." Black shook his head, then rubbed his temple, all while keeping the gun leveled at Judith.

"It's the perfect time for an ocean crossing. You could visit London and Paris. Perhaps even Italy. Wouldn't that be enjoyable, Judith?"

"Yes. Yes, it would. We could put aside the work here and spend the rest of the summer and fall in Europe."

Bert didn't seem to register what was being said. "I certainly won't be building that old man's block of marble memorials." Bert looked down at Judith. "She doesn't want that either. It's a complete waste of money."

"I agree." Roman nodded. "That would be a terrible waste. But what about the trip? Don't you think that would be an interesting prospect? If not Europe, you two could go to California or perhaps the Orient."

"I'd never considered the possibility," Black admitted. "It would be terribly expensive."

"Yes, but you'd have Ashton's millions to spend."

Roman silently prayed he could keep Black talking and get him to lower his guard. No matter what, he had to keep him from shooting Judith, even by accident. In Black's state of mind, who knew what he might be capable of?

Finally, everything was coming around right for Norbert Black. All his life he had known he was destined for greatness and wealth. He had been beyond excited when James Ashton spoke of making him his heir. He had come up with this as he shared his plans for the Ashton Block in downtown Minneapolis.

"I will have you in a position that will allow you to honor my wishes and benefit from them at the same time," Ashton had assured him long before deciding to bring Judith into his life.

It wasn't Bert's fault that the old man changed his mind. Everything that had led up to this moment was a hodgepodge of good and promising, as well as frustrating and intolerable. In the early days, Bert had felt confident that he could become invaluable to the man and win his absolute trust and confidence, but that wasn't the way James Ashton did business. He trusted no one. Ever.

Judith was another story. She was a beautiful woman with great compassion and trust. He could have a good life with her. He just knew he could train her to be what he needed. She was smart and capable. They could accomplish a great deal together. Maybe they'd move back to Philadelphia. He really had no desire to remain in Minneapolis, and in Boston, his father and brothers would only make his life miserable. Once they knew how wealthy he was, they'd be after him for money. They'd believe that Bert owed them. But he owed no one.

"You really don't need the gun anymore," Judith said from where she sat watching him.

He stood at her left side, gun in his right hand, the barrel still fixed on her. Of course he wouldn't shoot her now. Turner had relinquished his claim on her. If only Bert had known that Turner was causing such problems. It was no wonder that she wouldn't agree to courtship with Turner confusing her.

Where was that valet? He'd gone to get a bridal gown for Judith. They couldn't be expected to marry if she was still clad in black.

"Where is Winchell? Why is he taking so long?" Bert felt a growing sense of discomfort. What if Winchell had run off to bring the police? It hadn't occurred to him before now that the man might do something underhanded like that. Bert had been so happy about Judith agreeing to marry him that he hadn't thought of the servant being deceptive.

"Where is he!" Bert's raised voice brought Judith back to her feet. Her action took him off guard, and he nearly fired the gun. "Sit!"

"Please stop waving that gun around," Judith said, shaking her head. "You're making me positively sick to my stomach with worry." She put a hand to her abdomen.

Bert considered her a moment, then calmed. "I'm sorry. I just don't want to be made a fool of. Winchell should have returned by now. There's no call for him to take so long."

Judith smiled. It was such a pretty smile, and one intended only for him, not for Dr. Turner.

"Bert, there's a lot to be done. They'll have to sort through my things to find the proper dress, and then there are the undergarments and shoes. It will take a little time to gather everything together, and if the gown needs to be pressed, then that will also take time."

He hadn't thought of that. Of course, it all made sense. Confusion muddled his mind, and that never made for good reasoning. He needed a drink.

"Pour me a drink," he said, looking at the doctor. "Ashton keeps the liquor in that cabinet over there." He pointed to the cabinet near the entry to the billiards room.

Roman nodded. "What would you prefer?"

"Whiskey. Just whiskey."

Turner crossed the room with a backward glance at Judith. Bert felt his ire rise. "Don't look at her. She belongs to me. She's going to marry me. You heard her say as much."

"I did, indeed." Roman went to the cabinet and opened the door. "You're a lucky man, Mr. Black. Mrs. Stanford is a kind and gentle soul. You really shouldn't frighten her so. It could cause her to suffer apoplexy or something much worse. Fear takes a terrible toll on our bodies."

Bert frowned and cast a glance at Judith, who was still standing. "Please rest, my dear. Perhaps a sherry would help?"

"I don't imbibe in alcohol, Bert. I just don't like being frightened, and guns have always upset me. They're very dangerous and can go off without warning. I would feel so much better if you would at least uncock your revolver."

He really could hear the fear in her voice. "Very well." He raised the pistol to point upward and eased back the hammer while gently pulling the trigger. But his thumb slipped, and the gun went off, sending a bullet into the ceiling overhead.

Judith screamed, and Bert dropped the gun. Complete confusion washed over him. What should he do? He could take Judith in hand or reclaim the gun, but he could hardly do both. Already she was running toward the far door. Bert tried to move, but he couldn't. He didn't know what to do. Nothing made sense.

"Stop!" Bert yelled as he reclaimed the revolver.

Judith froze in midstep and turned. "I feared that gun might go off again. You could have hurt someone," she chided. "There's no call for guns. Please put it away."

She hoped he would be sane enough to register what she was saying. He was clearly confused about the reality of the situation. Judith kept calm, hoping she could keep him distracted enough to refrain from any more gunplay.

"I didn't mean to frighten you, Judith." He looked for a moment at the gun and then to where Roman still stood by the liquor cabinet. "Bring me that drink!"

Roman nodded and moved with slow, deliberate strides toward Bert. Judith knew that the gun was less of a threat now. Bert hadn't thought to recock it. Still, it was loaded and could end the life of anyone Bert chose to shoot.

"Please, Bert, just put the gun on the desk or even back in your pocket," Judith encouraged. At least those places would make it harder for him to use it.

"No, I don't trust Dr. Turner."

"Then send him away." Judith doubted Roman would leave her, but it was worth a try.

"I can't. We need witnesses . . . for the wedding. Where is Winchell? It shouldn't be taking so long. He might have run off . . . gone for the police."

"Nonsense. We would have seen him." Judith motioned toward the windows. She had pulled the draperies back that morning, and it was easy to see most of the front lawn.

Bert walked a few paces toward the windows. "Yes. Yes, we could have seen if anyone had tried to leave."

"As I said, Winchell is just busy. My maid is probably trying to find the perfect outfit. You do want me to look my best, don't you, Bert?" She smiled to put him at ease. It seemed to help.

"You always look your best, but I hate that you're wearing black for that abominable man. I should have killed him long ago."

Judith felt her stomach clench. Had Bert killed her grandfather? "What do you mean, Bert?"

"He was a terrible man, as you well know. I mean, his business practices were bad enough. He was wretched, and he didn't care who he hurt. I remember your father, Dr. Turner. I hadn't been here working that long when Ashton tricked him. He told me that property was the best in the city, and he would have it for himself. Of course, your father didn't wish to sell. He wanted to build houses . . . apartments . . . some such thing. He wanted to make it very affordable, but nice. I remember him telling Mr. Ashton about his plans. That greedy old man pretended to be excited about it.

"He had me write up a contract that would trap your father in a hopeless game. There was no chance of him ever getting to build those apartments or houses."

Bert rubbed his temple with his left hand, while the gun remained in his right. "Mr. Ashton cheated him. He had me set the terms differently than what was originally planned.

Your father signed the papers without going over them. He trusted Mr. Ashton, as far too many people did."

He grimaced as if in great pain. "There was no hope of your father making the payment due. None whatsoever. He tried. He went to his friends, but there was little that could be done. Ashton celebrated that evening with champagne. Did you know that, Dr. Turner?"

Judith looked at Roman, expecting to find him angry. Instead, he seemed perfectly at peace. She heard something. Footsteps. In the hallway just outside the door. Roman seemed to hear them too and hurried to keep Bert talking.

"It's good of you to share the details, Bert. I didn't know exactly how he cheated my father. But I can understand why you wanted to kill Mr. Ashton. I wanted to do it myself when I learned what he'd done." He brought Bert the drink and extended it. "Here you go."

Bert stopped rubbing his temple and took the whiskey. He downed it quickly. "I certainly thought about it for a long time, but then he got sick, and I figured I wouldn't have to do the job. But . . . well . . ." He smiled at Judith. "I was tired of waiting so that we could marry. You told me you couldn't even consider me while he was still alive."

"And that's why you killed him?" Judith asked. She heard murmurs of someone speaking low. She raised her voice slightly. "You killed my grandfather so that we could be together?"

"Yes. I had to do it. And the fight was gone out of him anyway. He was asleep, and I took a pillow and smothered him. He only tried once to push me away, and then he gave up."

Judith swallowed the lump in her throat. She looked at Roman, who, after having given Bert the drink, had positioned himself between Black and Judith.

"Would you like another drink?" Roman asked Bert.

"No. I want to be sober for our wedding." He walked closer

to the window, stopping long enough to put the glass on Judith's desk. "This will all be mine. The most beautiful house in all of Minneapolis."

"Would you like to live here once we're wed?"

Bert turned with an expression that suggested she was the one who'd gone mad. "Never. I would never live here. It's full of bad memories. No, we'll go to your home in Philadelphia or perhaps live in New York. I want to leave this wilderness for a proper city, where we can go out in society and really enjoy life."

"All right. We can certainly do that. Should we sell this house?" Judith could clearly hear activity in the rooms beyond the office. She had to hold Bert's attention. "I suppose with all the new people coming to the area it would be easy enough to find a buyer for this property."

"It's worth a small fortune," Bert said, glancing back outside again.

Roman motioned Judith to back up toward the rear exit. She nodded and took a step. Roman did likewise. When Bert remained fixed on the view outside, Roman motioned her to leave.

Go, he mouthed.

She didn't want to leave Roman there to be shot at but knew it was probably to his benefit if he didn't have to worry about her. She took another step and then another. She had nearly reached the door to the billiards room when several men rushed into the office through the living room entry.

Roman grabbed her and pulled her out the door and past another group of officers who had been waiting. She heard Bert cry out, but there was no gunshot. She fell into Roman's arms and couldn't stop the tears that fell. The shock of it all was more than she could endure, and her knees buckled.

"I've got you," Roman whispered against her ear. He carried her away into the private sitting room where the portrait of Caroline Ashton looked down upon them. Placing Judith on the sofa, he joined her there and pulled her against him.

Judith wept silently for several minutes. She couldn't believe all that had happened. While he was annoying, never had Judith imagined Bert Black had gone mad. He seemed so reasonable prior to this. There was nothing that indicated to her that he'd lost his senses.

Roman handed her a handkerchief, and Judith straightened to wipe her eyes. She drew a deep breath and finally locked her gaze with his.

"I thought he would kill you," Roman whispered.

"I thought he might kill *you*." She reached up to touch his cheek.

"Did you have any idea of him having killed your grandfather?"

"No." She dropped her hand and eased back against the sofa. Roman kept his arm securely around her. "I knew Grandfather was much weaker and presumed his heart had stopped on its own. I pray he didn't know what happened. It's just too terrible to consider."

A uniformed officer stepped into the sitting room. "Mrs. Stanford?"

Judith looked up and nodded. "I am Mrs. Stanford."

The officer came to where she sat. "And you are Dr. Turner?"

Roman stood and extended his hand. "I am."

"I spoke with your aunt, Doctor. She told us what had happened, but I'm still going to need to take information down from both of you while it's fresh in your minds."

"Did you hear him admit to killing James Ashton?" Roman questioned.

"I did, along with several of my men."

"He's clearly lost all reason," Judith said, looking up at them. She didn't trust her strength and remained seated.

The officer nodded. "We've taken him into custody. My

guess is that he'll end up at the Hospital for the Insane in St. Peter."

"Where is that?" Judith had never heard of the town, much less that there was an insane asylum available in Minnesota.

"It's about seventy miles from here," Roman offered. "The hospital there is fairly new. Just built in 1866. I serve on the board. In fact, when I first met you, I was in Philadelphia to visit area asylums."

Judith knew that if Roman was involved, it would be a good place and not one of those horrible prisons that did little but torment those who were already lost in their madness.

"I suppose that is where he belongs."

"It's the best place for him, Judith. It's on over two hundred acres with all sorts of things the patients might do to ease their long days, including tending sheep." Roman looked back at the officer. "I'm glad you were able to take him without further danger. He fired his gun into the ceiling."

"By accident," Judith felt compelled to say. Little by little her strength was returning. They were safe now, and hopefully there would be no further trouble.

Just then Mary appeared with the tea cart. "I heard them say that they would need to question you. I thought tea or coffee might steady your nerves."

"Coffee is exactly what I need." Judith waited while Mary poured her a cup and added cream and sugar.

"Thank you." Judith sampled the brew and nodded. It was perfect. She looked up with renewed confidence. "Now, what would you like to know, officer?"

Roman was relieved when the police finally left the Ashton mansion. He could tell that Judith was spent from the ordeal and suggested she take a lunch tray in her room and then a nap.

"I suppose a rest would be good since the afternoon has grown so warm."

Mary gave a light knock on the sitting room door. "Mrs. Markle is wondering about your lunch, as well as what you might have planned for dinner this evening. Would you still like her to make the crab cakes?"

"Well, that depends on Dr. Turner." Judith turned to him and smiled. "I just wondered if that impromptu proposal of marriage was sincere."

"What's that?" He looked at her for a long moment.

Judith laughed. "I seem to recall you telling Mr. Black that I was going to marry you. I just wondered if that was your offhanded way of asking for my hand?"

Roman laughed, and even Mary couldn't help but chuckle. Judith raised her brow as if to emphasize her question.

Without hesitation, Roman dropped to one knee. "I have no ring and no fortune, but my heart is clearly yours for the taking. Would you do me the honor of agreeing to marry me?"

The look on her face was one of absolute adoration and joy. "I will. Thank you very much for asking."

Roman got to his feet and swept Judith into his arms for a kiss. As he bent her back, Judith clutched at his arm for fear of falling.

"Don't worry," he said, giving her a wink. "I have you. Now and always."

She closed her eyes and wrapped her arms around Roman's neck as they kissed. He had never known such happiness, and to imagine . . . he was sharing that joy with an Ashton.

Mary cleared her throat. "There's still the matter of dinner."

Roman straightened, and Judith did likewise. She looked at him for a moment and then turned to Mary.

"Let's have all the Turners to dinner and share the news of our engagement, as well as the details of the deed transfers.

We'll make it all a true celebration, and you and Winchell will join us, Mary."

Roman considered the idea for only a moment. "I don't know of anything my family will be otherwise occupied with. I think that sounds perfect."

"Tell Mrs. Markle to whip up a feast and include the crab cakes. We shall be celebrating in grand fashion. I'll tell Winchell."

"And I'll head home and inform Mother and Claudette."

"Make sure she brings Daniel as well. It won't be complete without him." Judith rubbed her hands together. "Oh, I'm so excited. This shall be such a great occasion."

Seeing her so happy and safe blessed him, and Roman couldn't help but hug her close once again. "The first of many we shall have."

Judith found Winchell in her grandfather's room. He had been packing away the clothes at her instruction. They had discussed the matter and figured to donate the clothes to the poor. Her grandfather had worn quality garments but not overly fancy ones. He hadn't worried about keeping up with the times but rather preferred his wardrobe simple and modest. The pieces would be perfect to pass along to those who had nothing.

"I'm so glad that you're all right, Winchell. I feared we might all be killed before the day was out."

"As did I, ma'am." He set aside a stack of shirts, then gave her his full attention. "Is there something I can do for you?"

"Yes. We're having a dinner party tonight with Roman's family. I want you and Mary to join us. It's been a difficult day, and we deserve to celebrate the outcome."

"The outcome, ma'am?"

"Our safety, and my engagement to Dr. Turner."

"Congratulations, ma'am. That is good news and worthy of

celebrating. However, I hardly think it fitting that I be a part of that gala."

She went to where he stood and put her hand on his arm. "I want you there, Winchell. I was so glad that you didn't return to the room after leaving. I know that must have been hard."

"It was. I warned the rest of the staff and bid them hide in their rooms. Then I came and retrieved your grandfather's revolver but feared I might well just make things worse. I knew Mrs. Deeters would bring the law and decided it would be best to wait."

"It was the wise thing to do." She squeezed his arm. "There's something you need to know. Bert . . . Mr. Black admitted to killing Grandfather."

Winchell's eyes widened, and the look on his face was one of pure shock. "Did he smother him?"

"Yes. How did you know?"

"I found Mr. Ashton's pillow strangely positioned and wondered at it."

"Apparently, Bert felt that if he hurried Grandfather's death along, I would then agree to court him. I'm so sorry, Winchell."

"I should have been there with him." Winchell's eyes dampened. "He might have been safe had I remained."

"Perhaps, but only God chooses the hour of our death. Had Grandfather been meant to live longer, God would have made a way. We must accept that it was simply time. We have no way of knowing why one goes at a young age and another lives to be quite old. We don't know why one passes in violence and another in peace. But we can rest assured that God sees all and will be in control of our destiny."

A tear slipped down Winchell's cheek, and Judith reached up to wipe it away. "No more tears, dear man. We are going to celebrate. From this moment on, this will be a house of love and joy. And you will be a part of it for as long as you desire."

“I’m glad that these legal matters are finally settled,” Judith said as Roman helped her into the carriage. It had been nearly seven weeks since Norbert Black was taken to jail for the attack he’d made on Judith and the others, as well as the death of James Ashton.

“I believe the judge was wise to keep him at the insane asylum. I don’t think Mr. Black is a killer at heart. I think he simply lost the ability to reason and understand reality.” Roman settled into the seat opposite her.

“I would think that spending the rest of his life in a hospital for the insane is certainly better than hanging. Still, I can’t help feeling sorry for him. He looked so sad and confused in court. He once had a brilliant mind.”

“He’ll get the help he needs at the hospital. There are new therapies coming to light, as well as medications for people like him. Studies of the mind and personalities are up and coming. There are quite a few doctors who are turning to this area of study so that rather than simply leave someone in this state of mind, they may find a way to transform them. It might one day be possible to help the insane regain their sanity."

"I felt particularly sorry that his family refuses to have anything more to do with him. I would have thought his father would come to be with him, at least during the sentencing. It seems from the letter the elder Mr. Black sent me that he wants nothing more to do with his son. He asked only that I conclude my grandfather's arrangement with his firm and pay any remaining monies due. He was all business."

"It is sad. It's a special bond between father and son. I would give anything to have my father back in my life. And I look forward to one day having a son of my own."

"I hope that will be so. I want very much to have a large family. Of course, there is adoption, and I believe we should also consider that as well. After all, there are a great many babies without mothers and fathers to love them."

"I agree, and as I've told you before, I am perfectly happy with whatever size family you desire. I have enough love for a dozen or more."

Judith smiled and nodded. "I know you do. Oh, before I forget, I had a note from Reverend Knickerbacker. He said November fourth is perfectly fine with him for our wedding. We can just come to the parsonage, and he will perform thc ceremony there with our family and Mrs. Knickerbacker to witness it."

"I like the sound of that. Only, I wish it were going to be October fourth or perhaps the day after tomorrow." He grinned. "Or today. Waiting another two months or so was hardly my idea."

Judith laughed. "I apologize. I just wanted this affair with Mr. Black to be well behind us, and I had thought your sister and Daniel were marrying this month. Now that they've put off their wedding until after the new year begins, I suppose we could move our date up. However, I am making that trip to Philadelphia with Mrs. Van Cleve next month. I'd just as soon settle my affairs back east before starting up all my new ventures here."

"So now marriage to me is nothing more than a new venture?"

She could see the teasing in his eyes. "Yes, but it's the very best of all my new ventures."

He roared in laughter as the driver pulled onto the toll bridge. Traffic was rather heavy today as business carried on as usual. It seemed Minneapolis had grown even in the short time since she arrived.

"So what new business dealings are you up to?"

"You know I have made great progress with some of Grandfather's dealings. I'm trying out a man from church to help me manage shipping here in Minneapolis. The Knickerbackers recommended him. He'll coordinate the rail and river shipping. I've also purchased a steamboat right here in Minneapolis and ordered two more. I'm arranging for them to carry some of the Ashton lumber mill shipping, as well as freight for other businesses. One of the boats will be devoted to passenger travel."

"Sounds like you've been busy. I'm surprised you've still had time for your charity work, but Mother assures me you've been quite busy there as well."

"The needs are so great here. In some ways, even more than in Philadelphia. I suppose because Philadelphia is so much older and better established, its charities are firmly organized and used to receiving proper attention. Although I do remember lean years when the donations were quite limited. Right after the war, no one seemed to care about helping the less fortunate. They were just happy to be done with the fighting. It took quite a bit of encouragement to get people to attend the fundraisers and see the need for themselves."

"You'll find some good people here in Minnesota," Roman

said, glancing out at the river. "They have that pioneer spirit mingled with the Scandinavian and German work ethic. We're also seeing more Italians and Irish. We've become like New York City with all sorts of people. Of course, once they endure a Minnesota winter, they may well decide to move again."

"Does it get so very cold here?" Judith had heard several people talk about the upcoming winter and was beginning to think she'd better order some heavier clothes.

"When people write home to their families in other countries, they always encourage them to bring warm clothes. The temperatures can go well below zero in the winter. That's why it's so imperative to have places for those without homes to live, rather than see them try to make it outside or in tents."

"I can well imagine it would be. I'm thinking I should probably update my wardrobe, not with Worth gowns and frippery but with heavy woolen stockings and fur-lined coats."

"You wouldn't be sorry if you did. I know Mother mentioned something the other day about it as well. You might talk to her about where she and Claudette intend to shop." He looked at her with such an expression of love. "Thanks to you, they'll have what they need. I can't tell you how grateful I am for what you've done for my family."

"I'm so glad they agreed to move in with me once the construction is finished, which should be in another couple of weeks. Well before winter. After Claudette and Daniel marry, your mother would have been all alone, and that I cannot allow. She is much too dear."

"Well, the house we are building for Claudette and Daniel's wedding present is quite large. Claudette said she wanted it that way in case Mother wants to live with them."

Judith nodded. "I realize that, but they will be newly wed and need their privacy for a time."

"And what about us?" Roman asked, chuckling.

"The house is enormous, as you well know. And with the complete change to the third floor and remodeling of the second, we need never see another soul if we so desire."

"Well, for a time after we marry, you're the only soul I want to see." The look on his face was full of mischief, and Judith couldn't help but look away as her cheeks grew warm.

"You'll see me so much you'll be desperate to flee," Judith murmured.

"That will never happen. I want to be at your side every day for the rest of my life."

Judith sighed with sheer joy. "It's a good thing you feel that way, because I feel exactly the same."

At dinner that evening, Roman thought back on the years behind him. There had been such a hopelessness after the death of his father. In his bitterness and sorrow, he had allowed Satan a foothold, to be sure, and he didn't intend to ever make that mistake again.

"Have you settled on a wedding date?" Mother asked.

"We have," Judith said as she picked up her fork. "November fourth. Reverend Knickerbacker and his wife have invited us to come to the parsonage for the short service."

"You really should have a beautiful church wedding and invite the entire town," Claudette said, glancing with a smile at Daniel. "Like us."

"Well, we're not inviting quite the entire town," Daniel countered, "but with all my relatives, it feels that way."

"As much as Judith is doing to see people compensated for her grandfather's wickedness, I'm sure there will be hundreds of folks who would like to join in your celebration."

Roman was sure his mother was right on that account. Judith had been hard at work undoing the problems caused by her grandfather. Her generosity had dumbfounded the hardworking citizens of Minneapolis and St. Anthony. The newspaper had even written two articles on her deeds.

For himself, Roman could say that the actions of his betrothed had brought about healing. He was made keenly aware that even from an evil man, God could bring about good. And, just like Judith, Roman hoped that her grandfather had turned to God before drawing his final breath.

"You aren't even listening, Roman," his mother chided.

He looked up, trying to feign innocence. "Who me?" Everyone laughed, and it did Roman's heart good like a medicine.

"We were asking you about the reverend's charity hospital. Since you're involved with the plans, we wondered if everything had been agreed upon?" his mother questioned.

"Yes. The property is chosen, and the hospital plans were already drawn up." Roman had seen the final sketches just yesterday. "It's going to be built a few blocks from the church. Not far at all. The reverend thought it important to keep it close to the mills and railroad due to injuries that are commonplace for both.

"There will be a ground level, as well as second and third floors, although the third floor may be mostly storage. For the time being, we're planning to only have between six and eight beds."

"And the donations have been quite generous, I'm told," Judith added. "The Masons, workers in the machine shop at the Milwaukee Railroad, St. Mark's Parish, the Ladies' Aid, and the Brotherhood of Gethsemane Church have all donated various items and furnishings."

"It's true, and our own dear Judith recommended several marvelous ideas to secure continued support for the hospital after it's open. Lectures will be held, as well as concerts and a variety of other entertainments. On each occasion, there will be a small entry fee for the support of the hospital, and we're hopeful to find people who will donate their time and skills for the events."

"I already have a list of people and groups who have agreed to perform for free. We'll also host tables at the events where we can tell interested donors what our needs are and what they can do to help," Judith jumped in. "It's surprising what people will do to support a charity when they know more about it. That's the most important thing I've learned over the years."

"It's all too wonderful to imagine," Mother said, slicing into her pork roast. "And to think Roman will head up this new hospital."

"I'll be the head physician, but there will still be a board to answer to. I also plan to continue making my rounds to the various destitute neighborhoods. Not everyone with needs will think to come to the hospital."

"And we've plans for an orphanage as well. The Episcopal Sisters are already excited to help with that plan, as well as act as nursing staff at the hospital. We've even discussed the idea that in time we might expand and start a nursing school."

"And is this going to be part of your grandfather's block?" Mary asked.

Roman nodded. "It is. Judith and I have talked at length about where the location will be. It seems the area James Ashton chose for his memorial block is on land he confiscated under false pretenses. Judith is arranging for it to be returned to the original owner. They've already agreed to sell it back to her so that the plans laid out can continue."

"That is so very admirable, Judith. I'm proud to have you for a daughter-in-law," his mother said.

"Well, here's the remarkable thing about doing what is right in the eyes of God." Roman picked up a slice of bread. "Even as she has given away property and money, the Good Lord has blessed her investments, and she has managed to keep very nearly the same amount in the bank. It's like the loaves and fishes that were shared in the Bible." He looked at Judith and smiled. He couldn't begin to tell her how proud he was of her efforts to locate the people her grandfather had wronged.

"It's true." Judith returned his smile before looking at Roman's mother. "God has clearly been the orchestrator of all of this. It has been proven many times over to be exactly His will for me. I feel this was the reason He brought me to Minneapolis." Her gaze settled on Roman once more. "Along with finding my own dear love."

"We're so glad you followed God's prompting. I stand amazed at the way God has answered this old woman's prayer."

"Mother, you are not old," Claudette protested.

Martha Turner chuckled before returning her attention to her meal. "I'll admit, since Judith came into our lives, I've felt younger and healthier. She's like a balm of healing."

Roman lifted his water glass as if to toast. "I couldn't have said it better."

The next morning, Judith was ready when Roman knocked on the door. She hadn't told him the night before why she wanted him to come first thing, and he was more than a little curious.

"I can't help but wonder what you've got going on this early. The sun is barely up."

"That's the best part." She tied the ribbons to her bonnet. "Now come on. Mr. Manfre is waiting to drive us in the carriage."

"To where?"

She laughed and pulled his arm. "You'll see." She paused. "Oh, I nearly forgot my shawl." She retrieved it from the coat-tree and pulled it around her shoulders. "Now, I'm ready."

The driver was ready and waiting, just as Judith had said. They climbed into the carriage, and before Judith had even managed to settle herself, Mr. Manfre snapped the lines and put them in motion.

"Seems quite mysterious, this surprise of yours."

"I felt it was time you knew a little bit more about me and my life in Philadelphia."

"And you're planning to take me there?"

"Not exactly. But I thought it might be fun to show you a part of what I grew up with. This was pretty much my daily life for quite some time."

"I see." He folded his arms and seemed to consider what she had in mind.

Judith couldn't keep it to herself any longer. "I'm taking you on the river. Remember I said I purchased a steamboat? It's set up for passenger service, and I've been having it spruced up a bit. I talked to the captain, and he's going to take us for a trip down the river and back again."

Roman perked up at this. "That sounds more than a little bit interesting. I've never gone on a riverboat."

"Well, since you're marrying a riverboat captain's daughter, I think it's about time."

Twenty minutes later, they stood at the stern of the *Heritage*, a beautiful paddle-wheeler that reminded Judith of one of the ships her father had bought nearly a dozen years ago. He had called her one of the most beautiful ships ever built and named her for Judith's mother.

"What are you thinking about?" Roman asked, pulling her close as the boat made its way down the river.

"This boat reminds me of one my father purchased in 1858. He had her built special and named her for my mother. *The Waltzing Winifred*."

"Waltzing?"

Judith turned in his arms to face the water. She leaned back against him and spoke over her shoulder. "My parents first met at a dance. My father asked my mother to waltz with him, but she didn't know how. You see, the waltz was still rather scandalous, and my mother was just sixteen."

"So he taught her to waltz?"

Judith nodded and leaned her head back against Roman's shoulder. "He did. He said she took to it like a fish to water. He teasingly called her Waltzing Winifred in private moments, and this vessel is a very close duplicate of that boat."

For a few minutes, neither one spoke. Instead, Judith enjoyed the rhythmic whoosh of the water against the wheel. It was like a melodious reminder of her childhood. She was happier than she could have imagined.

"Your joy surprises me," Roman said, his breath warm on her ear.

"Why?" She turned to face him once again.

"Well, given you lost your parents to a boiler explosion, I suppose I find it strange that you should still love these boats as much as you do."

"My father raised me to know that danger lurks everywhere on a paddle-wheeler. You must always be aware of your place on it and keep in mind that without any notice at all, you may be fighting for your life. It gave me a healthy respect for the boat and the river, but not fear, and even in losing my parents, I couldn't hate it. My father and mother loved it so.

"For a time, my mother blamed the river for the death of my little brother. She stayed away, thinking her loss might hurt less, but soon enough, she realized it was in her blood, and she couldn't give it up. She came to understand, too, that God was in control of life and death, and that while it was heartbreaking to say good-bye to little Frank, she could hardly blame the river or the boat."

"That might have compelled her to blame God."

"I suppose for a time you could say she did. But she told me that she came to feel at peace with Frank's death and God's timing through her Scripture reading. She knew that faith required her to trust, even when it didn't make sense. I can only imagine the celebration when Mama and Papa joined their boys in glory. I do hope that Grandfather is there with them now." She glanced heavenward and smiled. "I somehow have peace that he is there."

Roman put his hand on her cheek. "I can't help but feel you are right. And perhaps he and my father have already embraced, and the past is set aside in the presence of our Savior."

Tears came to her eyes. "Oh, wouldn't that be glorious?" It was truly all she hoped for.

"You make the perfect bride, my dear," Sarah Knickerbacker declared, stepping back. She and Mary Deeters had helped Judith with all the finishing touches.

Mary led Judith to the cheval mirror. "Just look for yourself."

Judith studied her reflection for a moment. The gown of pale blue taffeta had two fringed tiers over the skirt that angled down to a point. The fringe on the skirt and bodice was done in a darker blue. The top of the gown appeared as a snug jacket with fitted sleeves. The bottom and the vee'd trim from the shoulders to the basque waist were fringed. It was exactly the fashion Judith had wanted. Simple yet elegant. A gown she could wear for other special occasions.

She turned to glimpse the bustle and then centered her gaze on the mass of brown curls pinned up in a very attractive fashion.

"Mary, you did a lovely job with my hair. Thank you both for all you've done to help me today."

"It was our pleasure," Mary said, looking to Sarah. She nodded most enthusiastically.

"I'm so happy." Judith pressed her hands to her heart. "This is just as I had hoped for."

"You make a beautiful bride, and Roman will be completely captivated," Sarah declared.

"He's already quite daffy when it comes to her." Mary chuckled. "I've never seen a man so in love."

Judith felt her cheeks flush. Roman had been most attentive, and she knew the love he felt for her matched her own for him.

"It's time we join the others and get this wedding started," Sarah said, heading for the door. "I'm so excited for you both and quite happy you chose our home in which to start your lives together."

Mary handed Judith a bouquet of flowers. "I'm still so touched that you asked me to stand up with you."

Judith gave Mary a hug. "You've been a dear friend to me since I arrived."

"Well, perhaps not that long. I was quite concerned when you first showed up. I wasn't at all sure why you were here or what you were after. I'm sorry to say, I was very suspicious of your plans."

Laughing, Judith gave one last look in the mirror. "I knew you were. I wanted so much to say or do something to put you at ease. I had no idea of how Grandfather had treated you and the others. I don't blame you at all for being apprehensive."

"Your character and devotion to God quickly proved themselves. It was humbling to watch you in action and realize just how wrong I'd been about you. I hope you'll forgive me my doubt."

"No need for forgiveness. It was wise to be cautious." Judith drew in a deep breath and let it out.

Mary wiped away a tear. "I'm so glad God brought you to Minnesota and to our family in particular. I know you and Roman are going to be so very happy."

"I'm still amazed at how it all happened. Back in Philadelphia, I often thought of the fundraiser where I'd met the elusive Dr. Turner. For years I had considered how I might get in touch with him, but then I chided myself. I figured if he wanted to know me better, he would surely have done something. So I told myself I was too old for such notions of romance and falling in love."

"You're never too old." They embraced once more, and then Mary opened the door of the room. "It's time."

Judith followed her out to the parlor, where the rest of the wedding party waited. Roman smiled as Dr. John Lester, his best man, gave him a nudge.

"Ah, our radiant bride. Come right over here and join hands with your groom," the reverend instructed.

Judith crossed the room as Roman held out his hand. She took hold of him and felt her heart beat faster with happiness. She thought of Alden and her parents and wondered if they, along with her brothers and grandfather, were smiling down from heaven. She liked to think they might know what was happening.

Reverend Knickerbacker led them through their vows. Judith pledged her life and love to Roman and let her tears fall. The very idea of spending the rest of her days with this handsome, kindhearted man was an unexpected answer to prayer. After losing her husband, she had accepted that she might well spend the rest of her life alone, but God had blessed her with Roman.

Judith prayed for God's protection and wisdom, knowing that the journey they were on would no doubt be fraught with many obstacles over the years. By the time they were instructed to kiss, Judith was ready to leave off with ceremonies and begin the dream.

"Congratulations," Roman's mother said as they turned to face the small gathering. She came forward and kissed Roman and then Judith. "I'm so happy for you both. I could not have asked for a more perfect daughter-in-law had I created her myself."

"I'm so happy," Claudette said, all but pushing her mother aside to embrace Judith. "I always wanted a sister, and now I have one."

Roman laughed and steadied his mother. "Claudette seems not to realize her enthusiasm can be dangerous."

"I'm glad she's happy," his mother replied.

"We're all quite delighted," Mary said, giving her nephew a hug. "I for one feared this day might not ever come. It seemed every hopeful prospect of a bride for you went completely unnoticed."

"I couldn't get Judith out of my mind," he admitted.

"Yes, but neither could you seem to do anything about furthering a relationship," Judith said, sounding as if she were annoyed.

Roman laughed and pointed his finger at her. "You could have come to Minneapolis. I was the only Dr. Turner in residence. A large part of the population here knew me."

She put her hands on her hips. "You could have come to Philadelphia, where your friends already knew how to put you in touch with me." She waggled her finger at him. "I was quite well-known there, and you wouldn't have had any trouble finding me."

Everyone laughed as Roman pulled her into his embrace. "Well, I've found you now, and I don't intend to ever let you go."

"If you will all join us in the dining room," Sarah announced, "we have some refreshments waiting." She pushed back the pocket doors to reveal a table overflowing with a variety of goodies. "Our ladies of the church made this for us."

Reverend Knickerbacker and Dr. Lester were first to make their way from the room. Sarah followed, chiding them to leave some food for the others. Daniel took hold of Claudette, and they made their way to join the others, with Mary and

Martha bringing up the rear. It left Judith and Roman alone for just a moment.

With her still in his embrace, Roman kissed her again. This kiss was leisurely, as if they had all the time in the world. Judith sighed and cherished the feel of his arms around her.

"I suppose we must join the others," he whispered against her ear.

"I suppose. If we were to just sneak away, it would raise quite the scandal."

Roman laughed and released her. "And we mustn't have that." He grinned in that impish way that Judith had come to love. He took her hand. "Come, Mrs. Turner, your family awaits."

There were a great many stories told about Roman as a boy, and Judith acquiesced and told tales about her own childhood. How she wished her parents might have lived to be there. Her brothers too.

"You look rather sad," Roman said as the others chattered away about the coming holidays.

"I was just thinking about my parents and brothers. I wish they could have been here; however, I'm blessed with my new family and the love they've shown me. I am quite content, not at all sad."

"I intend to make you happy every day of your life. Although, I know we'll have our moments." He grinned.

Judith shrugged. "We are both opinionated and rather fixed on doing things our own way."

"I am determined to seek God's will instead of my own. That alone should help immensely." Roman laughed, drawing everyone's attention.

"Did you say something we should all know about?" his mother asked.

Judith pressed her cheek to Roman's shoulder. "We were just planning for the future."

When they were finally able to return to the house, Judith saw the palatial estate with new eyes. She imagined it filled with children and great happiness. This house that had so long been a place of greed and devious dealings would now be one of hope and joy.

She smiled as the others disappeared to various rooms. They were making it easy for the new bridal couple to have their privacy. Glancing at her husband, Judith started for the stairs. She didn't say a word but knew he would follow her.

When they reached the top, he took hold of her hand. Judith led him down the long hallway without a word. She opened the door to her suite—their suite—and drew him inside.

"I hope you like what I've done with the rooms. Grandfather had them quite dark and brooding, but I took out all his things and gave most of it to the poor and crated up the rest, including the head of a most impressive stag."

"I'm sure it's perfect." Roman glanced around.

The walls had been painted in hues of light blue and yellowed cream and trimmed in wallpaper with a gold scrolling pattern and fleur-de-lis accents. The sitting area had a couch and two overstuffed chairs that faced the fireplace. Someone had thoughtfully lit the fire, and the large blaze set off the room in the perfect glow of firelight and muted sun from the windows.

Against the wall were sparsely furnished bookshelves and a window seat that allowed for comfortable reading and daydreaming. A few small tables and a mahogany Hepplewhite desk and chair rounded out the sitting room arrangements.

"I like that it's quite secluded here at the end of the wing," Roman said, closing the door and locking it. He leaned back against it as if shutting out the world and fixed her with a look of love that nearly caused Judith to melt into a puddle. Goodness, but this man had a way about him.

“I suppose it’s time to get back to our affairs,” Judith said as she finished dressing her hair. For the last week, she and Roman had enjoyed a honeymoon of sorts right there at the house. The weather had turned cold, and the first snows had left the area blanketed in white, so much of the time they stayed together in their suite, talking of the past and dreaming together for the future.

“I’m sure Dr. Lester is probably more than ready for me to reclaim my duties,” Roman said, watching her as she pinned her hair. “Although I find I could easily forsake it all to remain here with you.”

She laughed and got to her feet. “I won’t tolerate lies from my husband. I know you’ve been longing to return to your patients.”

He came and took hold of her shoulders. “It’s no lie that I would much rather linger here with you, my beautiful wife. You’ve quite bewitched me, and I find myself completely devoted to your company.”

“As am I with yours.” She stretched up on tiptoe to kiss him.

He wrapped her in his arms as she had known he would and kissed her quite thoroughly. Then without warning, he released her and went to retrieve his coat. “Come. I’m sure the others are awaiting us for breakfast, and if I stay here any longer, it will be lunch before I even attempt to leave.”

Judith gave an exaggerated sigh. “I suppose you’re right.”

Roman chuckled and slipped on his coat. He then headed for the sitting room, pausing only a moment to glance back. “I hope this day passes quickly.”

EPILOGUE

November 15, 1871

All eyes were on Judith as she took her place beside the mayor of Minneapolis. She smiled out at the gathering of citizens who had come to see her open the first of several new buildings that would grace the Ashton Block.

"Thank you all for coming today." She was glad she had thought to wear her fur-lined cloak instead of the plain wool wrap. The wind was a bit blustery, and the gunmetal gray skies looked ready to open up with snow.

"It is my pleasure to share this new building with the city of Minneapolis. We have long planned and worked to see this block developed as a memorial to my family. Therefore, I give you the first of four buildings that will comprise the Ashton Block."

She paused for applause and looked down at her husband, who stood faithfully awaiting her. He gave her a smile, which bolstered her courage to continue. She had both looked forward to this day and dreaded it, knowing that there were bound to still be those who hated the name Ashton.

"This building will house a new orphanage that will be run by the Episcopal Sisters. The facilities will also accept the help of volunteers who apply through the church. These volunteers are much-desired to assist with the children, who will need a great deal of love and kindness. I want to encourage you to seek more information by speaking to Mrs. Sarah Knickerbacker at the Gethsemane Episcopal Church. And now the mayor has a few words to say."

She stepped back and let the older man take charge. His words were thankfully few, probably because he wasn't dressed in the warmest of clothes. He did encourage the citizens of Minneapolis to remember those less fortunate, as the holidays were soon to be upon them and winter had already begun.

With the speeches concluded and her obligations met, Judith hurried to join Roman. "Let's hurry."

Roman signaled for the carriage and smiled. "We aren't much for being away from home long, are we?"

Judith gazed up at him and shook her head. "At home with my family is the very best place in the world. I long for nothing more."

Judith felt overwhelmed with gratitude for all that God had done in her life. So many times she had despaired that nothing good could be reborn from the tragedies that beset her. She was ever so glad to be proven wrong.

Once they reached home, Roman helped her down from the carriage, and Judith couldn't help but quicken her steps. Inside the house awaited the finest blessing of all.

"Are they awake?" she asked Winchell as he opened the door for them.

He smiled. "They were when I left them just a few minutes ago."

Judith glanced over her shoulder at Roman. "Hurry."

They raced upstairs to the nursery, where Roman's mother was watching over two very attentive babies. She held a rattle to keep their attention, but they seemed more than happy to be with their grandmother.

"I still can't believe you had twins," Roman said, shaking his head.

"I can't believe you never even suspected. I was as big as a house," Judith said, lifting their daughter into her arms. The baby immediately began to root. "I think we got here just in time. She seems quite hungry."

"Yes, I think they're both ready to nurse," Martha replied.

Roman picked up their son. "For two months old, I think they are quite advanced. Just see how he holds his head up."

Judith laughed as her son pressed forward for a moment and then fell back. "To hear Roman tell it, they are able to perform miraculous feats unknown to other infants."

She handed her fussing baby daughter to Martha and shed her jacket. She couldn't help but feel aglow in the wonder of motherhood and all that God had given. Once again, she found herself thanking Him for His goodness.

She settled into the rocker and unfastened the buttons on her blouse. Martha brought her the baby, and Judith gently arranged her to nurse.

"My little Evie. Such a precious gift from God."

At that, her son began to fuss, and Roman laughed. "I think he knows you're speaking about his sister and not offering the same praise in regard to him."

"Sweet Evan. You know your mother holds equal love for you."

"No two babies could ever be loved more," Martha said, heading for the door. "You know where I'll be if you need me."

Once she'd gone, Judith smiled and glanced at her husband as he made faces and babbled at their son. His face beamed with pride. She knew he'd never been happier because he'd told her that every day since they married. She had no idea of what the future might hold, but if their hearts remained faithful in the Lord, it was certain to be most satisfying.

Keep reading for a sneak peek
of book two
in the A MINNESOTA LEGACY series

Available summer of 2026.

PROLOGUE

June 1893
Philadelphia, Pennsylvania

"Nurse Turner, please come to my office when you're done."

Evie had her back to the older woman but nodded. She was focused on the porcelain bedpan in her hands. Why did she have to get sick to her stomach?

She sighed and straightened, feeling a little better. For all her years of nurse's school and advanced training, she still struggled to overcome her weak stomach. Since she was just a little girl, Evie had wanted to work with her father, the great Dr. Roman Turner, and she'd been working to become a nurse since she was seventeen. They spoke of creating a hospital for the poor and friendless, tending to those who couldn't afford the extravagance of good health. The entire community of Minneapolis knew about them and their plans. Unfortunately, no one counted on Evie's inability to deal with blood and injuries.

Even now as she cleaned out the bedpan, Evie wondered what in the world she was going to do. On top of everything, she was now going to have to explain herself to Nurse Conway and receive another lecture on being ill-suited for nursing.

She sighed, went to the dirty laundry cart, and disposed of her surgical robe.

How can I be so good at something and so bad at it all at the same time?

That question had haunted her for years. All this time, she had done whatever she could to hide that she had no stomach for the job. In the beginning, when much of their schooling had been book learning, it wasn't hard. But then came situations like disease and childbirth. Sadly, even the latter tended to cause Evie a bit of queasiness. She found that by focusing her attention on the instruments used by the doctor and then the infant, which was generally turned over to the nursing staff, she could manage to get through without vomiting. But at times when the birth was complicated and the outcome questionable, Evie had to fight against her body to maintain her decorum.

After that came more difficult situations. Traumas and injuries. Men and women who had suffered multiple wounds from accidents or attacks. Evie didn't manage those situations well at all. She remembered the first time she witnessed a man's mangled arm after a machinery accident. She nearly fainted. Thankfully, her supervisor noted her lack of color and moved Evie from the table before she grew worse. Evie had left the room in shame and promptly lost the contents of her stomach. She had nearly quit school at that point, but Nurse Conway encouraged her to stay. Perhaps now she would tell Evie how she regretted that decision.

Making her way to the head nurse's office, Evie smoothed down the apron on her uniform, then reached up to make sure her cap was straight. She knocked lightly on Nurse Conway's office door and awaited instruction.

"Come in."

Evie did and closed the door behind her.

"Take a seat, Evelyn." Nurse Conway usually addressed her

this way when they were alone, but Evie could hear something in her tone that left her uneasy.

She sat in a straight-backed wooden chair opposite the one Nurse Conway occupied. At least she wasn't behind her desk in a more formal manner. Evie forced a smile and took her seat.

"Are you feeling better?" Nurse Conway asked.

"Yes. Thank you, ma'am."

For a moment, the older woman just sat there looking at Evie. Her expression was one of compassion. Evie knew she cared a great deal about her students. She was strict and punishing when rules were ignored but equally compassionate and lenient when such actions were deserved.

"Evelyn, I know you're about to journey home. Have you figured out what you're going to do?"

Evie shook her head and gazed toward the ceiling. "No. I've prayed and asked for direction, but nothing ever seems to come to me. The entire city is counting on me taking up a nursing role with my father. Everyone there is so supportive. I've received cards and letters of encouragement, all telling me what a marvelous nurse I will be."

"You are a marvelous nurse. You simply have a weak stomach." Nurse Conway gave a hint of a smile. "Thank God in Heaven for peppermint oil."

Evie used peppermint oil under her nostrils and sucked on peppermint candies to soothe her stomach during difficult situations, especially surgeries. As a gifted surgical nurse, she was often requested by doctors who knew her skills. Without the peppermint, Evie didn't know how she could have made it through.

"I would have been lost without your suggestions," she admitted.

"But now the time has come that you'll return home, and then what? You can hardly fool your father. You have no joy in what you do, even if you are very good at doing it. Evie, you're going to have to stop lying to yourself and to them."

"I know. I just don't know how to face this. I hate disappointing anyone, but especially my father. He's my hero, and I know he's looking forward to me serving by his side. We don't even have that many years left to do so. He's already sixty years old and bound to retire before long, if my mother has her way. Maybe I can just force myself to do the job."

"We both know that isn't the answer, Evelyn."

Evie nodded and tried not to imagine the look of disappointment that her father would try to hide. He wouldn't want her to feel bad for this. He would be the first one to tell her that nursing was apparently not the right direction for her.

"They're all so proud of me." Evie returned her gaze to Nurse Conway. "The newspaper wrote articles telling about my progress, and they'd get quotes from my father about his ongoing plans for a charity hospital focused on women and children, since they haven't been comfortable at the current one. My father is even now readying the place to receive patients."

"There are other nurses, Evelyn."

"I know. And I know in time Father will be just fine working with someone else. But this has been his dream, and I hate putting an end to it."

"If he's half the man you believe him to be, he will manage to overcome his disappointment. He cares a great deal about the destitute and will no doubt put his focus there."

"I'm just so afraid it will change everything between us." That was the very heart of the matter. Evie feared not her father's anger, but his disappointment. She feared he'd stop talking to her about his desires and plans, that once he knew how nursing turned her stomach, he'd see her as less than desired. Seeing that look of disappointment in his eyes was more than she could bear. She'd witnessed it once or twice when he was dealing with her twin brother, Evan. He was far more of a wild card, sometimes really testing the limits set for him. He'd settled down after a time and now was a practicing lawyer, but there had been moments of concern and frustration, to say the least.

She didn't want to cause that pain for her father and mother.

"Perhaps you can write them a letter. There's still time for it to arrive before you do."

"No. I'm going to give this my best try. I made a promise, not just to my father, but to the entire town. I'm going to do what I can to fulfill that promise."

"Then I leave you with this." Nurse Conway got up and retrieved a small wooden box. She handed it to Evie. "It will help for a time."

Evie noted the stamp on top of the box. "Peppermint oil." She smiled. "I pray it will."

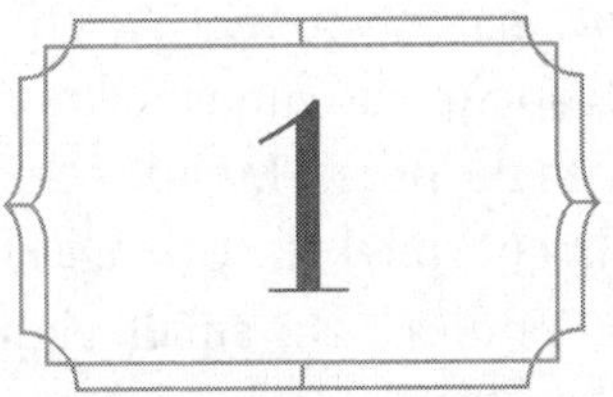

July 7, 1893
Minneapolis, Minnesota

How did a person keep lying to the people she loved and not be swallowed up by overwhelming guilt?

Evie Turner gazed at her reflection in the mirror, wondering where her plans went wrong as the maid finished dressing her dark brown hair.

At twenty-one, Evelyn had accomplished a great deal. She and her twin brother, Evan, had graduated high school and immediately sought additional education. Evan went to college and Evie to nursing school.

She had wonderful parents and nine amazing siblings too. After her twin brother, there were another eight children ranging down to nine years of age. Some were born of her parents and some adopted. Mother and Father had always done what they could for orphans. Mother worked tirelessly to find families who might consider adoption, and when those couldn't be found, she supported the orphanage and ensured the children felt cared for and loved. When their pastor, the Reverend David Knickerbacker, put together plans for the Sheltering Arms Orphanage, Mother had been the first one to write a check, drawing on a vast fortune left to her by her grandfather James Ashton Sr.

Evie admired her parents more than she could say. Father was an exceptional doctor and surgeon, known throughout the city for working with the poor. He had been faithfully involved in Minneapolis's first hospital, the Cottage Hospital and Home for the Sick and Friendless. The small, eight-bed facility had been the first dream of their pastor. Reverend Knickerbacker had done so much to improve the plight of poorer men. The Cottage Hospital was the first facility in Minneapolis focused on serving lowly paid railroad men and mill workers. It also became available to citizens. Ten years ago, it moved to Elliot Park and was renamed St. Barnabus Hospital, where it continued to operate as a private hospital. Now they had the small City Hospital on Eleventh Avenue South. It wasn't very big, but Father made rounds between the two places, as well as visiting the poor and downtrodden in their homes. It should all work together so perfectly, yet it didn't.

Evie had only been home for a week, but already she felt backed into a corner, trapped like a wild animal.

In a few minutes she would sit down with her parents and brother for a meeting regarding the various charities they headed up or supported. Evie would bring up the garden party fundraiser they planned to host in August. At least this part of her life wasn't a lie—raising money for the poor was something she truly loved—but so much else was pure deception.

The plan for Evie to serve with Father in a brand-new charity hospital had always been the dream. As a little girl, Evie had listened to his stories for hours on end, and when she mentioned plans to become a nurse and work at his side, her father had been delighted. She could still see the way his face lit up at the idea.

But as often happened in life, things hadn't worked out quite the way she'd hoped.

"Did you hear me, Miss Evie?"

Evie straightened and looked at the maid. "I'm sorry, Beth. I was daydreaming."

"I said that your mother sent word that they're waiting for you in the private sitting room."

Evie nodded. "You did a wonderful job with my hair. Again." She gave Beth a big smile. "I missed you while I was away. I swear I can't do anything but braid it and pin it in place. You always manage to arrange it in such clever ways."

Beth was already cleaning the hairbrush. "It's no trouble, Miss Evie. I love it. I used to love arranging your mother's hair in all sorts of fashions. Now most days she keeps it simple. I usually have her hair pinned in place before I have to think."

Evie's mother had become far more no-nonsense as she aged. She had just turned fifty-three in June and still ran the house in precise order, as well as her charities and the family business dealings. Judith Turner was a force to be reckoned with and probably always would be.

It was senseless to brood. Evie stood and gave a quick glance around. "It's so warm today. Please leave my windows open for as long as possible. I heard Cook say it was supposed to rain."

Beth put away the brush and pins. "Yes, and the skies have clouded up considerably since this morning. I think we're probably due for a thunderstorm."

Heading for the door, Evie glanced over her shoulder. "Then do what you think sensible."

With that, she headed downstairs to meet with her family. Evie wanted to let them know what she had arranged for the party so far. She also wanted to hear if there were any new changes to the economy. The country was not seeing a good time financially.

"There she is," Mother announced as Evie walked into the sitting room. Her father and brother were seated casually by the open French doors, while Mother was perched on the edge of an antique French gothic throne chair done in highly varnished chestnut. "You look quite lovely today, Evie. That pale yellow compliments your creamy complexion."

Evie smiled and glanced down at her watered silk gown. "I chose it for the short sleeves, to be honest. Summer has been quite warm."

"Yes, someone at the hospital mentioned it might well top one hundred degrees today," Father said, looking at Mother. "That's why I've suggested your mother take it very easy and enjoy the use of the new electric ceiling fan."

Evie knew her mother was given to fainting spells when overheated and nodded enthusiastically. "You need to stay in your room and wear something very light. Don't bother with a corset or extra petticoats. We have plenty of ice too. I'll make sure you have something cold to drink around the clock."

"Are you feeling all right now, Mother?" Evan asked. He looked just as concerned as their father.

"Goodness, you three. I'm fine for the time being. I'm drinking plenty of fluids and taking it easy, so stop fussing," Mother said, shaking her head. "Now let's get down to business. I want to make sure we're on top of everything that needs to be done for the fundraiser."

"I have arranged all the food for the party," Evie offered. "Mrs. Niedermeier and I have come up with a perfect plan. She really is the most talented of cooks. There will be a buffet set up under the trees where it will be cooler. We will have ice for the food that needs to stay cold and warming trays for the hot items. I've ordered the very best—rather lavish, if I do say so, but I want to impress upon the guests that nothing has really changed. Yes, we are experiencing difficult economic times, but they are still quite well-off and need to remember that the poor will suffer even more than usual if they don't continue to donate to the cause."

"How are things going in the country financially, Roman?"

Father shrugged. "Not good, that's for sure. More railroads have declared bankruptcy, and there have been additional bank closures. It's a worrisome time for rich and poor."

"But especially the poor. The rich might be less rich, but they're still better off than most. Look at us. We're still buying the luxuries of life—ice, electricity. We don't have to worry about food on the table or a safe place to sleep tonight." Evie crossed her arms. "The rich might not like losing some of their pet projects, but it's not causing them the trouble and pain that others are suffering."

"Evie's right on that account." Evan went to the refreshment cart and poured himself a lemonade. He held the glass up. "Anyone else want one?"

"I'll take one." Evie thought the cool liquid sounded wonderful.

Evan crossed the room and handed the glass to her before going back to pour himself another. "We had a meeting this morning at the law firm. Numerous banking clients came to hear our senior partners explain the legalities of what might occur in the future. The problem is the people are losing faith."

Evan took a seat and continued, "A great many people and businesses defaulted on their loans last month. This has caused the banks to falter, and citizens are making runs on the banks to pull their savings. It's hit the Midwest states quite hard. Over one hundred banks have suspended operations, and those same banks hold mortgages. The people fear the banks will demand payment in full, and the bank owners are afraid they will be left holding the bag for debts that will never be repaid."

"What did your partners tell them to do?" Mother asked.

"Hold fast. They're of a mind to sell off assets to cover cash runs, but that isn't going to bode well."

"And all of this because the US Treasury allowed gold reserves to drop nearly one hundred million dollars. People feared that the end of the world had come and rushed to change over their notes for gold," Roman declared.

"Among other issues. It's going to get much worse before it gets better," Evan assured them.

Evie frowned. "Then this party must raise enough money to help see the charities through for a good amount of time. If we're to see the economy struggle even more, the rich will tighten their hold on their wealth and the poor will assuredly bear the brunt of it."

"They are always the ones who suffer the most. When the economy struggles, the rich trade lobster and pheasant for fish and chicken," Mother began. "The poor who were already struggling on potatoes and pork fat are left scrounging for whatever scraps can be found."

"We need our wealthy friends to be very generous with their donations," Evie reiterated. "We'll give them a magical night with wonderfully lavish food, beautiful music, and delightful company. We must convince them that their money is more than secure."

"And that like most economic downfalls, it will reverse and recover," Evan added. "There is no reason to believe it won't. This is just one of those things that happens every twenty or so years."

****

Later that evening, Evie sought out her twin. Ever since Evie had returned from nursing school, she could see in Evan's eyes that he knew something wasn't quite right. She wanted to reassure him but wasn't yet ready to admit what was going on. Never had she refused to share her heart with him, but this time it seemed necessary.

Up and down the hall, their siblings moved from room to room getting ready for bed. Laughter and loud boisterous voices were common each evening, an expected cacophony that gave assurance that all was well. Fifteen-year-old Jim went rushing by with the youngest boy, Jared, in his arms.

Jared flapped his arms up and down. "Look, Evie, I'm a bird!" he shouted as they passed by.

"A bird who's going to bed," Jim added.

Evie laughed. She recalled a time Evan had done the same thing while Jim took on the role of bird. She loved the hubbub of their family and the great fun they always had. She paused in front of Evan's bedroom door. There was no one in the world she was closer to, and now, after several years spent mostly apart, they were together again. School had consumed them both, and then Evan had been busy learning the law while she'd been at nursing school. She supposed as they grew older, married, and began their own families they'd be together less and less. It was the natural order of things, yet she would miss him and all of this. She glanced down the hall at her siblings hurrying off to their quarters. Evie smiled and rapped on the door.

"I thought you would be coming to see me. Enter, please." He welcomed her into his room and motioned her to the dressing table chair. "What do you have to say for yourself? All evening at supper you looked as if you wanted to tell me something."

Evie laughed. "I just wondered what was going on with you. We've had so little time to talk and no time alone."

"It's true." Evan plopped down on the edge of his bed. "I've definitely missed you, and now you return looking as if something is amiss."

"Nothing's amiss." Evie hated lying. It soured her stomach nearly as much as surgery did.

"I know that something isn't right. As twins, we've always been able to sense that in each other. Why not just tell me what's happened?"

Evie shrugged. "I grew up. People said we'd experience change in leaving home and each other." She smiled. "I still adore you, brother dear, but I am a changed woman, and you are a man. We're neither one of us children. We've seen a great many things that have changed us."

Evan considered that a moment. "I suppose that does speak to the change in you . . . in me. I hope it won't put distance between us."

"Of course not." Evie sat down on the chair he'd offered earlier. "You and I will always be close. We have a bond that none of the others can understand."

"I agree. I just want to make certain that you know I'm here for you and always will be."

"And I for you." She smiled. "Now what else is on your mind? You wrote me about Carl Knutsson's sister Christina. How is your pursuit of true love?"

Evan grinned. "Well, she's beautiful and sweet and loves to read. I find that especially attractive in a woman. I asked what she particularly enjoyed in her reading choices, and she loves biographies and stories of adventure and danger. She also enjoys books that relate to the invention of various items and women's topics like fashion and romance."

"Oh, those are women's topics, are they?" Evie laughed out loud. "I suppose I must allow that they are. She sounds wonderful, Evan."

"She is. And Carl and I have been friends since boyhood. I've known her practically since she was born."

"Well, I hope she will make you happy."

"Whoa, now. I'm not proposing just yet. We aren't even formally courting."

"Why is it taking so long for you to get around to that?"

"I was establishing my career, like you. There are those who would say you've waited too long to marry. However, I do not feel that way at all. I believe reasonable, intelligent women are waiting longer these days to marry. They are looking at their circumstances and situations and figuring out for themselves what they might accomplish."

"Yes, and some of us simply haven't captured the attention of any good man." Evie shrugged.

"I know for a fact you've had your fair share of interested souls. Even Carl thought you might be the love of his life."

"Before he settled on my best friend."

"Amelia Bronson is a beautiful young woman. She suits the ideal of womanhood as many see it. Petite, blond, and blue-eyed. She also loves to read, as I recall, and she teaches Sunday school and loves children."

"Yes, Amelia is practically perfect," Evie said, standing and shaking her head. "I'm the one who is strange. I intimidate men. They don't know what to make of me. I'm studious and not only love to read but can probably hold my own in their conversations of current affairs. That doesn't bode well for a woman."

"Then mind your tongue until you catch a husband."

Evie laughed. "You know you don't mean that. Besides, I've already got a reputation in Minneapolis. People know our family's passion for the poor and friendless. They see me coming and grip their pocketbooks a little tighter."

Evan laughed and jumped to his feet. "Not everyone. You're a beautiful young woman from a wealthy family. Your pedigree speaks for itself. There are plenty of men who will, and have, come calling. A few I've tripped up before they could even speak to you because I knew they were bad news. The right one will come along, I assure you, sister."

Evie wasn't at all convinced. She patted his arm. "I've always liked Christina. Let me know how things develop between you two. Now that I'm home, I can also help fan those flames of romance."

He shook his head. "I've got this one under control. I just need your prayers and love."

She nodded. "You've always had that and always will." She bid him good night, pausing again at the door. "Please don't worry about me. I have changed, and there are issues, but I'm still your sister. When the time is right, I'll come to you and explain."

She headed back to her room. All at once Jared came barreling out of one of the bedrooms.

"Better slow it down, little man. You know how Mother feels about running upstairs," she chided.

"I can't slow down. It's almost time for Nanny to check that I'm in bed. I have to hurry, or I'll get in trouble again. I've been late to bed four times this week."

Evie laughed. "Jared, as far as I know, you've never in your life been in bed on time."

The young boy shrugged. "I can't help it. I have a lot of things to do."

Evie pushed him towards his room. "I've no doubt you do. Good night, little brother."

"Night!" He scurried off like a mouse desperate to avoid the cat. "Glad you're home, Evie."

Tracie Peterson is the award-winning author of over one hundred novels, both historical and contemporary. She has won the ACFW Lifetime Achievement Award and the Romantic Times Career Achievement Award. She is often referred to as the "Queen of Historical Christian Fiction," and her avid research resonates in her stories, as seen in her bestselling HEIRS OF MONTANA and ALASKAN QUEST series. Tracie considers her writing a ministry for God to share the Gospel and biblical application. She and her family make their home in Montana. Visit her website at TraciePeterson.com or on Facebook at Facebook.com/AuthorTraciePeterson.

Sign Up for Tracie's Newsletter

Keep up to date with Tracie's latest news on book releases and events by signing up for her email list at the link below.

TraciePetersen.com

FOLLOW TRACIE ON SOCIAL MEDIA

Tracie Peterson

@AuthorTraciePeterson